Chronicles of a Hustla:

GREED MASQUERADES AS AMBITION

....

Strictly Bizness

SED GREEN

Greed Masquerades As Ambition

This is a work of fiction. Names, characters, places, and incidents either are the product of the author's imagination or are used fictitiously. Any resemblance to actual persons, living or dead, events, or locales is entirely coincidental.

Published by: Honor Society Publications

Written by: Sed Green

Cover Design by: Tre Carter

Edited by: Megan B. Joseph

Joseph Editorial Services

www.JosephEditorialServices.com

Contact Author:

sed@honorsocietypublications.com

Contact Publisher: www.honorsocietypublications.com

Email: honorsocietypublications@gmail.com

Print ISBN: 979-8-9871404-0-6

Ebook ISBN: 979-8-9871404-1-3

Submission Guidelines

Submit the first three chapters of your completed manuscript to honorsocietypublications@gmail.com, subject line: Book Title. The manuscripts should be in a .doc file and sent as an attachment. The document should be in Times New Roman, 12" fonts, and doubled-spaced. Also, provide a synopsis with your full contact information. Sending multiple submissions must be in a separate email.

Do you have a story but no way to submit it electronically? You can submit it to Honor Society Publications. Send in the first three chapters, typed or written of your completed manuscript to:

Honor Society Publications
6120 Oakleigh Road
Montgomery, Alabama 36116

***PLEASE DO NOT** send the original manuscript! Must be a copy!

Provide your synopsis and a cover letter with your full contact information.

Thanks for considering the **Honor Society Publications.**

Your life is in your hands.
Stop waiting for further instruction.

~Rachel Wolchin

Dedication

■ ■ ■ ■

Dedicated to Sasha for being yourself, an inspiration. My parents, Charlie and Delia Green (R.I.P. Ma 4/6/2022). Thanks for allowing me enough reins to explore and make a few mistakes, then letting me figure my way out of them. Eternally grateful!

Table of Contents

Prologue

■■■■

June 2006

The sounds of Plies featuring Akon club banger "Hypnotized" resonated through The Rose Supper Club. The dance floor was crowded with an assortment of sexy women. Surprisingly the fellas weren't playing the wall. They're dancing with the women, having a great time.

Cortez, Boonk, and Bubba were upstairs at the bar that's towering the dance floor, enjoying the atmosphere. "Dis bitch jumpin'!" Cortez excitedly mentioned.

"Told y'all dis bitch was gonna be wall-to-wall," Bubba mentioned.

"I just don't fuck wit' dis spot for real," Boonk told them. "Everytime I come up in here, it's always some bullshit."

"Everythang good, my nigga. Let's find a section, get right, and fuck wit' dese hoes!" Bubba told him.

The guys went downstairs and maneuvered through the crowd, making their way to V.I.P. They instantly made their presence felt by ordering several bottles of Belvedere and Grey Goose. Before the first glass was poured, Big D approached their table.

"Fuck nigga, what's happenin' now!" Big D aggressively asked Bubba, eyes deadlocked on him.

Bubba immediately stood up acting off of impulse, "Pussy azz nigga whatever ya want to be happenin'! You know me, nigga!," he said clutching a bottle and easing around the table towards Big D.

Boonk intervened by stepping in front of Bubba, blocking the path toward Big D. He was completely confused because he knew both guys. Plus they're all from the same neck of the woods.

"Mane y'all niggaz chill the fuck out," Boonk commanded with a few spectators looking on. "Niggaz in dis bitch tryna have a good time, and y'all wanna bump? All dese bad broads up in here! I don't know what the beef 'bout and really don't care to know. But y'all street niggaz, so handle dat shit in the streets. These folks paid good money to get in here. Y'all let 'em enjoy demselves."

What Boonk explained must've carried weight because their tempers de-escalated a few notches. "I'mma catch yo' hoe azz in the streets!" Big D asserted.

"Fuck nigga you don't want dese problems, for real," Bubba nonchalantly replied.

Although they're all from the same area, Cortez and Boonk don't normally hang out with Bubba. Simply because they're well aware of his deception, and didn't want to get caught up in it. Also, they knew Big D's character. The type of behavior he had just displayed was abnormal for him. Big D usually was joking, laughing, and being relatable with the people. They had an idea of what may have taken place but didn't want to speculate.

To confirm his suspicion Boonk asked Bubba, "What's dat all about?"

"Talkin' 'bout I sent niggaz to his trap to rob him. Dese niggaz be trippin'. I'm finna get at dese broads, fuck dat nigga. He ain't talkin' 'bout shit my nigga," Bubba assured them.

Cortez and Boonk looked at each other. From past experiences, they knew he did it but didn't exchange any words about it. After about three hours of smoking, drinking, and partying, the guys wanted something appealing of the opposite gender to take to Drury Inn and Suites. A group of women Boonk invited to their section and had been feeding drinks to all night were preparing to leave too.

The one who'd introduced herself as Chandra had Boonk's attention. He decided to see if they could get better acquainted, "Y'all 'bouta breeze too?" Boonk asked reaching for her hand.

"Yeah," the slim thick beauty replied withholding her hand.

"Look here, me and my niggaz 'bouta have an after-party at the Drury Inn on the Eastern Boulevard. I'd truly be honored if you and your lady friends would join us."

"What kinda after-party?" Chandra asked.

"Somethin' exclusive, as always. V.I.P. type shit!" he boasted. "Tell ya what, y'all just follow us and we can go from dere. Ya, dig?"

Boonk gestured for the guys to come on as he engaged in a conversation with the women exiting the club. Boonk threw Cortez the car keys to pull his car around as he sealed the deal, "See dat white Lincoln, plain Jane," Boonk said pointing out his car as it made its way out of the crowded parking lot, adjacent to the club. "Just follow us, love."

Chandra agreed, so Boonk crept to his car and got into the backseat. When they got in front of the club, a burgundy Dodge Magnum, sitting tall on 26s, pulled up on the opposite side of them and opened fire. The .223s from the Bushmaster AR-15 riddled holes everywhere in the Lincoln Town Car.

Distraught by the ambush, Cortez finally got a grip on his pistol underneath the armrest. "Everybody straight!" he yelled over the screams and screeching tires.

"My arm!" Bubba bellowed. "I got hit in the arm!"

"Boonk… ya straight?" Cortez frantically asked.

No answer.

"Boonk!" he repeated before turning around in a panic.

Cortez immediately reached over the seat and grabbed his friend. That's when he noticed the back of Boonk's head agape and blood oozed everywhere. He let out a scream that might've been heard for blocks as he clutched Boonk in his arms. By this time, bystanders were assured of their safety and began to surround the vehicle with assistance.

A few days after Boonk's untimely death, Cortez, with a group of friends and associates met in Regency Park at Ma'dear's house. They came to share their condolences with the family and help plan the funeral arrangements. Cortez went out front of the house to clear his mind and smoke a blunt. He exhaled marijuana smoke leaning against his black Jaguar X-Type. Boonk's cousin, Lil' Derek from Orlando, Florida joined him.

"Dat ain't no reggo, is it?" Lil' Derek asked him.

"Naw dis Sour Diesel," Cortez somberly answered.

"I know y'all niggaz was like brothers. Ma'dear said you takin' it the hardest, too," he said, then bluntly asked. "Mane, who killed my lil' cousin and where dis nigga at?"

Hitting the blunt once more before passing it, Cortez answered, "Cuzz, dis nigga Big D used to be 'round the street on Wimbledon Circle. Nigga grew up wit' us, Cuzz! He was beefin' wit' another nigga dat was wit' us. But I look at it like dem niggaz tried to murk all of us how they dumped in the car. I was in the car! Bitch azz niggaz tried to murk me too!"

"Where dude at?" Lil' Derek curiously asked.

"Ain't nobody seen him," Cortez responded. "But the nigga gotta coupla traps in the Four-Way."

"Well, ya know how the game goes. And the game must continue to be played. I know you and Boonk were bizness partners and you had access to everythin'. It's yours: the guap, the work, all yours." Lil' Derek informed him.

"Word."

"What I wanna know, are you gonna continue to do bizness? Don't sweat Big D! Before I leave dis city, he'll be dealt wit'!" Lil' Derek assured him. "Scc you gotta live here, so make sure ya surrounded by people for yo' alibi. So, won't no heat come yo' way."

After the burial, again everyone met at Ma'dear's house for the repass. Cortez didn't stay long, but assured Lil' Derek he'd be getting in touch with him soon. Cortez made his way around saying goodbye to everyone, before heading to Boonk's apartment in Stone Crossing. This wasn't home, just a quiet spot where they broke down and bagged up packs.

He boxed up some sneakers and gear before sitting on the tan leather couch, for a money count. Cortez counted up a little over $200k. Placing rubber bands on the stacks, he positioned them in a Louis Vuitton tote bag, along with three kilos of cocaine. He casually made his way out of the apartment.

Cortez called Lil' Derek later that night to show him where Big D's spots were located. They sat out front in the parking lot of South Mall Apartments, a little over two hours talking numbers. Unexpectedly, a bronze Dodge Durango pulled up, and three occupants exited.

"That's him right there," Cortez anxiously stated squinting his eyes. "The big one! Those other two niggaz, I don't know 'em! Might as well do dese niggaz now!"

"Naw. I told cha I'mma handle 'em. Come on, drop me back off at Ma'dear house. Go 'head do somethin' good for your lady. Take her out somewhere nice. I got dis!"

"This morning's top story on WSFA-12 News: A triple homicide on the south side of the Capital City. Three unidentified Black males found dead from multiple gunshot wounds. Their bodies were found in the parking lot of South Mall Apartments. Currently, there are no suspects at this time. The case is under further investigation. If you have information regarding the homicides, call CrimeStoppers at 334-215-STOP. More on this story at noon," Valorie Lawson reported.

"Bwoy, ya for sho' wit' it," Cortez murmured staring at the television.

Chapter 1

■■■■

August 2010

Lying flat on his back with his hands behind his head, staring at the ceiling, Cortez re-enacted the dreadful events that led to him holding his closest friend's dead body in his arms. Light suddenly illuminated the cell, disrupting his train of thought. That's an indication it was morning, and the first shift was preparing to do a body count.

One might consider Cortez an insomniac because this had been his routine for the past two days, since he'd been detained in federal holding at the Montgomery City Jail. He might've got two or three hours of sleep a day. The rest of the time he focused on trying to figure out who was responsible for him being there.

"All rise. The Honorable Judge Calvin Williams," the marshal announced to the court.

"Good morning. Please be seated," Judge Williams instructed the court. "On the record. Case number 1385178, dm 126. The

United States versus Cortez O'Neal. This is a bail hearing to determine if the defendant should be granted a bail."

"Morning Your Honor. I'm AUSA Jonathan Adcock, and I'm assisted by AUSA Shametrice Cobbs."

"Good morning Your Honor. I'm Judith Kidd, lead counsel for the defendant."

"Morning Counselors," Judge Williams greeted them. "Would the Government like to be heard first?"

"Your Honor we have reason to believe the defendant is the leader of a local criminal enterprise, that's vastly spreading its reach," AUSA Adcock said. "His ties to the community are loose. Mr. O'Neal has wealth, resources, influence to murder, and the intelligence to flee. He should be held without bail, until trial."

"Would the defense like to rebut the presumption at this time?" Judge Williams inquired.

"Yes. Your Honor," Judith responded. "Despite the accusations by the prosecution, my client is a reparable businessman offering job opportunities, a father, philanthropist, and community activist... not a criminal. He has too much invested to flee. He's going to stay and clear his name, Your Honor."

"Considering the arguments of counsel, recommendations, and the pre-trial services report," Judge Williams explained, "the court finds there is no combination of conditions that can assure the defendant's appearance for trial. Bail denied. The defendant is to be remanded into custody to await trial. Court will be held in 3-C, Judge Thompson's courtroom."

Cortez replayed conversations in his head that may have led to someone cooperating with the Federal Government. He realized everyone loved the glitter and glam but wasn't willing to face the consequences once things went bad. Perhaps it was someone seeking a lighter sentence or trying to get a time reduction.

Whatever the case was, Cortez ultimately wouldn't be at ease until he knew of all the evidence against him. He couldn't imagine this being his reality. His days consisted of sorting through countless conversations, in hopes of finding a clue.

FOUR YEARS AGO

August 2006

Cortez's mind state was placid as he sat on the back patio of his home in Bell Wood, smoking a blunt. Clad in a white wife beater and charcoal Miskeen shorts, with his locs hanging down to his shoulders, his feet were propped up on the black, uniquely designed patio table, as he gathered his thoughts.

Still, somewhat topsy-turvy about the death of his ace and the sole responsibility of their operation now on his back, he felt that he had to prevail. Cortez embraced the quiet time to strategize his next move. What Lil' Derek mentioned about life going on, was indeed factual, so he relinquished his emotions.

Cortez decided his first obligation would be to get a few more traps. He was preparing to get off the work he anticipated receiving and intended to flood the city with. Taking advantage of a grand opportunity while he has this connection would set him up nicely. If executed properly, Cortez could just pick up, drop off, and collect his money. Melissa Grant came to mind with the thought of money dominating his brain.

She's an old friend from grade school that was ambitious, easygoing, and someone he deemed trustworthy. Also, Melissa was the owner of E-Tax, an independent financial-tax service, which has expanded throughout the city. He and Boonk shared aspirations of doing something big for the city to represent their people. Cortez understood this was his opportunity to do that.

For the type of money he envisioned acquiring, the people he chose to deal with needed to meet his approval. Also, these people must be knowledgeable in various fields, especially accounting, business law, taxes, and certified financial planning. People who have a unique knowledge of investments and the ones to avoid.

While putting everything in perspective, Cortez automatically knew he would adopt a son to go along with his two daughters. Boonk's four-year-old son, Buggy must be taken care of, and his mother wasn't able to do that. Not the way Cortez felt Buggy should be provided for. So, it was clear, Buggy had been added to the family as one of his very own.

Cortez flicked the roach into a butt can and then walked inside through the glass sliding door. He went directly to his bedroom. Cortez grabbed a black leather duffel bag off the floor in the closet, dumping its contents onto the bed. Once he finished counting, Cortez earned $340k over the past few months and combined that with the $220k Boonk had stashed.

Cortez removed $20k for living expenses or emergencies. The remainder he planned to turn over. He organized the money and put an all-white t-shirt on over the wife-beater, along with a white Alabama Crimson Tide fitted hat. He was serious-minded about his money skyrocketing to new heights. Cortez knew he needed to be more flamboyant to attract the major hustlers.

The private fence around the backyard he left ajar and removed the car cover off of a toy he normally reserved for the highway. A candy-apple red Ford F-350 sitting on 28" Lexani's. Exiting the driveway, he floored it. Cruising northbound on Eastern Boulevard, he reached on his hip to remove the Palm Centro from its case.

After the funeral, he turned his cell phone completely off because he needed some solitude. The first person he called was Po' from Newtown informing him he was in route and that they needed to talk. When he pulled up, Cortez observed a crowd of guys standing outside in front of the trap.

Lemme stunt on these niggaz.

Cortez purposely positioned the big rims, so the sun beamed directly on them. The glare blinded the sideliners. He checked for their reaction while grabbing his Sig Sauer .45 P320 from between the driver's seat and console, placing it in the lining of his shorts.

"Where Po'?" he asked walking around the front of the truck.

"Ahh— shit! Nigga ya killin' 'em!" Po' exclaimed making his way through the crowd of guys.

"Tell dese niggaz to catch up!" Cortez replied as they slapped hands, giving each other half hugs. "Hop in! Lemme blow at cha a minute."

They got inside the truck. Cortez sat the pistol on his lap and started rolling a blunt. "Dis bitch blowin' snowballs too, Cuzz," Po' mentioned, curious by the random visit. "What brings ya thru dis Nawf Side?"

"Guap," Cortez candidly responded lighting the blunt. "Money on my mind! I came into a blessin', so I gotta spread my hustle. Since I can remember Newtown been a million-dollar spot. Ya dig? Not to mention, you always been a hustlin' azz muthafucka. Only dis time, the works limitless nigga."

"Bwoy ya gettin' it in like dat!" Po' anxiously asked.

"You wanna get some real money?"

"I'm gettin' money," Po' answered, pointing to his car. "See dat Cutlass wit' six wet coats on it, sittin' on twenty-sixes, wit' the Gorilla Lift on dat bitch? My shit almost sittin' tall as dis truck!"

"Bwoy, stop! Almost is the key word. Check it out! I ain't knockin' the fact dat cha gettin' money. I am knockin' the fact you're in a position to turn down life changin' money," Cortez explained. "I wanna set up somethin' over here 'cause dis really the heart of the Nawf. All the major action flows thru here."

"What cha talkin' 'bout? Hard or soft?"

"Both! However ya want it."

"Whole bricks?"

"No doubt! Can you handle 'em?"

"I can handle whatever! You ain't said shit!"

"Tell ya what," Cortez said. "I'mma give ya a brick and see what happens. Shit go smoove, we'll go from dere."

"Bet my nigga! But you ain't said shit 'bout the split."

"Gimme thirty-three racks," Cortez told him.

Po' sat silently a moment in deep thought, weighing out the proposal.

"When ya comin' thru?" Po' asked after estimating the profits.

"I'mma get at cha. When I hit cha, just be ready!"

"Bet dat."

****

Cruising down Federal Drive making a left on Atlanta Highway, Cortez's cell phone rang. He glanced at the screen and recognized his two daughters' mother. Cortez lowered the volume on the Alpine iLX-507 digital receiver then answered, "Yo' what's happenin'?"

"Nothing," Mona replied. "I been calling you for the past coupla days and your phone been going straight to voicemail."

"Yeah— I just turned it back on. I really forgot about it."

"Oh okay," Mona said. "I just hadn't heard from ya, that's all."

"Everythin' good," he assured her then asked. "How my babies?"

"Kenya at school and Cheyenne laying across this bed. She's not feeling good, so I kept her outta daycare today."

"What's wrong wit' her?" Cortez asked out of concern.

"Probably ate something that disagreed wit' her belly. You know she long-eyed. If she's not feeling better by tomorrow, I'mma take her to the doctor."

"Cool. Tell 'em I love 'em and I'mma come get 'em soon. I'm still alive. I'll holla at y'all later."

"Alright. Bye," Mona responded.

Cortez dropped the cell phone on his lap while delayed at the red light, in front of Hardee's on Perryhill Road. Perryhill Road Plaza was located next to the fast-food joint. Cortez parked his truck front and center of the business. He got out of the truck and just before he entered E-Tax, clutching the handle of the glass door, he spotted two female stallions exiting Subway a couple of doors down.

He lifted his Prada shades to get a better view of the beauties that hopped in a rimmed-up, teal-green Nissan Altima. Melissa was the first person Cortez noticed entering the establishment. She stood 5'5, with a blemish-free peanut brittle complexion, physically fit, and an excellent grade of hair.

She wore the most recent line of Donna Karen's business suit, with matching stilettos and not much jewelry at all. Better believe the few pieces she was sporting were high quality.

"Cortez O'Neal, how are you doing?" Melissa asked rising from her desk to greet him.

"I'm good! How you feelin'?" he responded hugging her.

"Man, I'm just fine. Thanks for asking," she replied. "Your butt hasn't been to see me nor called for that matter. Come on, have a seat."

Cortez simultaneously greeted the other four women that sat at their respective desks. "Afternoon ladies."

"Where you been?" Melissa asked.

"Mel, I be movin' 'round. Stickin' and movin'."

"How's the girls?"

"They straight!"

"I saw your Mama a few months ago and I asked about you. I be so— busy Cortez, because that night when I saw her, I intended to call and check on you."

"Trust me, I understand," he whispered leaning forward on her desk. "Mel I need to talk wit' cha a minute."

Melissa's facial expression altered, due to his sudden whispering. "What's up?" she asked in a whisper.

He motioned his head for Melissa to follow him outside. Cortez pulled out a fresh deck of Newports and packed them before lighting one. He stepped aside avoiding the view of the women and began to take Melissa down memory lane. Cortez recalled how they met and out of mutual respect, they decided having sex would more than likely ruin their friendship.

Also, Cortez mentioned how important he believed that decision was toward cultivating their relationship. Which enabled them to be as close-knit as they were. He commended her on all the accomplishments and accolades, along with the ones he foresees in the future. With Melissa he understood being manipulative would be futile. She's very sophisticated but hood, too.

Meaning she's capable of recognizing game. With Cortez wholeheartedly trusting her, he chose to be honest. Melissa was aware of the majority of activities Cortez participated in and disagreed with. But she realized he was going to do things his way. His relentlessness was one of the things she loved about him, it reminded her of herself. Cortez began to expound on how he always desired to enter the corporate world.

He told her about the immediate impact he would have on the City of Montgomery with some innovative ideas. Which he had neglected for far too long. He continued to elaborate on ways of converting the city from what he considered a retirement town, to a place with substance. Melissa's excited, but not by his thoughts alone. She always knew Cortez was capable of making this transition.

The leadership qualities one needs to excel as an entrepreneur she felt were innate for him. Now that her close friend decided to invade Corporate America, she felt honored and compelled to assist him. Before she could form the words to ask what field he intended to pursue, Cortez revealed that he was ready to start five businesses now.

He instructed Melissa to get the essential start-up paperwork prepared. He needed permits and licensing ready for some vending machines, a pool hall, a car wash, a barbershop, plus a laundromat. Cortez promised each spot he began operating would become profitable. Only if Melissa would be the C.F.O., Tax Advisor, and Personal Advisor in certain areas where he lacks knowledge.

****

After the meeting with Melissa, Cortez drove to one of the most drug-infested areas throughout the city, The Bottom. Kelt has been hustling in The Bottom for numerous years. Anywhere on the West Side of town, Kelt was well renowned. He was just like many other hustlers were, delusional. Content with not slipping underneath a kilo and buying materialistic things that portrayed him as a certified D Boy.

Cortez commanded the narrow street, lightening up the block in the huge pickup truck. He parked halfway on the curb so passerby's could get through with ease and reduced the chances of accidentally hitting it. He left the fog lights on and put his pistol in the lining of his shorts. Scanning the scenery for any surprises, he jumped out of the truck.

Before making it to the front porch two youngsters directly approached, out of the darkness. Once they were close enough to recognize Cortez, they acknowledged him by slapping hands. The eldest of the two, Scooby Dum, yelled in the direction of the front door, that it was Cortez in the unidentifiable truck. All he could hear in the dismal darkness was the unlocking of the steel burglary bars door. Cortez looked onward at the silhouette occupying the doorway.

"Come on in, fam!" said a raspy voice.

The familiarity of the voice verified this was who he'd been looking for. "My nigga, you on point!" Cortez affirmed. "Dem bwoys appeared out of the dark, like mercenaries!"

"Ain't no doubt! Cuzz, ya gotta stay on point 'round here. Jumpstreet subject to come thru dis bitch, at any given time," Kelt stated letting Cortez inside before re-locking the burglary bar door. "I ain't worried 'bout no jackboys."

Cortez followed Kelt into the kitchen where the light pervaded halfway through the living room. From the looks of things, it seemed as if Kelt had just finished baking a cake. He was in the process of cleaning up the mess.

"What I do to deserve dis visit?" Kelt sarcastically asked. "'Cause nigga, you don't come thru dis bitch but on spells. When ya swoopin' up one of dese broads, and ya chunkin' the deuces den."

Cortez couldn't refrain from grinning. "Fuck you, nigga!"

"For real, nigga! Majority of the time I see ya on dis West, you're snatchin' up one of our bitches. It's all love though," he said laughing.

Kelt removed a sheet pan from the deep freezer before he took a seat at the table. Ten cookies of crack cocaine lay on the sheet pan, and he started reducing them to $20 slabs.

"Do it Cuzz, wit' yo' cookin' azz!" Cortez told him.

"Every day, I'm hustlin'. You know me!" Kelt replied.

"I'm already hipped. You gonna grind! How long it'll take ya to get 'em gone?"

"Rock for rock. A day or two. And I'm back in the kitchen."

"Bwoy, you remind me of me. Dig dis though. I gotta proposition for ya."

Kelt instantly cuts his eyes towards Cortez.

"Glad I gotcha attention. I know ya gettin' money over here. But a major opportunity to get more bread should interest every hustla," Cortez told him. "I know you're independent and doin' you. But cha should consider expandin'. Feel me?"

"What cha mean by expandin'?" Kelt curiously asked.

"A partnership. I can drop 'em on ya, fast as you can get rid of 'em. As many as ya can handle. Everybody chew good bwoy! If niggaz play they role, bread gonna be plentiful."

"Yo' plug on like dat?"

"It's my time to eat! We've known each other a hunnid years. We both solid niggaz. Either ya gonna blow dis opportunity and continue pushin' rocks. Or take advantage of dis golden opportunity and rise like yeast, my nigga."

"Bwoy— ya should've been a politician! 'Cause ya make it sound so sweet! I gotta fuck wit' cha, 'cause I know ya don't play no games."

"Cool. I gotta whole thang in the truck. I want thirty-three racks."

Damn bwoy you pimpin', too!" Kelt shouted as he continued chopping cookies.

"Cut dat shit out," Cortez quickly retorted. "You know damn well ya gonna grind it. Rock for rock! You gonna get the butter from the duck! Dis my play, so quite naturally I'mma get me. I'm takin' the risks. So, fuck the riffraff. Either ya in or out. I want cha in, but cha can be replaced."

"Yo' thirsty azz— ain't gonna let a nigga win, for shit!"

They sat at the table another half-hour discussing the formalities before Kelt followed Cortez back to his truck. Cortez reached behind the passenger seat and produced a neatly folded plastic grocery sack, with two kilos inside. He informed Kelt that he'll be back in a couple of days for the money, and that's when the real show begins.

"Ya got dese bwoys on smash, wit' dis one fam," Kelt told him admiring the truck. "She looks good, but is she runnin'?"

"Ain't no need for the outside to be right, and she ain't shit under the hood."

Cortez crunk the truck and revved the motor while putting some volume on the subwoofers. UGK's "3 N Da Mornin'" pounded the block before Cortez floored it. Just giving Kelt a general idea of how hard the truck ran.

****

Arthur O'Neal and Mary Surles met at a Raceway gas station back in the late seventies. That's when Arthur first started his truck driving career. Arthur's route had a stop or traveled through Montgomery. So, the two would oftentimes see each other. They quickly fell in love and got married, immediately taking up residence in Arthur's hometown of Milwaukee, Wisconsin.

The newlyweds conceived three children: two boys and a girl. Bryon, Cortez, and Rose, plus Mary being a housewife, justified Arthur staying on the road to provide for his family. With Arthur always gone Mary began to feel abandoned. In a brand-new state, just her and the kids, always being alone was depressing. She convinced Arthur to move them to Montgomery, where she'd have support from family and friends.

Cortez had just celebrated his fifth birthday when they moved to Montgomery. Arthur being gone weeks at a time, Mary got assistance from Bryon and Cortez spending a lot of time at her parent's home. Bryon wasn't fond of the country, but Cortez quickly adapted. Cortez embraced the unconditional love, Grandmama's homemade desserts, and also learned new things by observing his Granddaddy.

But after the death of his Granddaddy and the absence of his Dad, Cortez's interest began to shift in other directions. Arthur would come home for a weekend every month or so, leaving just enough money for them to survive until he decided to return. There wasn't evidence to prove the theory, but the family knew Arthur had multiple families.

From that point forward Cortez began devising ways to better his family's situation. He and his brother Bryon were polar opposites.

Bryon was straight as an arrow, do no wrong, and Cortez had that by any means mentality. Bryon had dreams of being an R&B singer to rescue the family. Cortez had aspirations of being a pro basketball player as a rescue plan.

Thorough training with intense basketball drills, weightlifting, scrimmages…. Those aspirations were short-lived once he and Boonk became friends. The two became fast friends, and their bond tightened once they realized they were in the same predicament. Cortez watched Boonk and others make their money.

Whether it was stealing from the hood stores, cutting grass, washing cars, breaking into homes of the more affluent, or boosting from the mall… best believe Cortez participated. That was their way of hustling until Lil' Derek came to town, and showed them this new game that Cortez had been playing ever since.

Now, at twenty-one years old, he stood 6'3, 215 pounds, with a light full beard and long thick locs that complimented his brown complexion. Cortez maintained his athletic build as if he was still training for the league. Also, those aspirations of success from his childhood hadn't vanquished yet.

Cortez has about $700k street money, two homes, sixty acres of land, five different autos, a testamentary trust fund inherited from his Granddaddy, and other material possessions. But it was the death of his best friend that induced him to reevaluate his aspirations, beyond criminal enterprising.

Predominantly all of Cortez's family on his mother's side resided or derived from Lowndes County, Alabama. A forty-five-minute drive west of Montgomery, according to how fast one drove. After his Grandparents' deaths, his visits were minimal once he became of age. On a hunch, he decided to show his face and see what the outcome might be.

So, after leaving Erskine Street he took I-65 to Hwy 80 West, merging left on County Rd. 21 into Hayneville. Cruising through town he noticed the new reconstruction since he last visited. Cortez did the speed limit through town because he recalled how the sheriff's deputies were eager to write speeding tickets. He wasn't in awe but was surprised by the transformation of the rural town.

A few miles up the road he made it to what's called a safe zone. A stretch where there are no duck offs for sheriff's deputies or state troopers to hide from speeding motorists. The straightaway leads directly to Mosses. Some considered Mosses the hub in Lowndes County for drugs, prostitution, murder, and gambling. Entering Mosses was a scene he's all too familiar with. The same downtrodden, poverty-stricken community of the past.

He slowly drove down the badly battered road, passing the gas station he and his cousin, Marcus, hustled at years ago. A quarter-mile past the gas station on the left stood Barlow's Lounge, an after-hours spot where they'd also hustled. Just past there, Cortez made a right onto his Auntie Betty's property. As usual, his Auntie sat on the porch, and any car that approached the house would draw someone to the front door out of curiosity.

Ain't shit changed.

Cortez gingerly got out of the truck trying not to show any concern. But he took every step with precaution to avoid getting red dirt on his all-white Air Forces. Cortez had changed some since the last time he saw his relatives. Most noticeably was Cortez's appearance. The closer he got to them, the more visible their confused faces appeared.

The young woman who was occupying the doorway burst out the screen door, "Mama dats Cortez!"

"Yeah— dis Cortez," he responded finally recognizing his younger cousin.

"Uh bwoy," Auntie Betty said. "You can't come see yo' family? I been askin' yo' Mama 'bout you."

"Auntie I be on the move so much I ain't been able to get down here," Cortez explained.

"Dem children been tellin' me 'bout cha when they see ya in Montgomery. All dat long hair on yo' head. Sit yo' azz down. Erica go in dere and brang him one of those cold sodas out the ice keg."

"I see Marcus and Jean sometimes. I ask 'em how y'all doin'."

"Jean ain't lie!" Auntie Betty said. "She said every time she see ya, you in a nice car. Know ya ain't workin' nowhere! How ya afford that fancy lookin' truck?"

"Dats a Ford?" Erica asked returning with the soda.

"Yeah. Cuzz what cha been up to? You ain't got cha no job in the Gump?" he asked avoiding his Aunt's initial question.

"I'm waitin' on Hyundai or Mobis to call me for an interview."

"'Til den you chillin', huh? Where yo' brother at?"

Might be in Montgomery. Ain't no tellin'," Erica answered. "Want me to call him?"

"Yeah, call him for me."

Erica called her older brother on his cell phone to inform him that Cortez came to see him. Marcus was in route back to Lowndes County, commuting from Selma. While he patiently awaited Marcus' arrival, Cortez reminisced and caught up on old times with his family. After thirty minutes of talking, Auntie Betty went inside to start dinner. Cortez and Erica moved off the porch, out to his truck. He kept the driver's door ajar and sat on the step bar, rolling a blunt.

"You never answered Mama," Erica reminded him.

"'Cause it ain't none of her bizness," he said before inhaling the marijuana.

"You know how folks gossip. Dey come home and tell Mama everythang. Say ya always in a sharp car. Ya stay clean, wit' expensive jewelry and stuff. Dey say Marcus tryna be like ya."

"I see Marcus every blue moon, shawty. How thangs look to me, seem like Cuzz doin' aight for himself," Cortez said looking up at her. "Straight up! And we never discuss what either of us doin'. We just ball! We ain't never spoke about nothin' illegal. So, if he's doin' anythang, I ain't make him do shit!"

"Why the random visit? You hadn't been down here in years. Outta the blue, ya pop up lookin' for Marcus."

Yo' Gotti can be heard clearly, but there are no visible cars. A few seconds later a Ferrari Red '73 Chevy Donk pulled in. "Dere yo' cousin," Erica told him.

"Lil' Cuzz why all the questions? We fam. What cha gettin' at?"

"Just want ya to know, ain't nobody dumb."

"Girl you trippin'."

Marcus parked next to them and got out, "What's really goin' on?"

Erica giggled, solidifying her point.

"Ya ridin' dirty?" Cortez asked.

"Naw."

Cortez locked up his truck, "Come on let's hit a corner," he told Marcus.

Cortez hopped into the car with Marcus. They proceeded clean past Central High School and made the right headed toward Gordonville. Cortez reached over to lower the volume on the Sony Bluetooth media receiver. Cortez was being truthful when he mentioned they hadn't discussed hustling. Although, he observed

Marcus' demeanor, attire, and the company he kept were key indicators. Also, Cortez sporadically heard Marcus' name in conversations.

"What Erica talkin' 'bout, I gotcha hustlin'?" Cortez asked him.

"Dis the country, Cuzz. You know how dis shit is. Everybody wanna know everythang 'bout cha bizness," Marcus answered.

"Yeah. You're gettin' money though. I been hearin' ya name buzzin' here and dere for a minute now. Marcus from the country. Marcus from the four-five…"

"I'm eatin'."

"Lemme rephrase dat. Is it any real paper still down here?"

"Cuzz, ya know it's paper down here! Dats why ya down here! What's happenin' wit' it?"

"Can you get off a brick?"

"Fuck yeah!" Marcus confidently replied.

Marcus drove into the local racetrack that would be packed if today was Sunday. Only a few people were out this Wednesday, and they're testing their race cars. Cortez hadn't been in this neck of the woods for years, so Marcus explained the interactions throughout the counties. Cortez wanted assurance that his younger cousin understood what was going to be expected of him.

Cortez sparked a blunt and then began to elaborate on the importance of this opportunity. "Cuzz I gotta play I put together and dis shit gonna change our lives for real!"

"Mm-hmm," Marcus uttered exhaling smoke from his nose.

"I remember how much guap was made down here when we was lil'. Granddaddy overalls stayed stuffed wit' stacks of hundos," Cortez admitted. "Remember the conversations we use to have about being worry-free about money? Sure, we ain't kicked it like we used to, but we needed to venture off to build our foundations, cuzz it's time to move to the next level. That level we talked 'bout as kids."

"I feel ya. How could I forget? Dem talks and sharin' of ideas motivated me to get up, and get to it," Marcus replied. "Dis shit gotta be worth it! Cuzz, my shit flowin' smoove, my nigga. I ain't finna' disrupt my program if it ain't makin' sense. Feel me?"

"I found a plug that'll gimme whatever I want nigga! I'm tryna spread my reach and monopolize the whole state! I'm fuckin' wit' solid niggaz. Niggaz that understand the rules of the game. Muthafuckaz who I can trust. Family!"

Marcus continued smoking as he nodded his head, acknowledging Cortez.

"Only difference between my team in the Gump and you, is we're really family. Two sisters' kids. But dese dudes I consider family, too," Cortez explained. "Dats how we rockin'! Like a family, my nigga."

"Word."

I'm comin' to ya wit' dis because I know ya capable of regulatin' the west side of the state. Selma, Greenville, Fort Deposit, Wilcox County, Demopolis…," he told him. "Yo' Big Cuzz can get whatever! Lemme say it, again. I can get whatever nigga! Wit' the squad I'm puttin' together, we gonna control the state. You're that final piece. You're that piece we need to win the chip, my nigga."

"What if I need ten of 'em?" Marcus inquired gazing out the window.

"I'mma drop 'em on ya! Cuzz, however many ya need, I'mma handle dat! Hopin' ya need more than ten. Eventually, the order will grow when the others get on board."

"What's the ticket?"

"Thirty-three racks. Ya wit' us or what?" Cortez asked, flicking the roach, and looking at him.

Marcus thought a second about the proposal, equating figures in his head. He then outstretched his hand, "Let's make it happen, Captain! All dem spots you named, plus plenty more duck-offs thru here."

Chapter 2

■■■■

In route home, Cortez thought about the structure of the team he formed and felt confident about them. He wholeheartedly believed he chose the right individuals to build this alliance. Cortez stopped by Shell's gas station to pick up a few things, before retiring for the night.

Cortez crossed paths with a gorgeous, petite beauty exiting the store as he entered. Her outfit alone lets him know exactly what season it was. *Summertime down south, ain't nothin' like it!*

"Yes sir!" Cortez stated making sure the young lady knew she had his attention. "Sure wanna ride wit' cha."

She looked over her shoulder enticingly with a smirk, encouraging further advances. Cortez stood motionless. He held the door wide open watching as she got in the passenger seat of a silver Honda Accord. As they drove past him, Cortez saw three more women inside and the passenger blew him a kiss.

Damn, I should've got at shawty.

That thought brought Cortez back to the fact that the past couple of weeks have been a whirlwind, and he hadn't had much loving.

This sudden urge for affection came over him. Clutching his cell phone as he searched his mental Rolodex, Cortez called Roslyn to invite her over. Not only was her sex game superb, but they genuinely have a great time together. Another incentive was she lived in Eagle Landing, only ten minutes away.

Removing a case of Heineken from the cooler he awaited her answering the phone, "Hello," she seductively answered.

"Hey baby!" Cortez exclaimed.

"Hey."

"What you up to?" he asked completing the transaction for the beer.

"Layin' down, watchin' tv."

"Dats it!" he replied sorting through his money. "Looky here. Want cha slide by the crib and come keep a nigga company. Gotta few bottles already, plus dat wine ya like and ya know we smokin' presidential. Meet me at the crib. You ain't gotta get all jazzy— 'cause we just loungin'."

"Cortez, I've been calling ya and you haven't been answering my calls. Now you wanna fuck and want me to come running."

Grinning from ear-to-ear Cortez told her, "I been dealin' wit' alotta shit the last coupla of weeks love. I just turned my phone back on dis mornin'. Straight up! Baby just come over and kick back, I'll explain everythang when ya get here. I need yo' company. Aight?"

"I'm on my way," she murmured.

Cortez had already downed two shots of Belvedere and was sipping on another one when Roslyn arrived. Opening the door, he immediately pulled her close and gave her a firm hug. She looked stunning in a pink and black Baby Phat sundress with the matching sandals. Cortez swiftly took her by the hand and led the way to the den, after closing the door behind her.

They've had this fling for about nine months or so now. One Saturday night last year the two met at the Martini Bar and Grill, and quickly grew fond of one another. One reason they probably related so well was their similar personalities. She's a female version of him and they complimented one another.

"Come on sit down," Cortez told her.

Roslyn gave a devilish grin then stated, "You must've been spending quality time wit' your girl."

"No—. My partner got his brains blown out in my lap at The Rose a few weeks ago," he sarcastically responded. "So, we had to lay him to rest. Dats why I ain't been having time."

"I heard about that! Who was he?" she asked.

"Boonk. Real name Deon Means."

"Ohh— I heard about that. I didn't know that was him though," she replied. "I'm so sorry to hear that. Where were you?"

"In the front seat!" he answered busting down a cigar. "Two niggaz was beefin' and Boonk squashed the shit. We're leavin' the club and niggaz aired us out."

"Damn! I'm so sorry to hear that. Glad you alright, baby."

"I'm straight. Just been helpin' his folks cope wit' the shit."

Kenny G lightly played in the background as the two furthered their conversation. Normally, while smoking and drinking they would've gone at one another by now. Tonight, Cortez chose to use her as an outlet to vent. They discussed several pressing issues. It was the first time they got this personal.

Roslyn got comfortable and kicked off her sandals, sitting Indian-style at one end of the brown couch. She was smiling, giggling, and full of uncontrollable laughter. Just like a schoolgirl having her first encounter with the opposite sex. Cortez got aroused glancing between her thighs at the swollen print sitting perfectly in a pink thong.

He eased towards her, running his fingers through her manageable hair. Cortez nibbled on her left earlobe and then gently kissed her neck. After heavy kissing, Cortez began to pull down the spaghetti straps on her dress. He took his time licking around her bite-sized breasts, watching the nipples get erect before sucking them.

He sat up on the couch as Roslyn stood directly in front of him. She slid the satin dress down to her cherry color pedicured toenails. Always in awe by how perfectly well put together her physique was, Cortez just sat there caressing her. *A true definition of an hourglass.*

Roslyn's small frame made her bow hips, and butt look unreal for her body. Cortez turned her completely around until her back was facing him. The grimace on his face would've been uncontrollable for any man. *How did her thong pull a disappearing act between those cheeks?* Still fondling and caressing her, he broke the silence, "Baby you fine as fuck!"

She poked her butt out a little farther, before looking back at Cortez like a vixen out of King's Magazine. Loose from the wine she began to vogue and maneuver like an exotic dancer. She sat in his lap, grinding, before switching positions. Roslyn straddled him on the couch. She guided her left breast directly towards his mouth, teasing him.

Roslyn got up off of him and kneeled in between his legs. She hastily unbuckled his belt before removing his shorts and boxers. Already erect, Roslyn took his manhood in her hand and gave him the most seductive look ever, before placing it in her mouth.

"Ooh— I likes dat," Cortez uttered.

"You like that?" she asked before deep throating him.

"Oh yeah," he groaned.

Roslyn stood up to remove her thong. Cortez reached on the floor to retrieve a condom from his shorts. With his mouth, he tore the wrapper and placed it on his tool. Roslyn turned around slowly and lowered herself down on his erection. She gyrated, grinding on his manhood. Cortez was thrilled by the sight from behind. Especially when the vodka took effect, coercing him to take control.

Roslyn was instructed to place her knees on the edge of the couch. Cortez propped his right foot next to her knee for leverage. He eased his manhood back inside her wet womb and gave her the business. He watched her big ass jiggle from his thighs smacking against it, every time he protruded inside her.

"Shit Cortez! Shit!" she exclaimed. "Ooh— I'm cummin'! Ooh—"

Around two-thirty a.m., Cortez awakened from the joyous experience he shared with Roslyn earlier. He glanced over his shoulder to witness her still asleep. He grabbed his cell phone off the nightstand and staggered up the dimly-lit hallway, to the den. Cortez flopped down on the couch, fiddling around for the television remote in the darkness.

The 55" Sony flat screen brightened the room. He laid back on the couch watching ESPN highlights. Cortez gathered his thoughts and placed a call to Lil' Derek. In the background, Cortez overheard loud music, along with several oohs and aahs. Without hesitation, Lil' Derek commended him for his eager response. A positive sign that Cortez was serious about acquiring some money.

Also, Lil' Derek mentioned he and his father were recently discussing him. Lil' Derek's father wanted to know his opinion on the matter. Lil' Derek alleged that his opinion was highly valued, also his father wanted to personally meet him. Lil' Derek suggested

Cortez come down and visit this weekend since he responded so quickly.

Lil' Derek explained to him to wait on a text message that would inform him of the flight's information. All Cortez would have to do is go to Hartsfield-Jackson Atlanta International Airport and board the plane.

****

Cortez sat on the tailgate of his truck eating a BBQ chicken plate in the parking lot of Cook Ma's Soul Food restaurant. Today, he had Bug riding shotgun with him. They're in a conversation on random topics which Cortez turned into a debate about women, merely for entertainment. He got his point across that Bug wouldn't have a shot with the type of women he dealt with.

Po' pulled up in the '85 Metallic Blue Cutlass Supreme he had bragged about with the music blasting. He parked beside them and got out, "What the deal?" Po' asked Cortez when they slapped hands.

"Mama don't play 'bout that loud music out here. Shid really don't want a mu'fucka out here for real," Cortez told him.

"Thought cha was gonna blow at me last night?"

"Cuzz I been on the move. I was tired as fuck once I got thru handlin' my bizness. I took it in and got my nuttz outta pawn."

After another twenty minutes of shooting the breeze, Cortez handed the remainder of the plate to Bug so he could dispose of it in the Waste Management dumpster behind the restaurant. With Bug occupied Cortez went to the passenger side of his truck, lifted the backseat, and came out with a neatly folded paper bag.

He briefly scanned the scene for anything unusual then handed Po' the bag. There were no words exchanged before Cortez stepped back up in his truck. He pulled around the back to pick up Bug and fled the scene.

"How everythang look in the hood?" Cortez asked Bug.

"Shits good," Bug answered strolling through MySpace on his cell phone.

"Action 'bouta pick up real quick!" Cortez informed him. "So, get the lil' homies ready to expand. We 'bouta spread our reach! Take dis muthafucka over! Trust me bwoy. I'mma take ya to the promised land!"

"Bruh, they on go! Whenever it's time to mob, we ready!"

"Just makin' sure the soldiers on point. I'm 'bouta make dis move, right, and if everythang goes like it supposed to a bunch of niggaz gonna be mad."

"Fuck 'em!"

****

Derek Means was a thirty-three-year-old native of Orlando, Florida. He's about 5'9, black as an ace of spade, and weighed 125 pounds soaking wet. Since a kid, Lil' Derek's been meager in stature, which provoked the older kids to add the "little" to his name. Also, as a kid, he was always receptive, which was a tremendous help in him becoming very knowledgeable about the drug trade.

What would you expect when he's been surrounded by this kind of activity since before he started grade school? Growing up in the eighties on the west side of Orlando had gotten so bad, that the residents called it "Warlando". For years he observed his father and uncle live lavishly, considering the circumstances. So, it was very likely that would be the route he pursued.

Lil' Derek took to the game like a fish to water. His father, Ron, truly didn't want him to be a part of the lifestyle. Therefore, Ron tested him to get a general idea of which direction his only son would pursue in life. One day after school when Lil' Derek was in the eighth grade, Ron intentionally dropped seven grams of crack cocaine on the kitchen floor. He wanted to see what Lil' Derek would do with it.

Just as Ron figured, Lil' Derek picked the dope up off the floor and kept quiet. He sat around a while before rushing to Beirut, a neighborhood that's infamous for this type of activity. Lil' Derek and Jason, a close friend, who later got murdered as a result of this lifestyle, sat out front of Jason's mother's house until all the work was gone.

Lacking the knowledge of exactly how dope was sold nor the prices, junkies hounded them non-stop. They made $270 that Lil' Derek evenly divided with Jason before heading home. Ron's subliminal messages, along with him acting like he's searching for the small package were ignored. Once he realized Lil' Derek wasn't going to come forth, Ron admitted his scheme.

Lil' Derek sat quietly while his father dissected the game for him. Ron wondered where the drugs were after their talk. Lil' Derek confessed to selling it and flashed the $135 he made. Ron took his son in his arms, laughing uncontrollably before he placed Lil' Derek under his tutelage.

****

Bug was at Cortez's home while he packed a few necessities for his flight to Orlando, Florida. Cortez sat on the couch and unmuted the volume on the Indianapolis Colts and Pittsburgh Steelers football game. He sparked a blunt and then began painting a picture for his friend. Cortez needed Bug to play an essential role, too. Bug must be competent enough to control the hood and all surrounding communities on the south side.

"Bug you been gettin' ready for dis shit right here, ever since Sherrell died and ya started runnin' wit' me," Cortez assured him. "We've ran dis south side for the past six, seven years, hands down. You was nine or ten, when ya started fuckin' 'round in the game. Ya got active 'bout the same age I did, and now it's time to move to dat next level."

"I feel ya."

"If you play ya position and listen to ya bwoy. You'll be the most bossed up young nigga in the city. I'mma need ya to hold shit down, my nigga!"

"Come on bruh. I got too much time invested in dis shit. Feel me?" Bug nonchalantly responded. "I been ridin' too long and everythang ya said so far, has came true. Talk to me, my nigga! What's happenin'?"

"I'm 'bouta go to Florida and get some understandin' wit' the Plug. But when I come back, nigga we gonna get rich!" Cortez said hyped-up, passing the blunt. "I need cha to take over my role. Oversee the hood, Woodley Park, Spring Valley, the Four Way…"

"I gotcha!" Bug said nodding his head in agreement.

"The same plays we been runnin'. Only difference is, you runnin' it now. My role done got bigger. So, I ain't gonna be able to be in the hood or makin' rounds. My rounds gonna be pickin' up from y'all, my lieutenants. Look at it like dis, ya just gotta promotion."

"Bruh I'mma hold dat shit down!"

"I'm already hip! I'm just puttin' ya on point. Look— you the only one I'm tellin' dis too. I'm flyin' down to Florida in the mornin'.

I'mma need cha to drop me off at the airport, in Atlanta. I can't be late either!"

"I gotcha. What time in the mornin'?" Bug inquired passing the blunt back.

"My flight at nine o'clock, so we'll leave here 'bout six-thirty. Dats more than enough time to get us dere."

Chapter 3

■■■■

October 2006

Whenthe plane landed a flight attendant announced, "Welcome to Orlando."

Cortez walked through the terminal and casually looked around. He tried not to look lost. This was his first time in the city. Lil' Derek instructed Cortez to only bring himself and not to worry about anything else. Cortez complied, except for the $4800 in his front pocket along with a tote bag.

When he stepped out the front doors of Orlando International Airport, Cortez took a deep breath, while basking in the sun's rays. He stood out front of the airport fiddling with his cell phone when a Malibu-Green Lamborghini pulled up.

"Hey bwoy! Come on!" Lil' Derek yelled through the passenger window.

Cortez rushed to the sports car. He lifted the door and slid into the passenger seat like a regular exotic car rider, "What it do!" Cortez asked doing his damnedest not to look amazed.

"Ya here now, nigga!" Lil' Derek told him. "So, now I know you for real 'bout dis money. We gotta sit down wit' my folks first. Den we can do our thang! Show ya how we get down in the bottom. We gonna ball dis weekend!"

"Cool," Cortez replied.

"Boonk use to love comin' down," Lil' Derek said speeding through the city streets like Dale Earnhardt Jr.

"He used to tell me how y'all got down," Cortez informed him.

Bay Vista Phase II, an upscale gated community for the well-endowed located in East Orlando, was where Lil' Derek's daddy, Ron resided. Ron and Randy, Boonk's daddy wanted to have a sit down with him. Basically, to get acquainted with him, and lay some ground rules to make certain everyone's on the same page. Once they entered certain districts in East Orlando, the homes became immensely larger and much more expensive.

Cortez didn't ask any questions. He knew in a matter of minutes all he wanted to know would soon be unraveled. They pulled up to a bland colored security gate as Lil' Derek explained Orlando to Cortez. Lil' Derek made sure the security guard saw his face, then the gate automatically eased open. Cortez was amazed by the luxurious mansions but refused to display any excitement.

Right where I'm supposed to be!

They came to another security gate. Only this one had an oversized mansion atop of a hill. Lil' Derek entered the access code and the gate mechanically opened. They topped the driveway and parked on the side of the mansion, where the other foreign and executive autos were parked.

"Come on," Lil' Derek told him guiding the way through the side door. "Lemme introduce ya to the two that made dis shit happen."

Cortez closely followed him. He didn't say much at all but was observant. They walked through a large kitchen, and out of some double doors that led to the backyard. Cortez stood atop of some white sculptured cemented stairs, astonished by the size of the place.

"Mane come on!" Lil' Derek shouted as he sat down at a table poolside.

Cortez made his way downstairs to join the men at the huge glass table, "How ya doing, my man?" Ron asked as he stood to shake Cortez's hand. "This guy here is my brother Randy, Boonk's daddy."

"Please to meet cha both," Cortez replied.

"Have a seat. I understand you was wit' my nephew when he was murdered. I got the full report of what took place," Ron told him. "Life experiences has taught me, we gotta take the bitter wit' the sweet. Unfortunately, it happened, and we feel compensated wit' the actions that followed. Also, we realize life goes on, too. So, no need of harping over dat tragedy."

"We're goin' to honor my son by lookin' towards the future. Ya understand what I'm sayin'?" Randy mentioned.

"Yes sir."

"Okay. You made a conscious decision to be affiliated wit' this family. We're men, makin' a verbal agreement, so we shouldn't have any problems pertainin' to dese issues. Also, lemme lay down some ground rules. You and Boonk were partners, so you're aware of the reach we have. We've been doin' dis before y'all were born and managed to evade the Feds. You got me?" Ron explained.

"Okay. I gotcha!" Cortez replied.

"Number one. Never speak of us, especially to any law enforcement agencies. Secondly, as long as you stick to the system we've created, your shipment and our money will flow like the Nile River," Ron expounded. "Basically what I'm sayin' is don't complicate things, and enjoy a helluva lifestyle. Derek take care of him and show him a good time."

"Yes sir. I understand," Cortez responded.

"I got him Pops," Lil' Derek stated. "Let's ride Cuzz! It's Friday evenin'! Lemme show ya how we ball dis weekend."

****

The guys headed to The Mall at Millenia after the meeting with the heads of the family, which gave Cortez a better understanding. Before Cortez's arrival Lil' Derek instructed him not to bring anything and he meant just that. Lil' Derek intended to take Cortez on a mini shopping spree. Also, to show him a good time, along with the rewards of hustling hard.

Cortez had officially been adopted into the family, so it's mandatory that he was treated as such. On their way to the mall, Lil' Derek gave Cortez the do's and don'ts as a member of the family. Also, Lil' Derek confirmed the exact amount of work Cortez planned to distribute, and exactly how fast he could distribute it. Their final discussion was the figures the family expected before Lil Derek suggested, not to worry about any of the above until Sunday.

This weekend was a celebration for them, so they enjoyed the moment. The sun had just set upon their arrival at the mall. Lil' Derek was instructed by Ron to take care of Cortez and make certain he enjoyed his stay in the city. The guys strolled through the mall. Not looking for anything particular but were certain that by the time they departed, they'd be more than satisfied.

With zero worries about expenses, they flirted and talked with multiple women. They were of different shapes, and nationalities, all having their unique sense of style and beauty. The women wore outfits that embraced their bodies, plus desired attention with open arms.

"I liked dem Prada sunglasses you was rockin' in the Gump. I might get some of 'em if I see somethin' funky," Lil' Derek told him.

"Shit I ain't bring but a coupla stacks. If I knew ya was gonna cash out, I would've brought some bread."

"Cuzz, I told cha you're straight!" Lil' Derek assured him. "Ya want it! Get it!"

The guys wandered through different designer stores and fashion boutiques. Cortez's trust and confidence in Lil'Derek grew tremendously throughout the evening. Everything Lil' Derek claimed he'd do, suddenly occurred. Lil' Derek spent $12k on Cortez buying Louis Vuitton, Roberto Cavalli, Versace, and other notable designer clothing.

There was no arrogance nor egotistical attitude displayed about showing Cortez some love. Matter-of-fact the deeds were done without a second thought simply exemplifying how the family took care of one another. Also, it showed the amount of money that could be made if the business gets handled properly.

Ron recognized Cortez as a good hustler. Under the right tutelage, he could become a wealthy one, too. Ron sent him with Lil' Derek to motivate Cortez, so he'll take this opportunity seriously, and exploit it. Cortez witnessed how they lived. Also, the way Lil' Derek splurged, should be enough to persuade him to seek things unimaginable to the average street hustler.

The same formula he tried instilling in his nephew. That's why Ron and Randy were eager to meet Cortez, so they could decipher if these qualities came naturally or had to be developed.

"You straight my nigga?" Lil' Derek asked.

"I'm straight!" Cortez answered.

"See muthafuckaz can cash out like dis when ya gettin' real money! You'll see once dis shit get to poppin'. Nigga ya gonna have so much money, it's gonna scare ya! Real shit! Key to dis shit though, ya gotta stay sharp, Cuzz. We gonna school ya. But tonight, we just gonna ball hard."

"Dats what's up! Dis my first time in Orlando. Make me wanna come back!"

Lil' Derek giggled flashing his eight diamond-encrusted gold teeth, "Nigga, I'mma make you wanna relocate. I'm 'bouta put ya up in a suite at the Omni somewhere for the weekend. And tonight, we gonna swoop some of the baddest bitches in the city."

Lil' Derek drove to the Omni Hotel and Resort to get Cortez a suite, for the remainder of his stay in Orlando. He paid for the suite, then went home to spend time with his wife and kids. Lil' Derek tipped the valet a $100 before getting in his car. Cortez exited the elevator on the twentieth floor in search of his suite. He felt this lavish lifestyle start to become rewarding and began to embrace it.

Cortez was always accustomed to the finer things in life, but intuition told him he's about to enter another realm, financially. He entered the spacious suite and stood in the middle of the floor relishing the moment. Cortez looked around the suite, then made his way to the kitchen and got a crystal drinking glass, placing a few ice cubes inside.

He poured up a stiff shot of Grey Goose. Cortez flopped down on the leather sectional and took a sip of the vodka, before sorting through his bags. Trying to choose which outfit he was going to wear tonight. He decided the black and lime green Armani Exchange denim jeans and t-shirt were the way. Cortez strolled back over to the bar and made another drink. He took a few more sips, before hitting the shower.

Buzzing from the Sour Diesel and vodka he consumed, Cortez was ready to mingle. He went downstairs to the lobby to scope the scene, also to get out the lonesome suite. His cell phone rang fifteen minutes into entertaining some women. These women were provocatively dressed in short skirts and tops, heels, and peep-toe wedges, showing their French pedicures.

"What it do?" Cortez answered.

"Come on down. I'm out front," Lil' Derek told him.

"Bet."

Cortez was slightly disappointed about having to abruptly leave these women. He definitely liked the direction the conversation was headed. Cortez started towards the exit but managed to get one of the women's cell number, until he finds the right opportunity to pick up where they left off. He gave respective goodbyes to the group of women and then pranced out the front of the hotel.

"Fuck! You ran down here?" Lil' Derek asked as he positioned himself in the driver's seat of the Lamborghini.

"I was in the lobby kickin' it wit' some white hoes," Cortez told him. "A lil' more poppin' nigga, and I would've had 'em upstairs. I did get one of 'em number though."

"You wanna fuck wit' some white bitches?" Lil' Derek asked handing him a blunt to light. "'Cause if dats what cha into, I know a spot full of white hoes! Like dey off Bay Watch!"

"Mane just take me to a spot dats jumpin'. I'll catch shawty later."

Lil' Derek slowly cruised the strip, scoping the scene at the local hot spot, Cleo's. He circled the block to get an idea of what sized crowd was there tonight. Cortez was slumped low in the passenger seat. He's smoking the remainder of the blunt, observing the people in line waiting to enter the club. Lil' Derek pulled up out front where only the ones with status parked.

Their automobiles were more expensive than the rest. So the car watchmen were considered incentives by the club owner.

"Come on. We V.I.P. Majority of 'em ain't gettin' in," Lil' Derek stated.

Cortez got out of the car preening. He brushed off any ashes on his outfit.

"What it do partner!" Lil' Derek asked the doorman.

"Lil' Derek, what's good baby?" the doorman replied.

"Just came out to unwind, ya know. My family came down, so we came thru to fuck off a lil' bit," Lil' Derek told him.

Lil' Derek led the way up a flight of stairs. The higher they got up, the music became clearer. When they walked through the double doors, more security awaited. Lil' Derek gave them pounds and nodded his head, indicating Cortez was with him. The energy in the club was electrifying! Obviously, Lil' Derek was a regular or very well-known throughout the city.

Men and women alike bum-rushed him from the second they entered, up until the moment they were seated in V.I.P. Women of all ethnic groups were up on the mirrored stage, exotic dancing completely nude. Lil' Derek led the way over to a dimly lit, secluded booth over in the far corner. Before they could sit down, a waitress dressed only in a black bikini approached.

"Lil' Derek what can I get y'all?" the waitress asked.

Eyes barely opened, Lil' Derek looked up smiling, showing his diamond and gold grill, "You wanna breeze when you get off?" Lil' Derek replied.

"I don't fuck wit' you no more! Do y'all want somethin' to drink?" she irritably asked.

"Oh, we gonna do plenty of dat! Eat a coupla beans, smoke dis bitch out, and do our thang! You know!"

"We ain't gonna do shit!" she snapped.

"Baby I'm talkin' 'bout me and my family right here," Lil' Derek affirmed pointing at Cortez. "Not you! I respect yo' mind, shawty. Shit just didn't work out between us. So, bring us three bottles of Dom. What else you drankin', Cuzz?"

"Two bottles of Belve and cranberry juice," Cortez answered.

"Bring dat for now but don't get too far. The nights young!" Lil' Derek mentioned.

When the waitress stormed off to go get the alcoholic beverages, Cortez inquired about her foul attitude, "What up wit' her?"

"We hooked up a coupla times, and I took her azz down thru dere. She wanted it to be more than what it could've been. I ain't wit' it," Lil' Derek explained. "I'mma married man! And I ain't 'bouta leave my wife. Especially, for a broad considerin' me a sweet lick. Nooo— daddy. Dese broads scandalous down here, Cuzz. You'll see."

"Bwoy you shot out!" Cortez told him.

"Real shit! Dese broads thirstier than dese niggaz. That's why I handle 'em like I do."

Cortez thought about the info Lil' Derek shared as the waitress returned with the bottles. Before she could— set up the table, Lil' Derek unexpectedly erupted from his seat in excitement and grabbed a bottle of champagne, out of the ice pan. He guzzled down some champagne before he took a glass and poured it up. Engulfed by the music, Lil' Derek was bobbing his head to the beat.

Also, he handed Cortez a bottle, toasting before they took a sip. The guys displayed an extravagant lifestyle. They popped bottle after bottle and showered the dancers with money. Lil' Derek set out the Sour Diesel and gave away x-pills like they were Skittles. Men and women gathered amongst the guys to indulge in party favors. He wanted everyone to taste the rainbow.

This wasn't new for Lil' Derek, just a day in the life. Cortez was impressed by the sudden sense of stardom, even though he's somewhat of a celebrity in his own city. He hadn't witnessed stunting before on such a major level. Cortez was under the influence. Still, he managed to maintain his composure, being observant, while flirting with the women that surrounded them.

Hours passed, and the club was winding down when Lil' Derek invited three young ladies to accompany them back to the suite, for an exclusive bash. Cortez was satisfied with Lil' Derek's selection. But there was one particular dancer who had caught his eye. He'd been eyeing her throughout the night, and she recently finished her act. She got dressed in her street clothes and was about to exit the club.

"Hey love one, lemme walk ya out. It's alotta weirdos out dere," Cortez said looking into her hazel eyes.

"Thank you. But I gotta escort already," Wanda calmly replied.

"Naw— I insist."

She stared at Cortez with a suspicious countenance.

"Perhaps you ain't noticed, but cha had my attention, all night! And not 'cause ya was naked either. It's 'cause I thank ya bad as fuck!" Cortez admitted.

Wanda tooted up her lips implying disbelief.

"Really though," Cortez continued. "I'd be lyin' like a mu'fucka! If I told cha there's another woman in the club tonight, I'm feelin' more dan you."

"This my job. I hear bullshit and good game regularly," Wanda replied with a smirk. "I don't look to meet men here. You and Lil'

Derek made it rain all night, and I know how he get down. Whatever lookin' right to him on any given night is what he wanna take home."

"I ain't Lil' Derek though."

"Baby, I was taught birds of a feather, flock together," Wanda retorted. "Man, you could have any woman in the club. Why you botherin' me?"

"Dat cliché ain't always true. Maybe ya got the wrong impression 'bout me. Cuzz just bein' hisself. And I'mma be me, and I ain't interested in just any woman. I'm diggin' you, 'cause you're more my tempo."

"Really? And what tempo is dat?"

"Versatility is a must dese days. Ya most definitely know how to flip it. Hustlin'! Bold! Knowin' when to go wit' the flow, and when to be the flow…"

"And you know this by talkin' to me for five minutes?"

"My sixth sense told me! The vibes I get from ya."

"You gotta slick tongue. I'mma give you that," she told him. "Where you from? Lake Mann Homes somewhere? I never seen you in here before."

"I'm from Alabama. I came down to fuck wit' my folks. I told Lil' Derek to show me a good time. To take me somewhere dats gonna make me wanna come back."

"And Cleo's the spot he chose? Typical Lil' Derek. Are you impressed?"

"It's straight baby," Cortez answered. "But the highlight of my night is dis conversation we're havin'. I get to kick it wit' the real you. All the entertainment and fantasy shit over."

Staring into his eyes, lips turned up, Wanda showed disbelief once more.

"Cuzz let's ride," Lil' Derek told Cortez with three women in tow. "Oh, ya wastin' time fuckin' wit' Wanda. She game shot!"

Wanda ignored Lil' Derek's allegations of her being paranoid, thinking every guy has ulterior motives.

"At least I know your name now," Cortez sarcastically said. "Well, Wanda we bouta go back to the Omni and finish where we left off."

"Mane let's ride!" Lil' Derek exclaimed.

"Just be cool fam! I'm comin'," Cortez told him. "Honestly, I'd rather be in yo' company and further our conversation. Ya dig me?"

"Like I said, dis my job. I don't leave work wit' men I just met. I understand alotta girls do that, but I don't. Not tryna mislead ya."

"Just conversation baby. A lil' unwindin' in a more relaxed environment. Ya don't have to be threatened. Leave when ya ready. What's misleadin' 'bout any of dat?"

Wanda contemplated everything she just heard then asked, "What suite number?"

"Twentieth floor, suite 2024," he said. "Better yet. I'll ride wit' cha, so Lil' Derek and dem girls can do they own thang."

Before Wanda exited the club, she informed an enormous bouncer he wasn't needed— to escort her out tonight. Headed to the car, Cortez and Lil' Derek locked eyes. Lil' Derek unhesitatingly gave Cortez this devilish grin, nodding his head in approval.

****

Although Lil' Derek spent all night and the majority of the morning partying. He was awake before most, setting up transportation for the narcotics. Top of today's agenda was organizing and making sure Cortez's load was safely secured in a '06 Chevy Suburban, and ready to be transported.

Once Lil' Derek solidified everything for the trek to Alabama, he went home for a shower, and a change of clothes making sure his family was intact. After a brief stint with his kids, Lil' Derek was back out the door in route to the Omni. He noticed everything was as it had been when he left. The first person Lil' Derek saw was one of the women who accompanied him after the club.

She was comatose, completely nude on the floor in front of the sectional sofa. Lil' Derek disgustedly shook his head. *Bitches wanna party wit' the big dawgs and can't fuckin' hang.* He went to the refrigerator and retrieved a bottled water. Lil' Derek went to the backroom where Cortez dwelled. Slowly he eased the door open and peeped inside.

He tipped–toed over to the king-sized bed. Lil' Derek didn't make a sound while admiring Wanda's full breast before tapping Cortez, "Playtime over daddy! Back to bizness!" Lil' Derek shouted.

Cortez gingerly raised up trying to regain complete consciousness, "What time is it?"

"Nine-forty," Lil' Derek answered, glancing at his diamond-studded timepiece. "We gotta go Cuzz."

The sound of their voices awakened Wanda. Noticing Lil' Derek, she immediately covered herself with the silk sheets.

"I ain't get the chance to bust yo' azz, but my nigga busted cha. Guess I gotta be satisfied wit' dat. And another thang, I finally gotta real close up on dem titties. Lawd!" Lil' Derek jokingly declared.

"Bwoy you a fool!" Cortez replied.

"Lil' Derek get the fuck outta here!" Wanda snapped.

"Too late now. I seen dem titties," Lil' Derek told her. "I'mma be up front Cuzz. Hurry up! We gotta make a move."

Cortez took a quick shower. He got geared up, then rounded up the women and they all exited the suite. Lil' Derek got in his car, waving goodbye to the young ladies in the cab. Cortez tightly hugged Wanda while whispering sweet nothings in her ear. When the women departed, Cortez took a seat in the passenger seat of Lil' Derek's '83 Lamborghini Yellow Buick Regal. Before Cortez could close the car door good, Lil' Derek handed him a blunt.

"Only thang I wanna know, is the pussy any good?" Lil' Derek eagerly asked.

"You wanna try shawty, don't cha?"

"Fuck dat! What the hoe sex game 'bout!"

"Bitch a bad bitch, ain't she my nigga?" Cortez playfully asked.

Lil' Derek irritably sighed.

"Shawty gets live! Real shit!" Cortez said when he exhaled the marijuana smoke.

"I knew it! She seen me bag so many broads at dat club, she refuses to be a victim. Least you fucked. I really thought cha was wastin' yo' time 'cause, she knew we were together," Lil' Derek expounded. "Those three young bitches, I Mr. Marcus dem hoes. We was rollin' too! You should've came in the room, and we could've slaughtered 'em."

"I started to but dem beans made me go hard for 'bout two hours," Cortez told him.

Lil' Derek wanted to be sure he made his point on how profitable this business could be. Also, the other avenues that are accessible if Cortez kept that in mind. Lil' Derek drove to a residential neighborhood where some young hustlers worked for him in a trap he'd established. Normally, there would be several people out, but it was still early. Many residents were recovering from heavy alcohol and drug consumption last night.

They pulled up in front of a brick house on Mercy Drive, which many of the occupants renamed Murda Drive. The guys exited the car. Walking up the driveway, they're greeted by two youngsters, Hot Boi and Glokk. The youngsters grew up in the neighborhood and were very knowledgeable about the activities they partook in.

Hot Boi and Glokk grew up watching Lil' Derek maneuver throughout the area, until Lil' Derek eventually groomed them. Once they turned fourteen years old, Lil' Derek fronted them a pack, and the rest was history.

"What's good O.G.?" Hot Boi asked Lil' Derek.

"Just makin' dese rounds," Lil' Derek answered giving them pounds. "Dis my fam from Alabama. Cuzz dese my lil' niggaz."

The guys greeted Cortez with dap and half hugs.

"What's been goin' on 'round here?" Lil' Derek asked them.

"Same ole shit. Gettin' dis money," Hot Boi replied.

"Dats what's up! Everythang good? The task force been ridin'?" Lil' Derek further inquired.

"Dats what got me throwed! Dem bitches ain't came thru in a coupla days. Dats crazy too, my nigga," Hot Boi eagerly replied.

"Stay on point! Whatever y'all do, stay on point!" Lil' Derek repeated. "Gone get dat bag, I gotta move 'round."

Hot Boi entered through the back of the house. He retrieved a gray Jordan gym bag and handed it over to Lil' Derek. Hot Boi assured him there was $44k inside. Lil' Derek didn't exchange any words and simply motioned for Cortez to get back inside the car. Lil' Derek glanced in the gym bag making certain everything was legit. Zipping it back up, he set it securely on the floorboard behind the passenger seat.

Lil' Derek popped the trunk placing the t–tops inside. He crunk the ignition and idled the accelerator to bring attention to the dual flow masters. Lil' Derek made a u-turn and mashed the accelerator, ensuring everyone knew the 350 small-block motor was responsible for the sound— coming from the exhaust pipes.

Lil' Derek explained how the cocaine would be transported to Montgomery. Big John, a reliable colleague of the family, whose job was to transport. He'll drive the Chevy Suburban accompanied by Cortez, somewhere he deemed safe. Not once was Cortez to get behind the wheel. By chance, if they happened to get arrested by the authorities, he was to keep his mouth closed. An attorney would be there to see him ASAP!

Lil' Derek was sure everything would be a success, but just in case he didn't want Cortez to panic. Big John traveled throughout the southeast region and hasn't had an incident occur yet. Lil' Derek reminded Cortez not to say a word. Also, he's not to call anyone, especially the family. Big John would take care of everything. Worst case scenario, Cortez could spend a day or two in jail.

On their arrival in Montgomery, Cortez should direct Big John to a discrete location. For Big John to unload the product. Cortez's expecting fifty kilograms of raw Colombian cocaine, and the rest would be on him to deliver.

First, they hit Raleigh Street. They made two pick-ups and then went directly to a trap in Carver Shores. Lil' Derek pulled out front and tooted the horn before going inside. Five minutes later, he was headed back to the car with a brown grocery sack underneath his right arm. Same as before, Lil' Derek glanced inside then neatly tucked the sack inside the gym bag.

From there, he drove across the street to Richmond Heights. Turning on Bruten Blvd they witnessed a large number of people wandering. Some tried flagging Lil' Derek down to no avail. His focal point at the moment was to pick up all money and get Cortez situated. He refused to be sidetracked.

When they arrived back at the hotel Lil' Derek didn't hesitate to call Big John. He informed Big John it was time to hit the highway. While Cortez gathered his belongings, Lil' Derek counted out $5k for Cortez to put in his pocket. They're out front of the hotel when Big John pulled up. Lil' Derek introduced the two while helping load Cortez's luggage in the back of the Suburban. Lil' Derek and Cortez slapped hands then half hugged before their departure.

Chapter 4

■■■■

Once arriving in Montgomery, Cortez navigated Big John to a distinct location in Macedonia. A rural area within the city limits, where youngsters stripped stolen cars, next to Mr. Mooney's property. Big John positioned the SUV and then began dismantling the rear end clip.

Cortez stood there watching as Big John worked his magic. Then, wallah, he held the neatly wrapped packs stamped with C-4. While Big John reassembled the SUV, Cortez was busy with some assembling of his own. He stored forty kilos in the bottom of two designer tote bags, covered with clothes. The remaining ten kilos he placed inside a Hermes backpack. Cortez left the bags on the backseat with the rest of his luggage.

Cortez sat in the passenger seat with his feet propped up on the dashboard. He worked his cell phone as Big John finished. Big John drove Cortez to Stone Crossing. They took the luggage inside the apartment and parted ways with a handshake. The first thing Cortez did once he was alone, was call Po'. Po' informed him, that he successfully got off everything and was eagerly awaiting to see him.

Cortez explained that he just returned to the city. He needed to get situated first, but tomorrow would be a better day. Cortez gave Kelt a call, too. Almost verbatim, Kelt repeated what he'd just heard from Po'. Cortez and Kelt held the same discourse. Next, he called Mona to come to pick him up. His final call was to Joe Seifert, informing Joe in advance, to be expecting him within the hour. And if there were any guests, to rid of them before he got there.

Mona dropped Cortez off at his home. He gave her the $5k Lil' Derek awarded him for her time. He took the luggage to his bedroom. Cortez, stashed all the kilos inside his washing machine, except what he planned to distribute tomorrow. Cortez grabbed his keys off the kitchen table and was out the door, in route to Ridge Crest. Cortez crept down Woodlawn Street, then pulled into Joe's driveway.

Cortez parked on the back of the house. So passerby's wouldn't be tempted to stop after they spotted his vehicle. Joe knew the random visit would be beneficial for him. Before he even got out of the car Joe Seifert was coming out the backdoor, "What it do hustla!" Joe excitedly greeted.

Joe knew this random visit would be beneficial for him.

"What's happenin' mane? Ready to go to work?" Cortez concisely asked.

"Yes sir!"

"Who in dere?"

"Nobody. You said to clear it out hustla," Joe responded.

Cortez followed Joe inside, locking the door behind them. He sat a duffel bag on the kitchen countertop. Then he removed his all-black t-shirt revealing a black Ruger P89 in the lining of his tan LRG cargo shorts. Cortez closed the blinds to the window over the kitchen sink, before removing any cocaine from his duffel bag.

"Oooh— shit hustla!" Joe shouted. "Dats why I love when you come thru. You don't be bullshittin'!"

"Nigga stop cappin'! I'mma straighten ya out. Looky here, I got, ten of 'em I need cha to Babyface 'em. Put your whip appeal on 'em!" Cortez informed him. "When I leave here, I want dis bag to have 450 ounces in it. Still, fire though! I came and fucked wit' cha, 'cause you the best chef in the city. Hands down."

"I feel ya. I feel ya," Joe agreed.

"Joe Seifert, ya know me mane. Don't play no games!"

Joe Seifert's an old-school ex–hustler who'd been tempted to try his supply and never bounced back. He's well-known for his whip game. Several hustlers would bring their packages through for Joe's whip appeal. Also, Joe is notorious for having a net in the pipe underneath the sink to catch dope he'd intentionally dropped, during the process of cooking. Once he was alone Joe would re-whip it and bring it back.

"Come on hustla. Ya know I wouldn't do you," Joe assured him.

"Shittin' me! If I let cha, you'll bust my muthafuckin' head. Gone hook dis shit up."

Cortez sipped on an Evian bottled water and chain-smoked Newport's while overseeing every move Joe Seifert made. They took intervals and in the kitchen Cortez kept his surgical mask on, not taking his eyes off him. It was daybreak once Joe finally completed the order. Throughout the night, Cortez devised many ways how he intended to invest his money. Plus, how he could capitalize from these investments.

Ten kilograms of powder cocaine had been converted into crack, bagged, and packed. Before Cortez stepped foot out of the house, he needed assurance for his conscience. He coerced Joe Seifert to unloosen the P-Trap pipe. Just in case Joe's hands really were quicker than the eye. Joe played fair, therefore he was compensated.

"I'll be back in a coupla days," Cortez told him.

****

Newtown's a close-knit, residential community located on the north side of Montgomery. It wasn't a downtrodden neighborhood that had fallen into ruins. There were some abandoned houses, but for the most part, the residents took care of their property. Newtown's five minutes away from the Police Precinct on North Ripley Street, and that never slowed the volume of drug trafficking.

Newtown has always been the heart of the north side. The neighborhood was an intricate part of the north side's economic infrastructure, also responsible for birthing some bona fide hustlers. Carlos Austin and Brenda Gordon were born and raised in Newtown. They've known one another their entire lives.

Carlos lived with both parents until his dad was murdered. He was shot in the back of the head by a hustling partner after scoring their biggest load. Carlos was eleven years old when this happened. Also, that's when a drastic change in his life occurred.

Brenda was high yellow complected with thick coarse hair, a straight-A student, with an average body that most boys overlooked, due to her exceptional beauty. Because of her looks, several girls found out the hard way that Brenda could fight after underestimating her. Her mama and three older sisters encouraged her to start using it to her advantage.

Carlos and Brenda messed around some in middle school but nothing serious. In high school, Brenda began to take her family's advice. She started showing genuine interest in Carlos once he began to gain notoriety, as a savvy young hustler. Things intensified Brenda's senior year of high school. March of 1984, she gave birth to their first child, Vanshon Gordon.

Vanshon looked just like his mama. Carlos was extremely happy his son was born healthy. He doubled down on his hustle and eliminated a few unhealthy habits, to make sure he could provide for all his son's wants, plus desires. Vanshon always had the latest sneakers, Starter jackets, fresh new fitted hats, and everything else a kid his age could want.

One night his parents threw a small gathering with family and some close friends. Carlos's female cousin made a statement about the home being nicely furnished. She was hinting toward Carlos's money, which prompted Vanshon to vouch they were poor. Everyone laughed in unison. It was the enunciation and pitch of how he used, Po'. Before you knew it, family and friends had dubbed Po' as his name.

Po's parents had two more kids after him and didn't much change in their lives. Everything was perfect for a few years until Carlos winded up incarcerated for Attempted Murder of a law enforcement agent. Jumpstreet raided his trap unannounced, and Carlos thought it was a home invasion, so he fired shots. Ironically, Po' was eleven years old when Carlos got sentenced to life in the state penitentiary.

In his dad's absence, Po' witnessed his family slowly dismantled. They went from the most coveted, to being the butt of many people's jokes. For years, Brenda relied solely on Carlos. Meaning she became complacent with being taken care of. So now she's obsessed with attracting the next drug dealer to fill that void. Brenda became a lush while barely making ends meet working at a Wendy's.

Po' began to venture into the streets as things got hectic at home. He and some of the neighborhood kids participated in some petty hustles. Like stealing from Mac's Tavern, breaking into businesses, houses… That was his hustle until Lil' Johnny Gaithers took him under his wing. Lil' Johnny was eighteen years old, and he had that work!

Po' immediately took a liken to him. He reminded Po' of his dad, that sense of security. Lil' Johnny liked Po' too. That's why he groomed Po' and took him everywhere he went. Lil' Johnny bought him sneakers, outfits, video games… One afternoon, Lil' Johnny got aggravated with Po' for repeatedly asking for some sneakers. Because he had just received a new pair, a week ago.

At that moment Lil' Johnny realized Po' was ready to get his feet wet. He enlightened Po' that moving forward he'd be responsible for paying his own way. Lil' Johnny kept Po' under his tutelage by letting him hustle at his spots. He taught Po' the game and simultaneously protected him from parasites. Also, that broadcasted their affiliation, just in case the jackboys had some bright ideas.

Po' quickly picked up on the hustle. He began to understand it wasn't about sneakers anymore, it's much bigger! Lil' Johnny caught a murder case. Which was self-defense, but District Attorney Ellen Brooks chose to capitalize on the publicity of the high-profile case. Lil' Johnny was found guilty and sentenced to twenty-five years in the Alabama Department of Corrections. By this time, Po' had grasped the game and began making it his own.

One evening Po' had a play in Dixie Court for four and a half ounces. Earlier that day he'd been grinding out of a half-ounce, that's been reduced to a quarter by this time. Po' made the transaction and got back in the car with his homie. Jumpstreet watched and waited on them to exit the apartment complex, before pulling them over.

His homie was driving and admitted to Po' he had a pistol in the car. Po' never admitted he had anything. Simply, urged his homie to remain calm. Slumped low in the passenger seat, Po' looked in the mirror to see how many officers approached from the rear. His homie was distracted by the narcs approaching from the front. Po' used that opportunity to slip the quarter ounce of crack cocaine underneath the seat.

The narcs used the oldest trick in the book to gain access in searching the vehicle. They claimed to have smelled marijuana. The narcs removed them from the vehicle and placed them in handcuffs before patting them down. Two narcs searched the vehicle and immediately found the pistol. Minutes later, they stumbled up on the seven grams of crack cocaine, too.

Po' and his homie stood handcuffed in front of a squad car, surrounded by narcs. The two narcs who discovered the contraband approached with the evidence. They wanted to know to whom it belonged. The pistol, his homie recognized but the crack cocaine he was clueless about. He looked at Po' whose tongue was still as his facial expression.

In Montgomery, Alabama whoever is operating the motor vehicle, was also responsible for what was found inside. Po' remained dumbfounded about anything that took place. The narcs placed his homie in the back of a squad car and were about to release Po' from custody. Another officer wanted to run Po's name for warrants, before cutting him loose. Waiting on dispatch for confirmation, the narc searched Po' again and found a small sack of rocks.

What ensued? Po' was escorted to another squad car and placed in the back. They were taken to the Narcotics Bureau for interrogation and from there, Po' was transported to Air Base Juvenile Detention Center. His homie was charged with Possession of an Illegal Firearm, and Possession of an Uncontrolled Substance then was transported to the Montgomery County Jail.

Po' could've been released in the care of Brenda, except he repeatedly lied to a counselor about his money. So out of spite, the counselor kept him until his court date. This was where Cortez and Po' first met. For possession of a burglary tool, Cortez was there until court, too. They became spade partners and regulated the cell block when it came to gambling.

From that, they began to build a rapport, which led to much deeper conversations. After they were released, they'd hook up from time to time. They would cross paths at a house party, Looney's Skating Rink, Brunswick Bowling Alley, Side Pocket, Movie Four, Club NXS, and other popular spots.

****

"Hey— Were you sleeping?" a woman asked.

Mind still in disarray, Cortez glanced at the screen to see if he'd recognize the number. "Yeah, but I needed to get up anyway. What time is it?"

"Twelve-ten p.m.," she told him.

"Lemme get my azz up," Cortez said once realizing who he was speaking with. "What's been good, Precious?"

DeAnn Peters was her real name, but Cortez called her Precious. She's an assistant bank manager for Well's Fargo. She and Cortez have been dealing with each other for a few months. Finally, he convinced her to approve his small business loan for $80k after putting some acres of land up as collateral. Precious upheld her end of the bargain, while Cortez procrastinated. He didn't know if he'd need her again in the future, so he kept things cordial.

"Mad at yo' azz!" Precious answered.

"For what?" he inquired.

"Got me sweatin' you! Blowin' yo' phone up!"

"Shawty I just got back from Florida last night. I been tryna get alotta shit straight. Ya dig?"

"Uh yeah."

"What's on your mind though?"

"I need some dick!" Precious bluntly answered.

Cortez grinned as he wiped the sleep out of his eyes, "Dats all I am? Some dick!" he asked.

"No— I wanna see you too."

"Sounds like you tryna use me for my dick."

"Bwoy please."

"Lemme know somethin' den," he jokingly said.

"Am I goin' to see you today?"

"Sure."

"When?"

"Lemme get up and handle my bizness. I'll hit cha later. How dat sound?"

"Sound like I don't have much of a fuckin' choice. Guess I'll see you later."

"For sho'."

"Bye," she nonchalantly said.

"Aight," he responded.

Cortez immediately got out of bed and took care of his hygiene. Feeling rejuvenated when he stepped out of the shower. Cortez put on a pair of indigo Evisu Jeans, a white tee, and all-white shell toes. He put on his gold Cuban Link with the diamond-studded Jesus piece, two diamond pinky rings, and a timepiece by Johnny Dang.

Cortez ruled out the bucket hat because he wanted his locs to hang out today.

He went into the laundry room to retrieve the work he stored in the dryer, that Joe whipped up. Then he reached on the shelf for his pistol, tucking it in the lining of his jeans. Cortez put on some Emperor Armani sunglasses and grabbed his car keys off the hook on the wall, then headed out the door. He turned up a Styrofoam cup filled with Belvedere and crushed pineapple juice.

Eastbound on the Northern Blvd it dawned on Cortez, that he and Melissa should discuss the direction of his start-up business ventures. He figured tomorrow they could meet for lunch somewhere and determine the best avenue towards progression. Cortez got out of the Jaguar in front of Po's trap, clutching a Styrofoam cup as he walked to the side door.

Cortez knocked on the door. He saw the curtains ease back a bit, noticing a piercing eyeball, "Who is it?" asked a raspy voice.

"It's Cortez. Where Po'?"

The door abruptly opened and Cortez stalled a second before he entered. The guy who opened the door informed Cortez that Po' was in the living room. He joined Po', and another guy who was grudging on the PS3, playing Madden '07.

"Nigga I thought cha was playin' games," Po' said.

"Fuck you mean?" Cortez asked.

"I was expectin' ya sooner."

"Do it matter when I come? Main thang is, I'm here. Right?"

"Guess so."

"I need to blow at cha."

Immediately the game paused, and the two guys were told to leave them alone. Po' escorted them to the door. He came back, giving Cortez his undivided attention.

"Damn I left the cigars in the car," Cortez mentioned.

"I got some," Po' told him, then went to the back.

Po' threw Cortez the pack of cigars as he sat on the love seat, "You got dat bread for me?" Cortez asked ripping the wrapper off the cigars.

Po' went back to the bedroom once more. He returned with two white envelopes and handed them to Cortez. Cortez took the stack of money out of one envelope, combining it with the other. He laid the envelope on his lap while placing the cigar tobacco inside.

"Dis the amount we agreed on?" Cortez asked.

"Yeah nigga! Cuzz, I don't play no games!" Po' snapped.

"Look mane, I just asked. All dat other shit obsolete," Cortez responded pulling a quarter ounce of purp from his pocket. "I'm tryna get some understandin'. What I wanna know, is ya able to get off dis work!"

"Cuzz, we gotta go thru dis shit again? What I told cha! One or two days, it's outta here. Money good. Bricks, I'll grind rock for rock. Day and a half! Nigga my trap's be doin' the watusi!"

"What about five?" Cortez asked, exhaling marijuana smoke. "Four hard. One soft."

"Where they at?"

"Just be cool, I gotcha. The numbers the same off each one. How fast ya get 'em off, determines how many ya get the next time."

"Ooh— my nigga done gotta major plug! Let's get it!"

"Don't misinterpret what I'm sayin'."

"What?"

"Don't try to get off 'em so fast, ya fuck 'round and get jammed 'cause ya ain't thankin' straight," Cortez told him. "Keep a level head and we'll put the whole city on smash. Feel me? Not bein' too flashy, but livin' life like we supposed to."

"I'mma handle me," Po' assured him passing the blunt.

"I know when niggaz start gettin' money, they'll start doin' outrageous shit, that'll attract the wrong kinda attention. I know ya a hustla. Why ya thank I'm fuckin' wit' cha? I just don't wanna fuck dis up!"

"My nigga, I gotcha!"

They finished smoking the blunt. Also came to an understanding, so Cortez eased out to his car and popped the trunk. Newtown has forever been a hot spot. The main reason he pretended to smoke a cigarette was to observe the surroundings for anything, out of the ordinary. Cortez flicked the cigarette and then got the work out of his duffel bag. He went back inside and sat the bricks on the coffee table. Again, Cortez reiterated his expectations, before leaving Po' to himself.

Cortez's main objective for the upcoming months was to accumulate supreme clientele. Understanding the worth, he thought it'll be more logical, not to mention a lot easier to distribute by forming a credible organization. He intended to expand on each side of the city, followed by the surrounding counties and cities that'd potentially get supplied.

He'll deal with most out-of-towners directly, for now, to build a rapport. As long as each member does their part, the pay-off would be rewarding. Cortez parked in front of a dilapidated duplex and popped his trunk to mix another drink. Kelt sat on the steps of the front porch strolling through Facebook.

"What cha sippin' on?" Kelt asked.

"A lil' Belve and pineapple juice," Cortez told him.

"Shid. Pour me up one."

Cortez took another sip and then handed over the Styrofoam cup, "Dis the last of it. You can have it, I'm good."

"Bwoy ya got dis mixed just right, too," Kelt told him.

"Ain't no doubt!" Cortez replied. "Everythang straight though?"

"Oh yeah! Come on in," Kelt told him headed inside.

Kelt locked the burglary bars door and then showed Cortez to the kitchen. When Kelt returned, he had bundles of money in hand. It was six separate bundles with rubber bands around them, $5k apiece. He sat the money on the tarnished countertop, in front of Cortez.

"Count it," Kelt told him.

"I'mma count it. I'm really on a mission right now, but you better believe I'mma count it," Cortez assured him. "I told cha gimme a coupla days, and I'll be back. I'm straight! Ya ready for a coupla thangs?"

"Hell yeah!"

"Can you grind 'em?"

"Cut it out!" Kelt disgustedly stated. "Cuzz, this West Side generates so much muthafuckin' guap, nigga it's ridiculous!"

"Can you handle five of 'em? Four hard, and one soft."

"Mane— let's do dis!"

"Come on," Cortez gestured to follow him, as he put the money in his front pockets.

They went back to the Jaguar, where Cortez went inside the console to retrieve a cigarette and popped the trunk. Cortez instructed Kelt to remove the duffel bag and take it inside the trap house. He was leaning against the car smoking a cigarette, when Kelt returned, placing the bag next to Cortez's foot. Cortez flicked the rest of the cigarette as he started laying down rules.

Like the things, he'd mentioned to Po', about the unnecessary attention. Cortez wanted the crew to be sure of whom they dealt with. Also, keep in mind the significance of this golden opportunity. He emphasized keeping their mouths closed. And last but not least, having his money in full!

****

Around dusk, Cortez had just made his way to Spring Park. He used the entrance off McInnis Road, by Walter T. McKee Middle School abruptly made a right in the dead end. Cortez immediately turned off the headlights, as he eased alongside the curb in front of his destination. He knew she made it home when he saw her silver Chrysler 300 C in the driveway.

Cortez got out of his car and strolled up the driveway. He observed the darkness of the house except for the dim-lit lamp in the living room window. He rang the doorbell, and a few seconds later the varnished oak wood door opened. Precious stood in the doorway with her hands on her hips, staring at Cortez through the glass storm door.

She tried to look menacing, but her seductiveness outweighed it. They gazed into each other's eyes a moment before Precious unlocked the door and walked away.

"Hey Precious!" Cortez exclaimed locking the doors behind him. "Expectin' somebody?"

Precious began lightening the living room and responded, "Yeah! You better go, before he gets here."

"Lemme jet den," Cortez replied turning towards the door. "Hate I wasted my time tryna come see ya!"

"Nigga sit yo' azz down and stop playin' wit' me, Cortez! I must be expectin' somebody. Yeah! For the past week or so. I'm shocked to see ya here, now, for real," she explained.

Cortez flashed that million-dollar smile, and tightly held her well-put-together frame. As he towered over her, Cortez looked her in the eyes and said, "I told cha shawty, I've really been busy. And I just got back in town. Sorry, but I gotta eat boo. Shit ain't gonna pay for itself."

"I know," she agreed.

"I'm here now! Let's enjoy dis time we have together, now!"

Cortez gripped her hand, and stood back off of her to thoroughly inspect the violet-purple Victoria's Secret nightgown she stood there glowing in.

"I was in the bed and had to use the bathroom. I looked out the window and saw your car. I'm about to go get back in it. Dem muthafuckaz worked the shit outta me today," Precious admitted.

"Go 'head baby, I'm comin'."

Precious swayed her bow hips as she pranced down the hallway. Cortez went to the kitchen and fixed a glass of orange juice, then he accompanied Precious in the bedroom. She's underneath the covers watching the Flava Of Love with her head propped up on a pillow, supported by the headboard.

Cortez removed his shirt and threw it on the rose-colored, Queen Ann chair sitting catty-cornered next to the bed. Cortez removed a cigarillo from his shorts pocket. He started busting the cigar down with his teeth sitting at the foot of the bed

"That's some reggo?" Precious asked eyes still locked on the television.

"Naw boo. Dis strong," he answered laying his shorts across the chair. "Wanna hit it?"

"Yeah."

"You smokin'!" he asked in disbelief.

"I'm kinda tense, shit," she coyly replied.

Cortez sparked the blunt before he joined her underneath the covers. They engaged in small talk, passing the blunt back and forth. After the marijuana was consumed, Cortez took another sip of juice, and placed the glass back on the nightstand. Cortez propped his pillow up against the headboard, too.

Precious scooted closer to him, burying her head in his chest, "I'm glad you came by," she confessed. "I needed to be comforted tonight."

Cortez sensed the marijuana began to take effect. He remained silent watching tv.

"Nigga you know you got me," Precious admitted. "That's why you do what you do. That shit turns me on. But, lemme ask you something?"

Still, he remained silent.

"What made you stop by here tonight? You ain't have no pussy lined up nowhere else?" she asked, and immediately nudged him for an answer.

"Like I told cha for the umpteenth time I been makin' moves. Dats why I ain't been 'round. Shits time consumin'! I got the chance to spend some time wit' cha, so I came thru. You done got blowed, now ya wanna trip and shit. I came to chill. Don't get the wrong impression. We ain't gotta have sex."

Precious raised up to look him in the eyes. She gave him a soft kiss on the lips, followed by a sequence of kisses on his chest and stomach. Deadlocked eye contact, she pulled down his DSquare boxer briefs. Precious planted a fervent kiss on his limped manhood, as gently as she kissed his lips. Cortez instantly became aroused.

"Don't take this the wrong way," Precious stated.

"Never," he replied.

Without hesitation, she wrapped her full lips around his tool maneuvering up and down, with precision. Cortez threw the covers back to witness what was making him feel so satisfied. He pulled her around and slid her thong to the side before he sunk his middle finger into an already moistened love passage. The more he rubbed her clit, the more outrageous she worked his pole.

Coming up for air, Precious removed a Magnum from the nightstand drawer. She's obviously in dire need of some good loving. Precious assumed the doggy-style position and braced her hands atop the headboard. Cortez eased in behind her and slowly inserted his manhood. The heat of her tight womb penetrated through the condom.

Slowly, but forcefully thrusting inside her, Cortez turned Precious over unto her back. He stood flat-footed before he commenced grinding inside her. Almost at his apex, he held her legs overhead using the mattress as leverage, to plunge up and down in her, until they reached ecstasy.

Chapter 5

■■■■

After Cortez awoke from the episode last night, the top priority today was to meet with Melissa, and discuss a few more ideas that bombarded his brain. He thought these ideas could be sound investments if properly executed.

Cortez took a quick shower. He sprayed on a few squirts of Curve, before getting dressed. Clad in a solid forest green Lacoste polo shirt, madras plaid shorts by the same designer, and a pair of white and green Nike Shox, he placed on some jewelry. He then checked himself out in a full-length mirror, on the closet door before starting the day.

Melissa agreed to meet him at Sommer's Place located on Vaughn Rd. First, Cortez stopped by Stone Crossing and paid six months' rent on Boonk's old apartment, because he decided to continue using it as a hub. He convinced the property manager that Boonk will be out of town for a few months, and he'll be attending to the apartment.

Cortez gave her $1k, along with his number if any problems arise. Also, if she noticed anyone besides himself snooping around the property, give him a call first and then notify the authorities. Navigating to the restaurant, Cortez smoked the remainder of the blunt he ducked earlier in the ashtray. This helped reduce tension and mentally relaxed him.

He pulled into the parking lot looking for Melissa's black Lincoln Navigator. Cortez parked on the side of the restaurant. He squirted Cherry flavored Blunt Power in his hands and rubbed them together, before wiping himself down. Exiting the car he casually walked to the entrance of the restaurant.

"Good afternoon! Welcome to Sommer's Place," a hostess greeted. "Table for one? The bar?"

"Naw. I'm expectin' someone else, but she hadn't made it yet. Can I get a table for two? By a window."

"Sure! Follow me."

The hostess guided Cortez to a table that was available with a front view of the restaurant. After he was seated, a young, energetic waitress approached, "Hi. My name is Taylor. I'll be your server today," she greeted. "Today's special's are Soup of the day, Chicken & Gnocchi. Entrees are chicken scallopini and our Alfredo chicken…"

Before she could finish explaining Cortez intervened, "You can just bring me a double shot of Belvedere, while I wait on my friend."

"Sure," she replied. Cortez phoned Melissa.

"I'm on the way, Cortez. I'm turning on the Vaughn Rd. now," Melissa told him.

"Cool. See ya when ya get here."

Cortez ordered another drink to sip as he awaited Melissa's arrival. Within ten minutes, Melissa was being escorted to the table. Cortez stood to hug her and removed her chair from underneath the table.

"People are so use to me eating lunch at the office. A client came in at the last minute and I needed to take care of him," Melissa apologetically explained.

"No problem! Ya good Mel," he assured her.

"It's been so— long since I had someone invite me to lunch. What did I do to receive this?"

"Come on Mel! You know how we get down. Everybody shine on my team! Plus, I wanted to take some time to explain the direction I wanna pursue," Cortez mentioned before taking a sip of his drink. "Ya know how far we go back. You're highly trustworthy, and rub elbows daily wit' some rather prestigious white folks in dis city. I'm interested in alotta thangs, and you know who's connected. The first thang I need to do, is, get a few homes; properties. Are you familiar with the real-estate game?"

"Somewhat. I have a few associates with Aronov Realty and ReMax..." she answered.

"Really!"

"I can make a few calls. What are you interested in, though?"

"Some starter homes, three bedrooms, two baths. Somethin' nice— I can flip quick, for a profit or possibly rent out. Duplexes, multi-unit, commercial properties... Anythang dat makes sense."

"Okay," she replied.

The waitress returned and introduced herself to Melissa, then asked were they ready to order. After placing their orders, they continued their conversation.

"I'll get a list for delinquent properties and foreclosed properties from my bank," Melissa informed Cortez as she instructed him where to sign the forms to legitimize his businesses. "Honestly, that'll be a sound investment. Owning property automatically gives you a bit of leverage."

"Mel dats just the tip of the iceberg. I got so many ideas to bring to dis city, dats gonna generate big money. Watch!" he assured her.

The waitress returned with their orders. They continued to converse about various possible business opportunities. Plus, bringing each other up to speed on where they were in their lives. Melissa sat there fascinated while Cortez strategized about future enterprises. What had her captivated was his savvy for business. She recognized it was immersed in him long before the conversation.

Melissa was so happy to be a part of this transition. They chatted briefly a little longer after Cortez paid the check before they dispersed. Afterward, he cruised the city looking for a fairly large venue to host concerts, and sizable events. Ideas were running rampant through his mind. All of them he thought could become lucrative, of course.

Cortez saw this as a grand opportunity to change his family's financial status, forever. Since the short duration of time in Orlando, he noticed how readily available large sums of money had become. Cortez figured with the money coming at such a fast pace, he was going to need larger legitimate establishments. Businesses that'll confirm how his money was being earned.

Cortez spent the last three hours hunting for a building big enough to hold 10-15k guests, to no avail. By happenstance, he came across some acres for sale off Fleming Road. Instantly, Cortez decided this location would be perfect for what he had in mind. He dialed the number on the signposted alongside the road into his cell phone, saving it. It'll be accessible once he's ready to follow up on this deal.

Cortez stood there a little longer, in a daze. Envisioning what he thought may bring more excitement to the Capital City. The sound of a passing motorist snapped him out of the trance.

****

"Leave the heat?" Bug asked Cortez about the pistol he held.

"Naw. And if one of dese country bwoys get stupid, ya better give 'em the bizness," Cortez informed him before they exited the truck.

They were the center of attention even before getting out of the truck. Residents were unfamiliar with the truck, not to mention, it's a guaranteed eye-catcher that had everyone curious. Marcus told Cortez to meet him in Mosses Projects that evening. Because that's where Marcus sponsored a block party for the community. They had four monstrous cast iron deep fryers that were cooking fish and chicken wings, plus fries, and hush puppies.

There were tables with varieties of liquors. A few kegs of draft beer, along with four plastic trash cans of imported beers, on ice. There's a slew of beautiful, scantily clad women, dancing to the latest jams the D.J. played. Cortez and Bug stood next to the truck.

Several sets of eyes watched them before Marcus appeared out of nowhere, "Glad cha made it," Marcus said.

"Look like we in the right spot too," Cortez told him. "Dis my lil' nigga Bug right here."

Marcus and Bug slapped hands. The residents paid more attention to them than Marcus, and he was hosting the block party. They were unfamiliar faces. Off the top, Marcus assured them there was no need to be alarmed. They're among some thorough people, "Come on. Let's get inside," Marcus suggested.

Marcus took them into a unit on the end next to the softball field where the festivities were being held. An instant sense of gratification overwhelmed them, as they entered the apartment. They entered the crowded living room and were bombarded by the smell of marijuana, combined with loud women chattering, getting high, and eagerly seeking enjoyment.

"Hey!" the women shouted in unison.

Cortez waved his hand to the women simultaneously scanning the room. They're watching a Boosie Bad Azz DVD on a 55" Sony Bravado flat screen. Marcus grabbed a glass bowl, containing a plethora of double and triple stack ex-pills, "Here Cuzz," he said, handing Cortez the bowl.

Cortez rummaged through the bowl in search of some blue dolphins. He ate two double stacks, then passed the bowl over to Bug. Bug downed three double stacks.

"Y'all bitches get up and let my peoples sit down!" Marcus commanded two women who occupied the loveseat. "Sharon fix 'em a plate."

"What's your name?" Sharon asked Cortez.

"Cortez," he answered.

"You used to kick it wit' my girl Kesa," she affirmed.

"Cuzz smoke one," Marcus told Cortez.

Marcus didn't have to tell him twice. Cortez really forgot about how much fun one could have down in these neck of the woods. Good food, fine liquor, great music, party favorites, and to top it off was the number of southern belles in attendance. *Now dis therapeutic. Gettin' away from the Gumptown, ducked off.*

The hiatus from visiting his relatives left him clueless about the influence Marcus now possessed. Although, he had knowledge of Marcus being in the game,Cortez didn't realize until this moment how he would overflow these rural counties with narcotics. The way Cortez and Bug were mingling, a person would think this was their stomping grounds for a lifetime.

The connecting link between them was merely the heavy consumption of alcohol, pills, and blunts of purp. The hospitality Marcus showed these two strangers from Montgomery, left the women intrigued. Bug rearranged the seating order. Cortez entertained a thick red one, who sat in his lap grinding. Of course, she intended to be seductive. Bug was on the sofa draped in between four women. He was nursing a Heineken and instigated as much humor as Cortez.

Marcus never intervened. He let them get acquainted, staking their claim. It was dusk, and the block party still was pumping just as much as it was when they arrived. Marcus and Cortez stepped out on the front porch. Cortez and Marcus's other first cousin, Adolph approached, "Yo', I'm finna start windin' dis thang down. Cool?" Adolph asked.

"Handle you," Marcus replied. "I'll be back in a minute."

Marcus motioned for Cortez to follow him. Cortez jogged back to his truck to retrieve a gym bag before they walked up the street. Cortez handed Marcus the bag containing three kilos of powder cocaine, and two hard. Also, he gave Marcus his expectations of fronting this work. Marcus' intentions were to show his cousin firsthand; this was his domain. If Cortez kept the supply of cocaine flowing, Lowndes County and surrounding areas would be a honey hole.

Sheriff Williams would get his piece of the pie for allowing the activity. Everyone else affiliated would live lavishly. It's not a high-risk situation like Montgomery, because when the task force does decide on their covert operation, they'll notify Sheriff Williams, and he'll alert everyone else. It's what Marcus considered a stacked deck.

"Who is it?" a female asked from a bedroom window.

"Me baby. Come open the door," Marcus replied.

The sound of latches being unlocked were heard before the door opened. Marcus opened the screen door and entered the unit. Cortez automatically began scrutinizing the well-furnished apartment. *Dis bitch plushed out, like Cuzz stayin' in dis muthafucka.*

"I'mma see if you remember her," Marcus told Cortez, as they stood in the well-lit kitchen. "Baby come here!"

The woman made her way up the dim hallway. Cortez could only make out the silhouette of a woman, with a curvaceous body. She called Cortez's name before he got a glimpse of her face. She revealed her identity in the kitchen. She modestly stood there in a Luxirie t-shirt and shorts set, displaying her perfectly toned legs.

"Megan," Cortez uttered. "Girl gimme a hug! Fuck—I ain't seen you… How ya been doing?"

"I'm good man. You remembered me?" Megan asked in disbelief.

"Girl please! Ya look just like—" Cortez momentarily paused. "Sophie. Where is Sophie?"

"She stay in Montgomery," Megan answered.

"For real? She probably forgot about me by now."

"Cortez, you was my sister first love! You know she ain't forgot about you."

Sophia was Cortez's first real girlfriend. They met after Charlie, Sophia's father, a Vietnam Vet moved back to his hometown. He intended to raise his two girls properly after his wife's death from breast cancer. Charlie returned to Lowndes County, so his girls would have respectable female role models to emulate, such as his mother, aunts, and sisters.

The girl's mother is a native of Paske, Laos. Automatically, they were the center of attention upon their arrival in Lowndes County. Their Loation descent, combined with unique beauty made them highly conspicuous. Cortez frequently visited his grandparents. The two met and quickly became tight knitted. When he was home in Montgomery, the telephone was their means of communication.

Also, they shared something most girls considered sacred. Sophia lost her virginity to Cortez. As time progressed after Cortez's granddaddy died, he was introduced to the streets, and they gradually grew apart.

"Y'all been together all dese years?" Cortez asked Megan as Marcus took the bag to the back room.

"Yeah, but this nigga don't wanna act right!" Megan proclaimed. "He'll rather be wit' these sack chasin' azz hoes, than me Cortez. So, I'mma let him be."

Marcus shook his head returning to the kitchen, ignoring her previous statement.

"Hey Megan. I don't know nothin' 'bout all dat right. How's Sophie doin' though?" Cortez asked shifting the heat off of his cousin.

"She alright. She's a Pediatric Nurse at Baptist East. She been working there maybe a year and a half now. Sophie doing good."

"Dats what's up. Tell my baby I asked 'bout her. What up wit' you though?" Cortez asked.

"Shit! A shopaholic," Marcus blurted out.

"Dats wifey Cuzz," Cortez proclaimed.

"That's right bro-law. Tell him again," Megan replied.

"Cuzz let's go back 'round here, so I can wrap dis shit up," Marcus told him. "Baby I'll be back."

"Uh huh."

"Megan it was good seein' ya again. Don't forget to tell Sophie I asked 'bout her too," Cortez said hugging Megan once more.

****

Cortez followed Marcus back to Auntie Betty's house to put something on their stomachs, after a wild night of partying and adult fun.

"Cuzz y'all must want me to move down here? I ain't balled like dat in a minute!" Bug admitted.

"For real mane, I really had forgot how they do it down here! Dis bitch used to jump every weekend! I needed to get away from dat madness in the Gump anyway. Even if it's only for one night." Cortez responded.

Bug was under the impression Marcus had informed Auntie Betty to be expecting company for breakfast, from the meal that's been prepared. Cortez explained to Bug that's how she cooked. There were grits, cheese eggs, Conecuh sausage, patty sausage, homemade buttermilk biscuits, orange juice, and coffee... Auntie Betty made the guys wash their hands before taking a seat at her dining table.

Erica's assistance was futile, although it was appreciated. Auntie Betty fixed the plates, while Erica took them to the dining room. The purp helped the guy's appetites in devouring the food. Not to mention, helped them ignore the constant accusations Erica repeatedly blurted out. Cortez could no longer conceal his menacing stare. Plus, his disgust for the useless conversations she chose to indulge in Auntie Betty's presence.

Surely, he's not trying to play on anyone's intelligence. Cortez understood his Auntie knew the activities he and Marcus partook in weren't legitimate. Also, she understood that she and Mary did the best they possibly could in raising their children. She could talk until she was blue in the face, still neither would stop due to her disapproval, only when they're ready or coerced to.

The guys left Bug with the women. They stepped into the backyard to discuss business. Marcus was unsure about exactly how many kilos Cortez could produce. Although, he had a hunch that his older cousin was connected with some major players. Out of respect for Cortez, and the game itself, Marcus refrained from probing about his affairs.

He only made suggestions on how they could financially gain. Cortez intently listened. Cortez wanted to get an idea of where Marcus's mind was. For a lot of the subject matter Marcus touched on, Cortez had already prepared ways to strengthen those areas. Cortez smoked a cigarette, gazing across the land, where he spotted an old school Cutlass next to his Auntie's property. He slowly walked over to where an elderly woman was hanging out clothes.

"'Cuse me ma'am," Cortez politely greeted the woman, not wanting to alarm her. "I was wonderin' do you or your husband wanna sell dat car?"

Mrs. Rudolph finished pinning her last garments before she turned to look at the car. She stared at the car a moment, then turned back toward Cortez, "Dat was my husband's car. He loved dat car. He passed almost eight years ago, and dat car hasn't moved," she told him reminiscing. "Hold on."

She grabbed her clothes basket and went inside for the keys. Marcus and Bug walked up, as Cortez patiently awaited her return, "What up?" Marcus curiously asked.

"Tryna knock off dis Cuddy," Cortez told him inspecting the car.

"Oh. Dat was Mr. Rudolph car. He passed away awhile back. That car been sittin' up for a minute," Marcus stated.

"Yeah. Dats what she said," Cortez replied.

Mrs. Rudolph returned with the keys in hand, "How ya doin' Mrs. Rudolph?" Marcus asked.

"Hey Marcus! You alright this mornin'?"

"Yes ma'am," Marcus responded.

"Marcus go get dat battery outta the utility house," she said, then handed Cortez the car key. "See if it'll crank up."

Cortez unlocked the door and got inside. He inspected the interior simultaneously putting the key into the ignition. The interior would be reupholstered once it's under his ownership, so that's obsolete. Cortez patted the gas a few times before turning it over. The car stalled once and the second time, too.

Marcus dismantled the carburetor to make sure the gas was passing through the gas line. Also, he switched out the battery, "Try it now!" Marcus shouted.

The car stuttered a few times before starting up. Cortez idled it up several times, before joining them in front of the car.

"It still works," Mrs. Rudolph stated.

"Yeah—. First, I'd like to say I'm sorry about your husband again," Cortez sincerely told her. "But Mrs. Rudolph, ain't no need for the car to just be sittin' up. A `72 Cutlass 442! Dis baby supposed to be on the road!"

"You ready to go to work on her?" Bug eagerly asked.

"Ain't no doubt!" Cortez answered.

"Will ya take care of it?" Mrs. Rudolph asked Cortez.

"Absolutely! Yes ma'am!" Cortez responded. "How much you want for it?"

"Since you so eager. And I think you'll take good care of it. I've held on to it long enough. Gimme $1500," she said.

Cortez unhesitatingly counted out the money. Mrs. Rudolph went inside the house again to get the title and draw up a bill of sale. Meanwhile, they thoroughly looked the vehicle over and weren't concerned about the few rust spots or any other blemishes. Cortez planned to fully customize it before the car even took to the road.

Chapter 6

■■■■

At home Cortez got his money's worth out of a newly purchased hands-free money machine, he separated his share from his partners down in Orange County. The truth of the matter is he's surprised by how much money they've accumulated. Especially in the duration of time, he's been back in town. Cortez was elated that everything was going as anticipated.

Everyone accepted their roles and was satisfied with the compensation for their services. As long as no one got greedy, they would be way ahead of the game in no time. Cortez sat in his living room putting rubber bands around the stacks of money. Melissa called to inform him that an associate from Aronov Realty located five delinquent and foreclosed properties.

These homes were in the Cross Creek, and Spring Valley communities. Three of them had asking prices between $50k-$60k, and the other two were around $20-$35k. Melissa suggested letting her check out the market value first. Because she could possibly convince the property owner's to take less. She wanted to do a little more research, in case there were clouds on titles…. Her job was to help him profit, not inherit someone else's debt.

Cortez configured the initial $1.5 million he projected making if he hadn't hired help. Which he was content with. Because the family's $1 million has been cleared, and he now stared at $700k, to the good. The most money he'd ever had in his entire life, at once. There were a few hundred thousand that needed to be collected, but at this point, Cortez was excited and extremely confident about the future.

He neatly stacked his partner's cash in their duffel bags for Big John to pick up. Cortez placed his portion in a separate Louis Vuitton bag, all except $120k, which he intended to drop off to Melissa in the morning, before leaving town.

****

Cortez called Lil' Derek coming through the terminal. He informed Lil' Derek that he'd just touched down. It's around three o'clock p.m. when he finally made it out front of the airport. When Cortez exited the airport Lil' Derek was leaning against a matte black '07 Corvette, with a red rally stripe sitting on 22" Forgiato Andata.

"What's the bizness? How was ya flight?" Lil' Derek asked him.

"Everythang good," Cortez replied.

"The game been good, ain't it?" Lil' Derek mockingly asked. "Ya shinin' nigga! I know money when I see it! Nigga ya smellin' like money! The cologne!"

Trying not to show his pearly whites, Cortez smiled.

"Now ya see what I been tellin' ya manifest right before yo' eyes. And ya lovin' it! Ain't cha?" Lil' Derek asked switching lanes.

"Nigga dis bread so— plentiful, it's scary!" Cortez exclaimed. "And everybody good. Long as everybody eatin', shit should keep flowin' smoove. Ya dig!"

"I hear ya. Just don't get too relaxed, 'cause unexpected shit happens. Niggaz get jammed and fold like bad poker hands. They'll rat on everybody and everythang, they can remember. Always remember dat!" Lil' Derek reminded him. "Muthafuckaz greedy. Forgettin' who put 'em in positions to get paper. So, like I said don't get too comfortable."

Cortez listened to the advice he'd just received and tried to decide if it was directed at him or was for general purposes. "Gotcha Cuzz," Cortez responded as they topped the driveway to the mansion. "You been back to Cleo's since I been gone?"

"You wanna know 'bout Wanda. I still ain't fucked her."

"Nigga, I ain't thankin' 'bout dat broad."

Lil' Derek uncontrollably laughed. He escorted Cortez to the study, where Ron was reclined in a burgundy executive chair, behind a wood office desk.

"Pop dis nigga in love with a stripper. The first thang he asked 'bout was Cleo's," Lil' Derek playfully teased.

"Ron what's happenin'? You aight?" Cortez asked. "'Cause Lil' Derek trippin'."

"Life's good, Cortez. I can't complain. It ain't gonna do no good, no way," Ron replied. "See you're back already! So I'm assumin' everything's marvelous on your behalf too."

"I couldn't have said it no better, Unc."

"That's what I like to hear." Ron said.

"Excuse me, Mr. Means," an attractive maid intervened. "Niguel's out front with the car to take you to your meeting, sir."

"Thank you, Candice," Ron replied then he stood up from the chair.

"I wanted to run somethin' past ya, but I'll catch cha later," Cortez informed Ron.

"Go 'head and speak," Ron retorted.

"I gotta bizness proposal."

"Okay."

"I'm lookin' to brang some excitement to Montgomery. A spot to host parties, special events, and mainly concerts. Also, dis spot would clean some of dis money, too. 'Cause pretty soon, it's gonna be hard to go undetected at the rate dis money comin'."

Ron burst into laughter.

"What dat, Unc?" Cortez asked intrigued.

"Money comin' pretty fast, huh? Carry on," Ron told him.

"Serious though. I need a partner to go in wit' me. I've already found some land that'll be perfect for what I got in store."

"Sounds interestin'. I tell ya what, lemme give it some thought, and you can call later wit' all the details. Then I'll let ya know if I'm interested or not. Fair enough?"

"Cool."

"Alright," Ron said leaving the study room.

"You thank ya ready to get off into somethin' like dat?" Lil' Derek asked Cortez.

"Cuzz, I'mma all around hustla. Fuck yeah, I'm ready! Better question, is the Gumptown ready?"

"Why you ain't come to me wit' it?" Lil' Derek inquired.

"You ain't off into shit like dis."

Lil' Derek stared at Cortez in disbelief, insulted by his statement, "Bwoy I love it when they underestimate me," Lil' Derek uttered.

Lil' Derek expressed his disdain for being deemed incompetent of operating a business. He and Cortez jumped back in the Corvette and were off for a night on the town. Lil' Derek promised him everywhere they go, he won't have to spend a dime and guaranteed he'd enjoy himself. The first place they went to was a soul food restaurant, called Lucy's.

Lil' Derek advised Cortez to eat something to coat his stomach. Lil' Derek led the way to the back of the eatery and selected a table. A big-boned woman named Keisha, who was acquainted with Lil' Derek, quickly approached them. They exchanged hugs after greeting one another. She started to place menus on the table, but before they were out of her hand good, she picked them back up.

Lil' Derek simply instructed Keisha to bring some of the restaurant's finest cuisine. He wanted to show Cortez why Lucy's the best soul food joint in Orlando, hands down. Keisha and a coworker did just as Cortez requested. They brought out fried chicken, fried fish, oxtails, curry goat, cornbread muffins, steamed cabbage, mac and cheese, creamed corn, and a pitcher of homemade lemonade to wash it down.

The women stood there momentarily watching in sheer delight, as the guys grubbed. The guys were stuffed. Although they couldn't begin to eat all the food. When the women returned, they stood there waiting for an indication of how good the food tasted. Cortez was so full, he couldn't even find the words to describe how good the food was. So, he simply gave two thumbs up, like The Fonz.

Lil' Derek drove in a parking lot where only the exclusive vehicles were located. He maneuvered his way up to the valet parking rope. Big Dave, head of security recognized the Corvette and hurriedly unlatched the rope, so Lil' Derek could park. "What it lookin' like?" Lil' Derek asked Big Dave exiting the car.

"It's pumpin', but it's still early," Big Dave told him.

Lil' Derek led the way to the front of the club. Bending the corner, Cortez witnessed a vast array of lights, people, and cars alongside the strip who anticipated getting inside.

"What's the name of dis club?" Cortez asked captivated by the crowd.

"Firestone!" Lil' Derek emphatically answered. "The hottest nightspot in Orlando!"

"Lil' Derek. What's good baby?" Crown asked when they approached the entrance.

"Slow motion, nigga," Lil' Derek replied, then asked. "How's it lookin' inside?"

"Probably another hunnid fifty guests before we maxed out," Crown told him.

"Okay. Dis my man right here. He came down to have a good time," Lil' Derek said pointing to Cortez.

Cortez and Crown, the muscle-bound doorman, gave each other pounds. Lil' Derek lured him away from the overcrowded entrance. Lil' Derek came up with a cigarette and offered Cortez one. He's still infuriated by the fact that Cortez thought he was incapable of owning something legitimate. That thought has been festering throughout the night. Still, Lil' Derek made certain Cortez had a blast before forcing him to recant his presumption.

Lil' Derek flicked the remainder of the cigarette and entered the club. They entered untouched. Lil' Derek simply gestured with a nod, indicating the guy closely following was with him. As soon as they passed the admissions booth, Lil' Derek captured the attention of some club's occupants. He didn't exchange many words, just gave a few pounds and gentle hugs to the women.

D.J. Pro Styles mixed the music with a variety of the summer's hottest hits. D.J. Pro Styles automatically gave Lil' Derek a shout out, once they hit the door. Lil' Derek chunked the deuces, as he continued making his rounds. He wasn't saying much to anyone because he wanted the vibrant energy to ooze out, and swallow Cortez whole.

Lil' Derek managed to avoid the individuals who wanted to occupy his time with idle chatter. He went upstairs to the V.I.P. section and gave D.J. Pro Styles a pound when he topped the stairs. A considerable amount of people were partying, and mingling. The three bartenders made certain no one went unattended.

V.I.P. happened to be star-studded tonight. A few Orlando Magic players, a couple relevant R and B singers, along with some rappers. Lil' Derek went over to the long, maroon couch, where Juvenile and his entourage was lounging. Juvenile's scheduled to perform, and Lil' Derek wanted to make sure he was getting the royal treatment. Juvenile introduced himself, as did Lil' Derek before he expressed everyone's expecting a stellar performance.

Pumped up by the brief meeting between the two, Cortez couldn't quite make out what was discussed, due to the loud music. With a bottle of bubbly in hand, Lil' Derek headed down a narrow hallway to his office. The office was guarded by Big Chief, another member of security. Lil' Derek punched in an eight-digit access code then closed the door behind them.

"Have a seat," he told Cortez.

"Dawg dis yo' shit?" Cortez bluntly asked.

"Yeah, nigga!" Lil' Derek arrogantly replied.

"The soul food joint?"

"Mine— too!"

Lil' Derek popped a bottle of Louis the XIII and poured up two glasses. He handed a glass to Cortez. He grasped the other one as he reclined in a black swivel chair, and kicked his feet up on the desk, "Made cha eat dem words," he told Cortez. "Cuzz, ya think I'm out here bullshittin'? Naw nigga! I make moves! Flexin' is for show. To attract dese niggaz and bitches. I just look like dis."

Cortez sat speechless. His perception of Lil' Derek was the same as the majority all the other hustlers he'd encountered. Mostly arrogant, ego maniacs, influenced by the fact that they have money, but have no viable idea of what do with it, now that they have it. They've worked so long and hard to get money, just to lose it in a matter of minutes. Intrigued by this shocking revelation, Cortez sincerely apologized for his misconceptions.

"I learned at an early age, not to put much expectations on muthafuckaz, and to never underestimate the next man. Pop instilled that in me early," Lil' Derek told him.

"True!"

"Now 'bout the proposal you ran 'cross Pop earlier. He's gonna tell me to lace ya up anyway. Truth is Cuzz, you don't need no nigga. You can handle dat by yo' self. I respect where yo' mind at. Ya way ahead of the game, where ya tryna to go," Lil' Derek explained.

"Gotta have other avenues. I'm tryna beat dese crackaz, without any major sacrifices."

"Facts! We was tryna get Boonk off into somethin' legit, but Cuzz was more concern wit' the glamour part of the game," Lil' Derek admitted. "You got the right idea, though. I'll guide cha thru it, where necessary. Cuzz, I'm always here for dat. You can handle dis on your own though. I know dat! We'll chop it up later. Right now! Let's blow big and check out dis show."

Lil' Derek invaded the D.J. booth, and D.J. Pro Styles shut the music off, handing Lil' Derek the mic. Mic in one hand, glass of champagne in the other, Lil' Derek addressed the crowd, "Hey mane! I'd like to thank everybody for comin' out tonight! Hopefully, everybody enjoyin' themselves, so far. Comin' from New Orleans! Here to spread some of dat Louisiana love! Give it up, for my nigga, Juve!"

Juvenile opened the set with Balla Blockin'. He then randomly ran through his catalogue, according to the reaction of the crowd. He performed a little over an hour before he and his entourage returned to V.I.P. Lil' Derek and Cortez accompanied them in the middle of several groupies running amuck.

****

Cortez was comatose the majority of the morning. As he set on the side of the king-size bed, it began to dawn on him where he stayed last night. Cortez was in a guest room at Lil' Derek's home. He got dressed, then sluggishly descended the stairs. Hearing the laughter of a few people, he opted to follow the sound.

"Hi, you finally got up?" Kim asked sitting at the dining table with the kids. "Derek had to run a few errands."

"Okay," Cortez grumbled trying to perk up.

"Have a seat. Lemme fix ya something to eat," she said.

Cortez introduced himself to Lil' Derek's kids when he sat down. Unfamiliar with Cortez, they bashfully told him their names. He looked at both of them, amazed by the eldest one, Tia's facial features. She's a spitting the image of her father.

"Here you go," Kim said placing a plate and glass of orange juice on the table.

"How long Lil' Derek been gone?" he asked her.

"About an hour or so. He called a few minutes ago and asked had you gotten up. He'll be back shortly."

Cortez devoured his breakfast while talking with Kim and the children, awaiting Lil' Derek's return. Kim offered seconds before she left to go groom her kids. Cortez was picking over the food when Lil' Derek walked into the kitchen. Lil' Derek greeted Cortez and informed him he had to attend to something urgent. Lil' Derek got a bottled water from the refrigerator before leading Cortez to the west wing of the 7,500-square-foot mansion.

They entered another huge room with impeccable wooden floors. The walls were filled with customized portraits of some world-renowned icons. Such as Miles Davis, Angela Davis, and Marcus Garvey… A full-size bar sat to the left of the room. There were two 55"flatscreens, and a Brunswick Billiard professional pool table embellishing the center of the room.

"You gotta decent stick?" Lil' Derek inquired racking the balls.

"I got a helluva stick!" Cortez retorted.

Lil' Derek pointed to a bundle of cue sticks in the corner, "Yo' break," Lil' Derek told him, then sat on a barstool.

"Dis yo' spot. You break," Cortez replied.

"Cuzz. Ya might don't get a shot."

The beginning of the match was competitive for them, back and forwards. After the fifth game, the competitiveness slowly diminished and Lil' Derek took the opportunity to explain some things, "Look— I thought last night about cha idea on the amphitheater," Lil' Derek admitted. "So far it sounds like a good idea, but I gotta get my people to do some research. If everythang check out…"

"You fuckin' wit' yo' bwoy!"

"Yeah, I'mma fuck wit' ya. We family now! After givin' it some serious thought, I believe it'll bubble too," Lil' Derek told him.

First on the agenda was how often they were going to start transporting the work and money. Big John would make regular trips every other week or whenever necessary. Secondly, Lil' Derek agreed to be a silent partner /investor in his project, at least until it's sustainable. That way Cortez could verify the whereabouts of the capital used to help fund this project. Precautionary measures in case the IRS wanted to probe.

Once the venue began to generate its own money, Cortez could purchase all the shares back. Making him the majority owner. Lil' Derek warned Cortez this move might place him under severe scrutiny. Perhaps ruffling the feathers of some city and state officials, and possibly government agencies in Montgomery. Lil' Derek assured to back him if he was serious about pursuing this because there's not much that can be done if everything's accounted for.

This time money wasn't the motive for him. Lil' Derek sincerely wanted to help guide and assist when necessary. He's experienced blow back from some who felt he didn't deserve to be in his position. Lil' Derek understood all too well that some people were offended by someone looking like himself and rubbing elbows with some of the upper echelons. He just hoped Cortez comprehended this fact.

Chapter 7

November 2010

Judith Kidd's one of the top and most respected attorneys in the state. She has licenses to practice law, state and federal, throughout the southeast region. Judith stayed true to her word in being relentless, with her efforts of getting Cortez released. She finally convinced the judge that her client has no intentions of doing anything egregious or fleeing the country. Cortez was coerced to hand over his passport, also he agreed to a leg monitor.

She advocated that Cortez believed in the system to rectify these injustices. Those determining factors enabled him to be reunited with his loved ones. Cortez had to momentarily readjust his eyes when he stepped out of the jail. He was detained for ninety days without any fresh air or sunlight. Cortez stood atop the stairs with both hands in front of him, admiring his loved ones on the sidewalk.

Sophia rushed into his arms, kissing him uncontrollably. Marcus and Bug gave him dap, and half hugs showing their excitement for seeing him released. They had many questions, but not enough answers to what led up to his brief stint. Out of respect for Sophia, they opted to wait until they were amongst themselves before tackling the matter.

Right now, everyone just wanted to cherish this moment and get out of the winter weather. So, they all loaded into the 2011 Cadillac Escalade EXT and fled away from there. Cortez realized there were several things about this dreadful ordeal, he couldn't begin to understand. Sure, he was blind-sided but he could only imagine how his crew felt. What happened? Were they next? Also, they're unaware that he's still in search of answers.

Regardless, they're going to have to wait for the details, tomorrow's a new day. First, on the agenda, Cortez went to Judith's office to get enlightened on the nature of the government's case. Cortez considered his faculty to be a tremendous asset. He checked with his managerial team and saw the legit businesses were operating as expected.

His people in Orlando were probably worried because he's certain they've gotten word of what's taken place. So, Cortez anticipated tomorrow to be a long dreary day. When they arrived at Cortez's home, he informed the guys that he needed them to bear with him, until tomorrow. Right now, he's exhausted and wanted to spend time with his wife and kids.

Cortez stepped out of a black-on-black Range Rover. He's draped in a black Ralph Lauren RLX sweater, with the matching toboggan to help fight the cutting wind. He swiftly pranced to the door of Judith's office, located downtown on South McDonough Street. Entering the heat influx lobby, he was immediately greeted by a receptionist. Cortez told her his name and informed her that Judith should be expecting him.

The receptionist called on the phone for confirmation. Within a matter of minutes, Judith emerged, gesturing with her hand for Cortez to follow her to the office. Inside her office, he glanced at the expensive décor, also the eighteenth-century artwork that adorned the walls. He took a seat in one of the two leather chairs that occupied space in front of her freshly polished cherry oak wood desk.

Judith closed the door to her office, then strutted to her desk like a runway model. She wore a gray skirt, with a silk turquoise shirt and a pair of turquoise stilettos. She sat behind her desk looking the part of a power attorney. Glancing at some paperwork, Judith assured Cortez she took her job seriously. Also, she explained that her investigative team unraveled some information, that could be detrimental to the outcome of his case.

That statement provoked an attentiveness from Cortez she hadn't recognized before. She informed him that he might've stepped on some sensitive toes of the elite in the city. Different lucrative businesses they wanted in on, and he wouldn't conform, which caused them to conspire on his downfall. They were mainly irate over the O'Neal Amphitheater.

That establishment alone has caused the Montgomery Civic Center a tremendous deficit, which caused the city to lose money. City officials were unable to steal money to support their lifestyle if there was none to take. So, as his attorney, she was obligated to inform him of this conundrum. She hadn't received the discovery to see exactly what kind of evidence the government has that warrants the RICO Act.

Judith assured him as soon as she received the evidence, he'll be the first to know. Meanwhile, she warned him to be cautious of who he spoke with, especially about the case and his affairs. Cortez left Judith's office puzzled trying to comprehend the info he'd just heard.

For him, it was unbelievable that he'd catapulted to such heights. That public officials would plot against him, simply because he wouldn't let them in on his game.

All the money he donated to these crooks and their projects. Cortez became infuriated, the more he thought about this treacherous ploy against him. He immediately called Melissa to meet him at his loft downtown. Cortez parked in the parking deck to evade speaking with anyone. As he rode the elevator up to his loft, Cortez devised ways to shed light on these corrupt officials planning his demise.

He stepped off the elevator before entering the loft and picked up a couple of weeks' worths of Montgomery Advertisers. Cortez dropped the newspapers on a caramel-colored leather sofa, grabbed the remote, and flopped down next to them. While glancing at the cover story in the newspapers, he turned on the 60" Toshiba flat screen that hung on the wall. Cortez came across a newspaper with his mugshot on the front page.

Tryna assassinate my character too, huh?

Cortez laid back on the sofa and pulled out his cell phone to check the emails he received, while he was confined. Although, the seriousness of his current situation can't be compared. Cortez was proud to find out his staff was competent enough to conduct business, even with his absence. Melissa came inside with a dubious facial expression and sat down in the matching recliner.

Melissa was aware of what Cortez recently encountered but was unaware of whether the charges were true or not. She reclined the chair, elevating her high-heeled snow boots, and sat in silence with him, "Word is, dem crackaz hatin' 'cause of the Amphitheater," Cortez disgustedly said. "City councilmen, state reps, and shit. Dem shiesty bitches you introduced me to at dese functions ya drugged a nigga too."

Melissa sat up, "Are you serious! You're blaming me for you getting arrested?" she asked in disbelief.

"If—"

"Nigga, I just tried to help you. In every way possible," Melissa bellowed as she sprung up from the chair towering over him. "Shit, I introduced you to the ones who sign the permits, and licenses and authorize the inspections... Tryna give you some leverage! And this the muthafuckin' thanks I get!"

Cortez clutched his face in the palms of his hands, for a second. He looked up at Melissa who was holding her ground, with a noticeable scowl on her face. What just took place finally registered, so he stood up and hugged his friend tightly. Wanting to vent, he understood she's not the one at fault here. Everything she said was nothing less than the truth. Everything she contributed was for his advancement.

Their tempers subsided and Cortez offered his deepest apology. He began to fill Melissa in on the info he received a couple of hours ago. Melissa wasn't shocked by what she heard because she knew they were capable of such a vindictive act. Especially, if you're not greasing their palms to their likening. Also, she knows about the skeletons hidden deep within some closets. Whether it's bribery, extortion, fraud, drugs, or a fixation with expensive call girls.

Any of those offenses could lead up to some federal prison time, or at least cause turbulence in their careers and personal life. Either way, their reputation, and credibility would be tarnished. They collaborated in an attempt to find the unseen hand behind this scheme, before revealing secrets. Melissa vowed to find out who was responsible and also assured him all his finances, and investments were still intact before she left. Cortez made the call to his people in Orlando, Florida.

****

July 2007

Business as usual was the mind frame of Cortez upon his return to Montgomery. His clique distributed the work, and he collected his money. Cortez called the owner of the land off Fleming Road. Mr. Antonio Ferguson informed Cortez that the land belonged to his father, who recently passed away. Mr. Ferguson claimed he just had the land appraised, and wanted to get rid of the property because he had no use for it.

Also, he explained there are 3500 acres, at $1500 an acre. Cortez was a firm believer in the buy low, sell high theory. He tried to see if he could get the land lower, finalizing the agreement at $1200 an acre. Cortez agreed to meet with him to close the deal, as soon as his people do their due diligence. He was overwhelmed with excitement that the ball was in motion.

He called Bill Watson, one half of the tandem Watson and Watson. Two brothers head their own independent architectural company, located downtown Montgomery. Bill and Cortez became associates two years ago. When Bill revealed his desire for crack cocaine, along with a vulnerable woman to accompany him.

Cortez instructed Bill to immediately begin designing him a state-of-the-art venue to house 10k-15k occupants. Also, he needed a design for an exquisite home. Cortez gave Bill some ideas on how he desired the home to look and allowed Bill's creativity to explore. He never mentioned the price for Bill's services, only to be prompt with the completion.

In route to Melissa's office, Cortez called, alerting her he was on the way. He casually walked into the office and removed his sunglasses before collectively greeting the women in the room. He gestured with his head for Melissa to follow him. She followed Cortez to his car, where he apologized for the disappearing act. Cortez hoped he didn't cause any inconvenience by not showing up to the meeting spot.

Cortez raised the trunk and produced a backpack containing the money to purchase the houses. Without delay, he came out of his pocket with $10k for her duties. Cortez told her to email him all the info on the houses before they dispersed. Preoccupied with organizing his affairs, Cortez unintentionally neglected his kids. With some time on his hands, Cortez took Kenya, Cheyenne, and Boonk's son Buggy to Fun Zone.

His way of staying relevant in their lives, plus it gave their mothers a break. They went to Eastdale Mall and spent nearly two and a half hours in Aladdin Castle, playing video games with them. Cortez purchased all of them clothes and shoes. Also, they sat in the food court eating pizza and talking. He enjoyed the opportunity to connect with the children. These were tangible moments that Cortez knew they would cherish forever.

****

"Derek, what'd ya think about Cortez's production?" Ron asked satisfied with the portion of money he just secured in the safe. "Seems like dis kid is serious 'bout the game. In full payments! That was a nice first load!"

"Pop, he on point," Lil' Derek replied. "What gets me, is he ain't fascinated 'bout none of dis shit. They been doin' fly shit, but not on dis level though. What I peeped, was comin' down here witnessin' all our shit, motivated him to hustle harder and get his own."

"That's a plus. What was the outcome of his lil' project? Or did it fizzle out?"

"Oh— After givin' it a second thought Pop," Lil' Derek exclaimed. "Cuzz might be on to somethin'! Brilliant idea to clean up a helluva lotta money. He confident 'bout it. Really, Pop I like it. We chopped it up 'bout how to get it off the ground and whatnot. Pop, I thank I'mma partna wit' him."

"Ummm. You must really like him, huh?"

"Pop, the nigga real. Ya know I ain't fuckin' wit' him if he ain't," Lil' Derek earnestly stated. "I been knowin' Cortez for 'bout ten years. Goin' to the Gump fuckin' wit' Boonk, Cortez was always dere wit' him. Pop, he certified."

"What exactly is it?" Ron inquired.

"An amphitheater. A concert hall, for real," Lil' Derek explained. "I'mma have our people do some research, and make sure everythang checks out."

"Okay. Makes sense. Where is it gonna be located?"

"I thought he was gonna lease or buy a building. But he talkin' 'bout buyin' land and comin' from the ground up."

"Hmm. That's gonna cost somebody quite a few coins."

"Like I said, I don't have all the details, but once he lemme know his move, I'mma get our people down on it," Lil' Derek told Ron.

"Son, dis, what y'all talkin' 'bout, gonna cost millions," Ron clarified. "How do ya plan to invest without attractin' attention?"

"Kinda difficult to give dat answer right now because I ain't got all the facts. If it ain't right, I ain't fuckin' wit' it," Lil' Derek replied. "Depending on the cost. If it's a huge number, then I'll work thru the venture capitalists group. Totally legit! If they liked the concept and decided to put some money behind it."

"Okay. I see ya thought it through."

"Come on, Pop. Dats why we committed to the group, right?" Lil' Derek boastfully asked. "My John Hancock ain't on none of the paperwork. If it goes bad for any reason, I walk away squeaky clean."

"Keep me posted, son."

****

"Yeah, shit was crazy the other night. Jumpstreet swarmed the hood. Just so happen ain't none of my team get jammed up," Po explained leaning against his newly purchased Cadillac Escalade talking on the cell phone. "They jammed up Taylor Made, TD, and some more niggaz scrabblin' for Willie P. But look here, I'mma blow at cha later though."

For every individual affiliated with their crew, the hustle game has been lucrative. Po' stood firm on what he prophesied. Every kilo Cortez delivered, he easily distribute them all. He took the initiative to expand, by setting up traps throughout the main hoods on the north side. He had two in his hood, Newtown, two in Charlestown, a few in Chisholm, Brookview, the Vadoc…

Po' eluded most foolishness to keep the hustlers complacent, and haters from overdoing their job. He made sure everyone got a percentage of money. His way of giving back to the hood. The frequent meetings with Cortez and getting a glimpse of his lifestyle, influenced Po' to make a transition that was new for him. He noticed with his affluence, came more generosity from both genders.

Po's a regular old school driver, who deferred to driving more luxurious automobiles. Sure, he turned heads in the old schools. But now he got notoriety from the people who normally wouldn't be in his presence. A pearl white Mercedes Benz E Class parked directly in front of his SUV. Po' walked over to the car. Sherry stepped out clad in Rock and Republic jeans, a t-shirt by the same designer, and a pair of Christian Louboutin peep-toe pumps.

She removed her Chanel sunglasses while placing her long dark brown hair behind her ear. Without hesitation, Sherry buried her head in his chest as she tightly hugged him. The affection she displayed was reciprocated, "Ooh— I missed you so much," Sherry admitted.

"I missed you, too," Po' replied palming her butt.

"I had to meet you here because my husband has so many friends, and I can't have this getting back to him," she explained referring to the crowded Winn-Dixie parking lot.

"That wouldn't sit right wit' him, huh? A young black man, wit' a strong back, fuckin' the shit outta his wife!" Po' jokingly asserted.

Sherry blushed, but her pondering revealed that she was imagining her husband's reaction if he'd ever found out.

"Shid—. Don't none of his friends grocery shop?" Po' asked.

"Of course, baby. Not on this side of town," she replied.

"What's so urgent you couldn't tell me over the phone?"

"I must admit. I just wanted to see you. I need you to ride to Birmingham with me," she said. "I know you may have plans but, baby I promise to make it worth your while. I'll take care all expenses."

I know bitch!

"I'll just feel safer. More comfortable with you beside me. Plus, we'll be able to spend some time together. You wanna be with me, don't you?" Sherry asked.

"What about yo' husband?" he asked.

"He's on a job in Louisiana. He'll be back at the end of the week. Just go with me, please. Don't worry about him."

"Shittin' me!" Po' snapped. "I don't wanna have to do nothin' to him. 'Cause he approach me, I'm gonna defend myself. I love me, way more than I love him."

"Don't worry baby," she assured him. "He's a pussy. I got him under control."

"Aight. I'mma leave my truck here."

"Fine."

Po' went back to his truck for his pistol and a sack of Purp in the console, "Pop the trunk," he told her placing the pistol inside a shoebox before reclining the passenger seat to his likening. "Let's ride."

Chapter 8

■■■■

Darren Smith the younger brother of Sherrell Smith, was a friend of Cortez's since they were eleven years old. She died in a car accident with her dad one evening coming from cheerleading practice. Cortez took a liken to Darren and out of respect for his sister, he vowed to keep a watchful eye on the kid.

He felt that was the least he could do. Darren and his mother stayed around the block from Cortez, so they saw one another daily. Kind of like the younger brother he never had. Although Darren was four years younger than Cortez, he still hung out with him and his crew. That's around the same time he was dubbed Bug, due to his abnormally big eyes and small stature. Bug didn't like the name at first, but it grew on him.

Bug learned first-hand about hustling from watching and listening to Cortez. He understood their friendship. The importance of being receptive, and playing his role put him where many of his peers wish they were. Getting out there early developed a cleverness that groomed him to oversee Regency Park, while Cortez coordinated other things.

There's nothing that took place in the hood that doesn't get his nod of approval. Everyone knew Bug's resume, and that he earned his stripes. He cruised down National Avenue and made a left on April Street. He whipped up in his '06 Dodge Charger Hellcat behind a chain of cars parked alongside the street. It's Sunday evening, and some of the city's most prominent hustlers are gathered at Nay Nay's gambling spot.

"Here come Bug," Ed informed the doorman over a chirp.

"Ten-four," Lee Harris replied before he relayed the message to the house.

Bug made his way past the cars, approaching the porch, "Is dey gettin' money in dis bitch!" Bug asked.

"Most definitely! Alotta major gamblers came out," Lee Harris answered scanning Bug with a portable Garrett metal detector.

He then patted Bug down, assuring he hadn't missed any weapons. Lee Harris unlocked the security door, allowing Bug to enter. Once Bug was in the front door he saw a crowd of men, with stacks of money in hand looking at the green dice on the pool table.

"Seven out! Next man wit' money!" Vic shouted, then announced, "New money in the house! Everybody Bug just joined us! What's happenin' baby?"

"Came to get at dis bread," Bug told him before upping a stack of hundreds from his jeans pocket.

Bug worked the room. He slapped hands with Shankman, Pork Chop, Big Eye, and a host of others. Bug went over by Cortez and Nay Nay to get filled in on how the dice had been reading. They shot $50, passed a $100, and betted whatever they liked. Whatever one's vices maybe were available too, compliments of the house.

"School 'em. School 'em again. I'm gone," Cortez informed Vic.

Cortez hit two licks before he caught a nine as his point, "Bet! Whoever don't like it, drop somethin'! Five or nine a $100 Shankman!"

He shot at the nine awhile. In the process of shooting, he threw a few fives and elevens, then fell off. Bug had patience that most guys his age couldn't begin to fathom. Sipping on a Corona he attentively watched the dice. He'd gotten a sense of what points regularly appeared, which determined how he bet his money. The dice rotated four, five times before Bug took a shot.

Bug brought an indescribable energy to the game that everyone secretly adored. The demeanor combined with his dialect intensified the game, making it more competitive, "Put down!" Bug said before he even touched the dice. "I'm shootin' $50, and $200 on the come-out."

Bug had $7500 in hand. He dropped $1800 of that on the pool table to bet on the come-out, plus $250 for the fader. He caught a six on the first roll. He peeled off an additional $1800 for the point. Bug schooled the dice, then took off.

"Shid— dice need more money!" Bug affirmed before dropping $1800 more on the pool table.

Bug rolled the dice once more. He then went into his other pocket and pulled out another stack of hundreds, "Bet!" he demanded dropping $1800 more. "Cortez told y'all, don't nobody move but me, when I hit dis muthafuckin' six."

Bug brought the six back, five, ace.

"Get money, young nigga!" Cortez shouted.

Just as Bug predicted, no one moved but him. He swiftly gathered the money off of the pool table and shot at another point. The prior routine Bug repeated. Besides, that was his purpose for coming to the spot. Bug brought $30k to either win or lose. The evening turned out to be very profitable, not only for him but for Cortez, too. Once Cortez noticed Bug's shot was on, he covered all side's bets.

****

Sherry Knox's a forty-two-year-old, 5'8, brunette, who's very high maintenance and has a physique like Pink. She married into a wealthy family and had some resourceful connections in several states throughout the southeast and east coasts. She's a CPA for the trucking company Wiley Sanders. This lifestyle was new to Po', but very familiar to her though.

They met at the Shoppes at East Chase about seven months ago, when Sherry got out of her Mercedes as Po' simultaneously exited his automobile. Sherry wore a yellow summer dress that was perfectly fitted and a matching hat by Chanel. Stevie Wonder couldn't resist the temptation of taking a peep at her. The difference is that Po' wasn't Stevie. He's from the slums and not going to peep, more like stare.

Sherry's aware Po' liked what he saw. She sensed his attraction and flaunted more. They made eye contact but didn't verbally exchange words. To Po's knowledge, it was coincidental they crossed paths again when they entered Dillard's department store. Sherry gave eye contact, with a slight smile as Po' opened the door for her. A simple hello had her intrigued about what it would be like, to be with a man like him.

Surely, she witnessed guys that looked like him on television but never had she intimately interacted. She's flattered by the fact she commanded his attention. Po' casually browsed around the store, until he found the right opportunity to approach her. *Dis white bitch bad! Act like she diggin' a nigga, too. Might just be my mind trippin'.*

Shawty ain't gonna fuck wit' a street nigga like me. Fuck it! No nuttz, no glory.

It went a lot smoother than he expected and they kicked it off. Browsing turned into a twenty-five-minute conversation before they exchanged numbers.

Today, after doing some shopping at the Riverchase Galleria, Sherry was ready to relax. Driving a little further north, she got a room at Valley Hotel in Homewood. They carried upstairs a few outfits they'd purchased. Sherry kicked off her stilettos as soon as she entered the suite, dropping two bags on the floor. Po' opened the curtains, permitting the sunlight to pervade the living room area.

He stood there, staring out the window that overlooked the ongoing traffic. Sherry eased up behind him, wrapping her arms around him while resting her head against his upper back. She desired the comforting feeling of their bodies being entwined, "Come take a shower with me," she said in a muffled tone, rubbing his chest underneath his t-shirt.

Sherry maneuvered her hand down his boxer briefs, stroking his tool a couple of times before removing her clothes and heading to the shower. Po' went to the refrigerator for a sip of water which allowed her time to have the water adjusted, before joining. Po' shed every remnant of his clothing in the hallway. He slid back the translucent shower door and was captivated by Sherry's figure.

He stared as soap suds ran down the crack of her butt. *She damn near twice my age, and body bangin' harder than the bitches my age.* Soon as he got inside the shower, Sherry reached behind her in search of his manhood. She turned to face him once she felt him becoming aroused. Po' pulled her close and planted a passionate kiss on her lips.

One hand cupped a 34C, the other palmed her round derrière, simultaneously darting his tongue in and out of her mouth. Without a doubt in her mind, Sherry knew her body was picture-perfect. As much as she prided herself on staying fit, she equally prided herself in sexual fulfillment. Sherry squatted down as the water plummeted on her. She began teasing Po' by licking his head with the tip of her tongue.

Sherry proceeded with this until he stood at attention. Po' guided how far down he intended her to go when she took him in her warm mouth. Sherry looked up at him with sheer seduction to see if he was enjoying the lip service, at the same time rubbing her clit in a circular motion. Po' pulled her off his erection by the hair and gave her a hard kiss, then proceeded to suck her firm oval-shaped breast.

Well aware that's her hot spot Cortez also slid two fingers in her moistened womb. Sherry's moans were delightful. Her moaning and shivering made him eager to penetrate. Po' lifted her with his arms underneath both of her legs and her back in the corner of the shower for support. Sherry clutched his tool, slowly inserting it.

Elated by how hot and tight her box was, forced Po' to thrust deeper with every stroke. She uncontrollably moaned and gyrated to the best of her ability. The more emphatic her moans were, the more rapid and vigorous Po's strokes became until neither could resist the imminent pleasures. Po' realized this relationship between them could benefit him.

Sherry's fixation for a street guy like himself, and the fact that her husband was not giving her the sexual attention she craved. Po' decided to give her the most rugged sex she's ever experienced, in return for her philanthropy. Sherry dried Po' off with a large white towel and he did the same for her while giving his body time to recuperate from the prior session.

Round two. I'mma put yo' ass to bed.

In the process of drying her off, his hands wandered underneath the towel, indicating it wasn't quite over yet. Fully nude they dropped their towels right where they stood, and Cortez took her hand leading directly to the bedroom. He stood behind her smelling the aroma of Vidal Sassoon hair conditioner, while she grinds her butt on his tool he squeezed both breasts, nibbling on her neck.

Aware that her hormones were raging, he pushed her in the back onto the king-size bed. Filled with anticipation of her throbbing hole being plugged once more, Sherry assumed the position on all fours, "Come on, fuck me," she gasped looking at him over her shoulder.

Po' crawled onto the bed behind her and without hesitation inserted his erection. First, he gave her long stiff strokes, then wrapped his hand in her long damp hair. With her head pulled back, Po' proceeded to vigorously pound her.

"Shit! Shit!" Sherry repeated after each thrust.

"Dis what cha wanted?"

"Yeah—"

"Huh?"

"Yeah…" she managed to slur.

I'mma dig off in dis pussy. Touch some spots she probably ain't never had touched before.

"Rollover," Po' commanded assisting her onto her back.

Sherry willingly spreads her legs and pulled Po' by his tool, fiending to put out the fire between those hips, "Lemme look ya in the eyes while I'm puttin' dis dick on ya," Po' expressed as he plunged inside.

"Ooh— baby. Fuck me baby," she pleaded.

Po' went from sucking her breast, to her lips, neck… while still grinding inside of her. He made certain his shaft rubbed her clit with every stroke, which made the pleasure unbearable until she erupted, "Oh my God! What are you doing to me! I'm cummin' again! Oh my God!" she delightfully shouted.

Chapter 9

■■■■

December 2007

Cortez felt remarkable because everything was going swell. His lieutenants were on top of their game. Just as he planned, all he had to do was collect the cash. Which came much faster than he anticipated. Two of the homes he purchased, were flipped for an adequate profit. Which urged him to buy more properties.

Under Melissa's advisory, he recently acquired a loan from Liberty Bank and Trust to purchase four mint conditioned Peterbilt eighteen-wheelers. He leased two with Walmart, and the other two with Jim Bishop Cabinet Company. Cortez's hustle smoothly flowed, and he looked forward to purchasing some commercial properties. The trucks stayed on the road. So, they're starting to pay for themselves, but he anticipated acquiring a few more.

The vending machines and cash-only businesses turned out to be productive. He even started putting ATMs in several local convenience stores, also in all of his establishments. He acquired knowledge of some business owners that were in financial binds, and desperately needed assistance they couldn't receive from banks. For his assistance, Cortez brokered deals that made him a partner in that business.

The architectural designs Bill composed for Cortez's home were marvelous. He loved the design so much, that it became a priority in making it come to fruition. Still, his most significant endeavor will shortly be completed.

"Hello."

"Good mornin', Mr. Ferguson. Dis Cortez O'Neal," Cortez informed him.

"Mornin' Mr. O'Neal. What can I do for you?" Mr. Ferguson asked.

"Hope I didn't disturb you, but I'm ready to close on the land. I've consulted wit' my people and everythang checked out. I was wonderin' could cha meet wit' us, so my attorney can review the paperwork?"

"Sure! What's a convenient time for you, Mr. O'Neal?"

"How's one o'clock sound?"

"Perfect!"

"Are you familiar with South Lawrence Street?"

"Yes sir," Mr. Ferguson replied.

"It's 261 South Lawrence Street. See you den."

Cortez never realized the influence money had in dictating the outcome of certain situations. How much easier it was for him to get certain things done, by simply greasing the right people's palms. For instance, the first time he set foot in Marquitette's Exquisite Jewelry. He wore a navy-blue Dickies work outfit with a bucket hat. He looked like your stereotypical street thug according to some media outlets.

The employees gave ridiculous stares and presumptions as to why Cortez even entered the fine jewelry store. It wasn't until he produced $7000 to buy a pair of gold two-carat diamond-studded earrings they became cordial. The second time he was dressed the part of an exec, wearing a $2700 Valentino suit, with $550 shoes, instantly becoming Mr. O'Neal.

This time Cortez was treated with courtesy, and respect, receiving multiple compliments. Just one of many scenarios to his recollection. After closing the deal with Mr. Ferguson, Cortez went to visit Bill Watson. Mainly to see the progression he's made in the architectural design for the amphitheater. Cortez took the elevator to the third floor, and he noticed the changes made within the past few months.

"Hi. How are you?" Cortez greeted the receptionist. "Mr. O'Neal here to see Bill Watson."

The designer suit, minus the locs made it difficult at first for the receptionist to recognize that this was the same guy from months ago draped in urban streetwear, "Mr. Watson, there's a Mr. O'Neal here to see you. Okay sir," Hannah said with a smile before ending the call. "Mr. O'Neal he'll be with you shortly. I like your new look."

"Thank you. And forgive me for my rudeness," Cortez replied looking over his Cartier frames. "'Cause every time I come here, you're lookin' wonderful and always professional."

Hannah tried to refrain from blushing as the two engaged in conversation while he waited. Bill walked up the hallway trying his best to decipher who the gentleman was in the designer suit. As he got closer, Bill realized this was his supplier. "How's it going?" Bill greeted Cortez shaking his hand with a perplexed facial expression. "You cut your hair! Gotta new look, huh?"

"My profession requires my attire to be casual," Cortez told him, "I'm venturin' off into domains where some be intimidated by dat lions mane. So, I cut mine just to infiltrate dese domains but ya better, believe me, I'm still a lion!"

Bill led the way back to his corner office as Cortez followed. He glanced in each office on the hallway through the glass fronts, "Close the door, and have a seat," Bill told him before sitting behind his desk. "I've been done with this almost a week now."

"A rush job," Cortez retorted.

"Whatever your profession may be, you consider yourself to be good at it, right? Well, this is my profession! I'm not exaggerating when I say I'm the best in the state!" Bill expounded before walking to a drawing board, revealing the blueprints. "Come over here. You asked for state-of-the-art. Here you have it."

Bill went in-depth about the designs, enabling Cortez to not only see a visual but opened his mind's eye to his creative genius. Also, Bill estimated how much he'll be looking to invest in the project being structured. Bill recommended the best company for the job. Cortez listened attentively as Bill expounded on every detail.

"What I owe ya, Bill?"

"When I give you a call, just don't forget this," Bill said rolling up the blueprints for him.

****

Sophia recently moved into a quiet neighborhood out in Pecan Grove. She's content with her selection, as far as the location and neighbors minding their business. Marcus and Megan saw the white Oldsmobile Alero snugly parked underneath the car porch when they pulled up. Marcus eased up the driveway and tried to avoid damaging his 28" rims, on the Donk.

He topped the steep driveway and parked midway, so he'll have a complete view of his car looking out of any front window. Megan rang the doorbell as she playfully rubbed her butt against Marcus. Sophia saw them through the storm door, "Y'all came to the wrong place, for all that," Sophia jokingly stated then welcomed them inside.

"Hey—big sis!" Megan bellowed hugging Sophia's neck.

"What's good sis?" Marcus inquired.

"Hey Marcus," Sophia responded.

The sisters are real tight-knit, stemming back to their childhoods. After the death of their mother, especially for her age, Sophia understood the significance of being a positive influence on her younger sister. Sophia never got angry with her sister even when Megan wore her clothes and makeup… Sophia loved her dearly and whatever she had, Megan was more than welcome to it.

Marcus followed Sophia into the kitchen, leaving Megan alone in the living room. "Sis you aight stayin' here by yourself?" Marcus asked rinsing out a glass he removed from the cabinet.

"Yeah. Why wouldn't I be?" she replied.

"You ain't scared here by yourself? Or lonely?"

"Hmmm. I don't really think about it. I've been by myself so long; I'm used to it."

"Oh, Sophie you wouldn't guess who came to visit us a few weeks ago," Megan said when she entered the kitchen.

"Who Megan?" Sophia asked.

"Cortez," she answered.

Megan looked to see if her sister had completely gotten over him. Sophia paused cutting the bell pepper. The knife was suspended in midair before she realized it, then continued dicing the vegetables. That alone, was adequate for Megan. Who knew there would always be a place in her sister's heart for this guy?

"Yeah," Sophia nonchalantly answered. "How's he doing?"

"Bruh good! He told me to tell ya, he asked about you, and for you to call him."

Marcus dropped a couple cubes of ice into the Martel and coke, then mentioned, "He said to give ya his number."

"Call him over here," Megan told Marcus.

"For what, Megan!" Sophia rhetorically asked, not sure what else to say.

"I'mma give her the number and she can do what she do," Marcus said jotting the number down on a memo pad. "And yo' azz always tryna play match-maker."

With an enormous smile on her face, Megan retorted, "Your azz just don't get drunk. How about dat!"

Both women laughed in unison.

****

Cortez picked Bug up from a female friend's house in West View Garden. As they rode along, Bug teased Cortez about his new GQ look. Cortez assured him that he needed to get used to it because he'll be seeing a lot more of it. Cortez never expressed the fixation he's had with the businessman type, since childhood. Cortez admired the cleanliness, combined with the power that exuded from these types of guys.

Also, Cortez correlated to the fact that some came from nothing to create their wealth. Mainly from their ambition, dedication, and willingness to succeed. From life experiences to reading about people like A.G. Gaston, Cortez had all the motivation needed in making this dream a reality. He figured he'll use the same format from the streets, and simply readjust his approach.

Cortez whipped the Jaguar into Sufficient Automative parking directly out front. He stepped out cleaner than most had ever seen him. Bug followed Cortez closely as they entered the shop. They found Lightbulb in a small office, facing the entrance of the shop with his feet propped up on a gray iron desk. It's lunchtime and Lightbulb's devouring a seafood plate courtesy of Destine's Connection.

"Dis nigga gettin' money!" Lightbulb exclaimed jumping from his seat at the sight of them, licking Destine's sauce off his fingertips.

Cortez stood before him with an aura that resembled the Dapper Don, as he playfully preened and jacked his slacks. Lightbulb slapped hands with both guys. He stood there astounded by the sight of his old comrades. "Cortez where ya headed, Cuzz?" Lightbulb bluntly asked.

"I'm workin' hustla. I gotta lotta major bizness I'm takin' care today. And dese type folks I'm fuckin' wit', a nigga gotta represent in every sense of the word. Feel me?" Cortez candidly explained.

"I feel ya! I know ya bwoy! You got somethin' up yo' sleeve. Bug what cha gonna do wit' him?"

"He a muthafucka," Bug retorted. "Say dis his new look."

"Do you Cuzz. Come on," Lightbulb told them leading towards the garage adjacent to the office.

Once Lightbulb unveiled the car, they were blown away. With the new look of the '72 Cutlass 442, Lightbulb was the only man for the job, hands down. They could hardly believe this was the same car brought up from the country, seven, eight weeks ago.

Lightbulb did a complete makeover on the vehicle and proceeded to run it down to them, "It's only a handful of dese in the city. I know you a different kinda nigga Cuzz, so I set cha apart from dem other dudes," Lightbulb immediately clarified. "I sprayed her PPG Radius Blue, wit' a white rally stripe."

"Word! I like the color, too!" Cortez replied.

"You don't want yo' rims too big 'cause that'll effect yo' performance on the slab. So, I sat her on some 24" Asanti's wit' the Hankook tires," he explained, kneeled next to the front tire pointing at the chrome rims.

"Dem bitches sittin' perfect up under dat hoe mane!" Bug exclaimed.

"Straight up Cuzz!" Cortez admitted.

"Appearance ain't shit, if dis hoe can't get nowhere," he explained lifting the hood. "Gotta 350 Rocket, and a 350 transmission. She'll shit or get bruh!"

Lightbulb sat in the driver's seat. He cranked the car before he tapped a button, removing the top. "In case ya hadn't noticed, you can show dem titties on dese kinda days," he told Cortez with a gigantic smirk on his face. "Blue carpet, white and blue accents, Dakota digital dash, Alpine IDA-X305. Gotta have the guts lookin' just as good as the outside. Dats for the bitches. Make 'em kick off them slip-ons and get comfy. Ya feelin' dat!"

Cortez and Bug were still awestruck by the job Lightbulb did on the old school. Lightbulb turned on the music so they could hear the sounds, then he stepped out and closed the door. Lightbulb informed Cortez this was a $65k-$70k job for anybody else, but since they had such close ties, he deducted $15k. Plus, Lightbulb never knew when he might've needed a favor that required a lookout from him.

Bug scampered back to the Jaguar and retrieved the backpack Cortez had on the backseat. Cortez counted out $50k for Lightbulb. He then instructed Bug to drive his newest toy. Lightbulb lifted the garage door and Bug peeled off in the customized Cuddy.

****

February 2008

On the porch of the dilapidated duplex, Kelt scanned up and down the block. He was looking for Jumpstreet as his neighbor, Shep sold $2 shots of corn whiskey. Every $20k Kelt made, he put inside the trunk of his '96 California Gold Chevy Impala. The season has made its transitioned, that was the main reason he wore a black Jordan hoodie, black Dickies, and the black and red patent leather Jordan 11's.

Kelt's mentality was ghetto. Being raised in the slums of the city, places where the odds of someone becoming successful were rarely unheard of. Although, this was where he felt most comfortable. Coming from nothing to being in a position to show the community love, whenever necessary.

It began getting dark and the temperature started to dwindle around the mid-forties. The kind of weather Kelt preferred hustling in. A ritual of some sorts, because these were the months he adopted tunnel vision about money. He stood on the porch kicking it with Shep. The entire time gripping an all-black snub-nose .357 Magnum, inside the pocket of his hoodie.

Anybody pulled up wanting to cop, must get out and come to him. Besides, they did come to see him or his crew. Kelt turned this trap into a Quarter House, no less than $9k per visit. Tonight, was pumping with a plethora of customers, and a lot of people were wandering up and down the street. Kids were still out playing, and if any law enforcement was spotted they would yell like it was a four-alarm fire.

Kelt was cool as a cucumber amid all the chaos. He chopped it up with some young hustlers, did a bit of flirting with a couple of hood chicks, and shot the breeze with the young ones. Still, he managed to watch the traffic that frequented his domain. His two protégés, Scooby Dum and Dae Dae roamed the strip while tending to everyone's needs.

Grinding was the kind of hustling Kelt's accustomed to. Getting that dollar was the same way he'd always hustled. Cortez had been aware of Kelt's willingness as a bona fide hustler because they ran together in their earlier years. When they parted ways, it wasn't on a bad note simply had to find their way, that's all. Occasionally, they'd come together as a tribute to their brotherhood.

Cortez knew he needed someone with a similar mindset to see this vision and help him sell the cocaine. Someone reliable that's going to help him manifest the vision. Someone capable of holding his own, along with the same mentality for his own money. Kelt's always been cleverer than most of their peers, especially when it came to bettering his situation.

Driven by the thrill of being able to attain whatever he desired, Kelt found gratification in the respect given once he set foot into someone's establishment. That feeling is one he strived to sustain.

Kelt got off the last four ounces he had with him. Without hesitation he went inside the house and vacated with a duffel bag, to add with the earnings of today's grind. He informed his team that he was gone for the night, placing the bag in the trunk of his car. After a day's grind, he wanted to relax and relinquish a little tension.

Kelt dropped off the majority of the money at his stash house. He then drove straight to West Gate to see Pep. He copped an ounce of Purp, plus Pep smoked one with him. Kelt chunked the deuces, then stopped at the Petro gas station on Fairview Avenue. He bought a box of cigarillos and a six-pack of Heineken. With no particular female companion in mind, Kelt chose to spend the night with Monesha in Gibbs Village, since he's in the vicinity.

He parked in front of the housing unit and casually walked up the sidewalk. Kelt met Monesha and Corey exiting the apartment as he reached the front porch. The deer caught in headlights expression Monesha displayed was an indication he showed up at the wrong time. *Dis what I get for just poppin' up.* Corey was furious and gave them both verbal tirades.

Kelt desperately tried maintaining his composure. He even tried to de-escalate the situation, to no avail. Corey was irate and jumped down off the porch at Kelt. Corey attempted to kick him down, but Kelt managed to avoid it. He took a swing at Kelt and his knuckles grazed Kelt's nose, forcing Kelt to no longer be reasonable about the issue. Kelt lifted the snubbed nose and didn't hesitate to squeeze.

Kelt shot him once in the side. Corey fell to the ground clutching his wound. Monesha's scream combined with the sound of the gunshot seemed to have garnered attention. People began turning on lights and peeping out of windows. A clique of guys stepped from the side of the unit. Some of them clutched pistols, and a couple had assault rifles. Kelt immediately back-peddled to his car.

Once the guys realized what happened they opened fire at Kelt. He let off four shots in return, buying him enough time to get out of there. Ducked down in the driver's seat he could hear a couple of bullets hit his car. His only objective was to get away unscathed.

When Kelt turned out of the housing projects, onto Air Base Boulevard, he floored the Impala.

Knowing someone might call the authorities and he may not make it to his destination, especially in the recognizable car, Kelt wiped off the .357, tossing it and the marijuana out the window. The traffic light in front of Maxwell Air Force Base was red when Kelt approached it. He noticed MPD's finest backed in at the Citgo gas station.

He decided to make a left on Day Street to take the back road to Prattville, avoiding the police. Cutting his eyes at the squad car Kelt realized it was positioning to stop him once the light turned green. Knowing the inevitable, Kelt had to decide whether to stop and play the game or make them earn their money. He chose the latter.

When the light turned green, Kelt proceeded with the flow of traffic which was minimal at this hour. His eyes were locked on the rearview mirror until the squad car appeared. Blue flashing lights erupted, and he floored it. *Fuck it! Y'all hoes gotta catch me!* Kelt topped the hill at high speed before slowing down, due to the winding road. When he came out the last curve, Kelt misjudged the oncoming traffic and got derailed. Causing the car to flip multiple times.

****

This newly developed partnership with Malik, a property inspector, enabled Cortez to learn the procedures and key essentials of home inspection. They're in Forest Hill inspecting a piece of property Cortez considered purchasing. A four-bedroom, two-and-a-half bath brick home, Cortez planned to give to Bug as a token of appreciation. Malik was showing him the technique on how to check the efficiency and durability of a pipe system.

Amid the demonstration Bug ironically called him, "Yo', say Kelt shot a nigga last night and took the white folks on a high-speed chase. The car flipped over a few times, but he straight. Broke his arm and shoulder, but he'll survive. He's at Baptist South."

Cortez thanked Bug for the information. His mind began to run rampant. *Would his name come up in this madness? Why did Kelt shoot someone? Did he try to rob Kelt? Where did it happen? How the law got involved?* Cortez chose not to rack his brain about what might've transpired. One thing he was certain about was that his friend, a key member of his organization was in trouble.

So, Cortez did the only honorable thing he knew to do. He gave Raymond Johnson a call. Raymond's a criminal defense attorney Cortez kept on retainer for situations like these. Raymond informed him that Kelt's charged with assault one, eluding the police, and reckless driving. His bond was set at $80k.

Cortez instructed Raymond to post Kelt's bond for the misdemeanors, once he's transferred to the Montgomery County Detention Center, so Kelt won't go any further than booking. That way, Kelt could still handle his business as Raymond prepared for his defense. Cortez refused to speculate not knowing the facts. His focal point was to have his friend free and safe.

Since transitioning into a legitimate entrepreneur, Melissa had introduced Cortez to some powerful people throughout the city. It was a strategic move to establish these relationships, for the near future. Licenses, ordinances, and permits were mandatory for some of his projects in the works. They're only pawns in a much bigger chess game.

Melissa was accompanied by Cortez to an annual benefit for Cerebral Palsy at the Renaissance Hotel and Resort. Ray Thornton hosted this event every year, trying to bring awareness to this dreadful disease. Also, to commemorate his mother whose life abruptly ended from this very disease. This year they have a couple of specialists to enlighten everyone in attendance. Plus, some guest speakers to share how this disease has impacted their lives.

The cost was $1500 for dinner plates, also voluntary donations were accepted. Cortez pulled up to the Five Star Hotel driving an all-white Range Rover. He got out looking splendid in a black tuxedo. He went around to the passenger side and opened the door for Melissa. She complimented him perfectly, wearing an elegant yellow evening dress by Jimmy Choo with matching heels.

Cortez tipped the valet attendant and accompanied Melissa through the entrance of the lobby. Where they met this guy who escorted them to the conference room. The extravagant setting gave Cortez more confidence in being included in something of this magnitude. When they entered the room everyone was chattering, sipping champagne, and having a festive time.

Melissa observed Cortez to see if he was nervous. It was hard to tell because he had on his poker face. She assured him he would blend in perfectly. When introducing Cortez she introduced him as her boyfriend of a year, and his profession was the owner of a trucking company. Melissa advised him to take advantage of a rare opportunity and be sure he made everlasting impressions.

Before Melissa got her words out, they were approached by State Representative Derrick Graham, and his lovely wife Alexis. They've gotten familiar with Melissa from prior events. Alexis took a liken to Melissa a while back and referred many of her colleagues to her for professional services. They socialized with the Grahams a moment before working the room.

Cortez was introduced to people such as Mayor Bobby Bright, Alvin Holmes, Blount Strange, Local and State Representatives, a few Congressional Leaders, and the host Ray Thornton. Out of everyone he met, there's one that stood out the most: Milton McGregor, the owner of VictoryLand Casino in Shorter, Alabama.

There was something authentic about Mr. McGregor, an undeniable connection between the two. Everyone else seemed to have secretly sized him up or have ulterior motives behind their questions.Milton was very down to earth, and not pretentious at all. After the dinner and ceremony, Milton rounded back giving Cortez a contact number.

****

Regardless of how much Sophia tried staying occupied, the reoccurring thought kept emerging. For the past week and a half, this has been happening to her. No matter how much she tried focusing on other things. Once her mind drifted she was back where she started daydreaming.

"Girl, you alright? You actin' like somethin' bothering you," her co-worker asked.

"I'm good," Sophia replied.

"Let's go to the deli for lunch. My treat."

"I'm good girl. I'm just gonna relax in this break room."

She didn't think it was noticeable to anyone, especially since no one had the slightest idea of any prior relationships. Well, perhaps Megan recognized the moment she mentioned Cortez's name. The only way to get the closure needed was to confront the issue.

"Hello," Cortez answered.

"Hi," Sophia gently replied.

"Hi," he acknowledged her.

"You know who you're speaking with?"

Cortez pondered a moment before placing the voice, "Sophie!"

"Yes," Sophia said, overwhelmed with laughter.

"All the time we spent talkin' on the phone, I can't forget dat voice!" he stated, obviously elated to hear from her. "I was at Marcus spot and Megan came from the back. I ain't seen her in a minute! I was glad to see dem still together. You must've got my number from 'em?"

"Yeah."

"She told cha what I said?"

"Uh huh."

"What she say?"

"Tell my baby I asked about her," she told him.

He grinned, then asked, "So, how's my baby for real?"

"I'm okay."

"What been happenin' wit' cha though?" he eagerly asked.

"Just working. Cortez I go to work and back home. They too wild in Montgomery. I don't be out like that. I love me," Sophia told him. "I went to nursing school and put in the work. Now it's starting to pay off for me."

"Dats what's up! You always wanted to be a nurse."

"Uh huh. My mom put me on that early. Only difference is I'm going to be a pediatric nurse. Help these babies!"

"Word. A nurse is a nurse. How many kids do you have?" he asked.

Sophia giggled.

"Zero kids! I gotta get my shit right first. You?" she informed him.

"I got two girls."

"Really! How old are they?"

"Kenya's six. Cheyenne's three," Cortez explained. "Yo' nigga aight wit' yo' plan?"

"Zero nigga, too."

"Sheesh! Well, want you lemme take ya out somewhere nice. We too young for all work, no play baby. Take ya out, so you can let your hair down. What cha say?"

"When, Cortez?"

"Whenever you're free."

****

The O'Neal Amphitheater wasn't quite ready to open its doors to the public. The outside of the building was finished except for the parking lot and landscaping. The interior still had a ways to go, some electrical work, seating, plumbing… Only a few minor details needed to be attended to before it'll be completed. Cortez contacted his team to meet him there at ten o'clock a.m. sharp.

He chose that spot because it was Saturday and all the workers were off, plus he wanted to show them the amphitheater. Kelt was out on bond and met Cortez there a half-hour earlier. Cortez sat in the Range Rover smoking a blunt when Kelt pulled up next to him. Cortez clicked the button, unlocking the passenger door to let Kelt inside.

Cortez turned down the volume, handing Kelt the blunt as they sat silently for a few minutes. Cortez broke the silence, "Word in dese streets you shot dis muthafucka 'bout his bitch," Cortez calmly stated. "But, I know how niggaz get shit twisted. What happened, my nigga?"

"Cuzz," Kelt said hitting the blunt a couple more times. "Dats true to a certain degree. Not like dese hoe azz niggaz makin' it sound though."

"Yeah. Dats why I came straight to the horse!" Cortez eagerly replied.

"I been fuckin' on shawty for the past nine, ten months or better. Cool lil' hood bitch. I'll go thru swoop her up, get a bite to eat, sip on somethin', blow some trees, freak off, shit like dat," Kelt explained to him. "Dis night I shut down shop, I dropped off the stash, went and got some strong from Pep, a six-pack from Petro, then I shot to her spot."

"Okay—"

"Nah, I fucked up by not hittin' her up first. I just popped up when they was comin' out the apartment and her dude went in flip mode!" Kelt recalled. "Nigga jumped off the porch like Jimmy Fly Snuka and rushed me! What choice I had? I ain't 'bout to let dem niggaz catch me down bad. I'mma gangsta my nigga, better him dan me. So, I gave him one."

"So, the nigga forced yo' hand?"

"Exactly!" Kelt exclaimed. Niggaz started comin' from under rocks and shit! Comin' from everywhere, lettin' loose!"

The crew started arriving at the end of their conversation. Cortez instructed Bug to take everyone inside the amphitheater.

"Aight, I don't expect ya to let a mu'fucka hurt cha. 'Cause, I might've clapped his stankin' azz too," Cortez revealed. "My purpose for callin' dis meetin' was to discuss shit like dis. You gotta stay on point and lay 'til dis shit straight. Raymond Johnson said he'd be able to make the eludin' and reckless drivin' charges disappear, but ain't no guarantees on the assault."

"Bet dat," Kelt replied.

"We just gonna offer dis nigga some bread, so he won't show up for court. Ya hear me?" Cortez suggested to him. "If his hoe azz won't take the money, we'll get the groundhog to deliver his mail to him! Let's go in here, so I can lay dis shit down mane."

As they entered the building Cortez reassured Kelt that everything was going to be fine. He locked the door behind them in search of his clique. The others were in the spacious auditorium probing the exquisite high-tech concert hall. That's when the idea materialized to show them what he'd been investing his money into.

Cortez jogged to the control booth and slipped in a DVD, with various hip-hop music videos in the DVD player. When he returned the guys were in awe, gazing at the Jumbotron. This jubilant feeling overcame Cortez witnessing his peers fascinated by his creation. Hopefully, this motivated them to create their own situations.

Once Cortez had their attention he took the four guys up to his office. Sitting on the window seal Cortez opened the blinds, so the crew could see the eighteen-wheelers aligned behind the amphitheater. The others took seats at the conference table and began bombarding him with questions about the state-of-the-art facility. Cortez intentionally refrain to answer, instead, he focused on why he called the meeting.

Kelt's incident brought about concern for productivity and the mentality of the crew. He decided not to openly share the details of what Kelt had done because at this point it's irrelevant. Although, Cortez did use it as a scenario to demonstrate the point he was trying to get across, which was how easy it was to get caught up in nonsense.

True they all were street and knew the streets, but Cortez wanted to remind them that others wanted their spot. They're doing numbers like Sudoku, and haters disliked that. Outsiders going to do everything in their power to dismantle or stagnate their progress. Therefore, everyone must stay mindful of that. Also all frivolous acts definitely won't be tolerated.

Cortez clarified what he meant, so his words won't be misconstrued. If someone's threatening or disrespectful they'll take care of that because their reputations are at stake, too. If it could be obviated then that's the route they were directed to take. Their only objective was the money. With that understood, Cortez began to answer the questions asked earlier about the amphitheater. Sharing his visions with them.

****

The Embassy Suites was one of Po' and Sherry's rendezvous spots. After their sexual escapade, they rode off in her Infiniti G35. Almost everything about Po's livelihood had been unraveled. Sherry knew how he earned his money. Considering her upbringing, all of this was new for her, although she was intrigued. Po' informed her that he's really from the streets, and there are rules when dealing with someone like him.

Po' revealed his status along with his rules. He commenced cultivating Sherry's mind. Enabling her to see his vision was also an attempt to influence her. Po' paid close attention to Cortez and noticed exactly which direction he was headed. He was doing his best to emulate that same format. Perhaps, that's why his wants and desires suddenly became more stupendous.

"Listen, I don't normally let folks in my bizness," Po' informed her. "We've gotten close over dese months and been spendin' so much time together. I gotta be real wit' cha, so you'll be on point in case somethin' does happen."

"Of course, baby! We must be truthful with one another," Sherry agreed.

"Dis shit dead serious! One slip-up could cost me my life. Feel me?" Po' earnestly asked looking into her eyes.

"Yes baby!"

"My team growin' every day, money comin' faster and in much bigger stacks. I been watchin' the moves one of my partnas been makin'. He been speakin' on shit to clean money for a minute, but I wasn't hipped," Po' admitted. "Now, I understand the blueprint he was layin'. Wit' the laundromat, trucking company, and pool hall shit, he cleanin' the street money for a bigger purpose. Dats the route I need to take and dats where you can help."

"Baby, I don't know anything about the streets, or anything about that lifestyle. Except for what I've seen in movies!" Sherry replied.

"Dats the beauty of it! You're not a member of the team, nor do you have any knowledge of what's happenin'," Po' told her. "It's wise to keep ya separate from dat side of the bizness. The less ya know, the better you're protected. Ya understand?"

"Yes," she answered with uncertainty.

"Well, trust me baby! It's good to know, it's more to us than just fuckin'. 'Cause ya sure don't mind lettin' me know how much you love me den," Po' expressed to her. "I'm a firm believer in, love is, what love does. We're in love wit' each other, I'm askin' for help and you're ponderin' whether to help me or not? For real, all I need from you is to use yo' image. I got my own money, so I'll pay my own way."

"You need my image. What do you mean?" Sherry inquired.

"Look, I don't have any work history, no kinda accounts. Any of dat shit they do to keep tabs on yo' money," Po' admitted. "Dats why I need your image, plus you're an accountant baby. You more than qualified for leasing a spot. I'mma need assistance wit' the bookkeeping and shit, bizness loans… I'll have to jump thru too many hoops and loops, just to get fucked in the end."

"I understand."

"Not to mention, I don't wanna draw the wrong kinda attention from the IRS. You can make me whole by helping me build a relationship wit' dese people to establish my own accounts. You co-signing for me helps it become a reality."

"Basically, you want me to be your legal front?"

"In a nutshell. At least 'til I get my shit established and could do it on my own."

"What kind of business would you start?"

"Now dats a good question," he admitted. "I gotta give dat some more thought baby. I got the blueprint from my dawg, but I don't wanna do exactly what he's doing. I been thankin' 'bout a tire shop, auto repair shop… Whatever it be, I gotta make it mine. Feel me?"

"Yeah. You need to come up with something then."

"So, is dat a yes!"

"Yeah, I can do it. Sounds like a good idea. Just don't get me caught up in nothing."

"Appreciate it baby!" Po' exclaimed tightly hugging her. "Tonight, I'll sit down and come up wit' somethin' dat makes sense. Yo' it's rules to dis shit, too!"

"I'm sure it is," she sarcastically replied.

"Yeah! My main reason for keepin' ya far, far away from dis shit. Can't have you being implicated in nothin'. Dis way, ya were paid for yo' services and tried helpin' a local business grow," he elaborated. "No affiliation wit' dat side excludes you from many rules, but I have my own. Number one, what we got goin' on ain't nobody else bizness. I don't see it happenin', but in case it does, you have no knowledge of the other side. Our relationship is strictly bizness! Aight!"

"Okay baby. I'll be telling the truth."

"Right!"

They stopped by Jack Ingram Porsche, and Po' inspected the Porsche's aligned out front. Some 911's, Carrera's, but Po' was captivated by the Cayenne. He liked its sportiness, and it was something unique. It abruptly clicked for Po'. To solidify their agreement moments earlier, he cracked Sherry to co-sign for a Porsche Cayenne.

Mainly to see if she's truly committed to the cause. There shouldn't be any problems, because Sherry's net worth was well over $80k annually. Plus her husband's in another tax bracket. Without a blemish on her credit report, there shouldn't be any hang-ups with her cosigning.

"I like dis! Dis muthafucka hard right here!" Po' ecstatically expressed.

He and Sherry peeked through the glass, trying to capture some of the vehicle's interior design and features. Fabrizio's a well-groomed Italian sales representative who approached them with anticipation of his first sale for the day. Po' was engulfed by the design of the auto and envisioning himself in it.

Sherry engaged in a dialogue with Fabrizio until Po' made it known he desired the Cocaine White Cayenne S, "Dis it!" Po' promptly stated. "My man, where's the keys!"

"Hang on a sec. Let me run to the office. I'll be right back," Fabrizio told him.

"Is this the one you want?" Sherry asked.

"Yeah! Dis me, baby! What you thnk?"

"I like it. You'll look good behind the wheel."

"Look— the ticket is $72k, but when the time comes, tell him ya got $10k cash right now! Just to see what kinda deals lil' buddy willin' to make for dis money."

Fabrizio returned and tossed Po' the keys after unlocking the vehicle. Po' sat in the driver's seat. Sherry stood next to him with Fabrizio in the passenger seat, who began running his reel. Fabrizio touched on every aspect of the vehicle. The leather interior, its features, alloy wheels, the horsepower.

Although Fabrizio made the vehicle sound undeniable, Po' knew his adrenaline wouldn't subside until he put the Cayenne S on the interstate.

Chapter 10

■■■■

October 2008

It's dusk once Cortez and Bug finished cruising the city. It had been a while since they've rode out, smoked trees, and kicked it. Bug showed up unexpectedly at Cortez's home that morning because it was his twenty-fourth birthday. Bug wanted to show his partner some love.

Cortez didn't put up any resistance. He got dressed and jumped in the passenger seat of the Cuddy anticipating what was in store. The day wound down as Bug drove to Norman Bridge Road, taking a right onto the service road into The Gambler's parking lot.

"Gotta taste for some of dem chicken wangs," Bug bluntly stated when he parked in front of the entrance. "Dat green got me hungry as fuck!"

"Damn, dis bitch blowed early! What the fuck they got goin' on in here tonight!"

Bug locked up the Cutlass before they entered the establishment. Bug's leading the way inside as Cortez followed. Cortez checked a text message he'd just received which read: SURPRISE! Before the message could register, Cortez was startled by the crowd's outburst in unison with Happy Birthday. He was certainly surprised, gazing around the bar at the faces of family, friends, and many associates.

Cortez turned and looked at his friend. "Mu'fucka, dis why ya been fuckin' wit' me all day!"

"Happy Birthday, bruh. It was a surprise. Nigga I couldn't tell ya," Bug uttered in his ear.

Po', Marcus, Kelt, and numerous others bum-rushed him with gifts in tow. Megan greeted him with a bottle of Moët before she hugged his neck and wished him a happy birthday. Bug escorted Cortez over to a section they had set up for him. D.J. Nest-O crunk the music back up. Many guests swarmed the dance floor, while others came over bestowing gifts and showing their respects.

Several people took pictures with the birthday boy. Many of those people hoped attending this birthday party would gain them favor in the future. Blunts rotated throughout the party, but Cortez has always been skeptical about smoking what he hadn't seen rolled. Once the attention dwindled and the first opportunity presented itself, Cortez slipped outside to blaze a blunt.

Leaning against the backend of the Cutlass 442 smoking a blunt, Cortez got approached by someone he could never forget. Regardless of how much they've aged since last seeing one another, Cortez immediately recognized her. He cuffed the blunt behind his back trying to conceal it.

"I seen you smoking that blunt," she admitted. "Plus, loud as it smells, is a dead giveaway."

Cortez smiled and stared at Sophia in sheer astonishment. Scrutinizing her from head to toe he noted, *Sophie ain't changed much at all.* As far as facial features were concerned, she had acquired some key assets body-wise. Cortez flicked the fire off the blunt and sat his bottle of Moët on the ground. He removed his gold Cartier frames for a better view of her.

"Gimme a hug," he said approaching her arms outstretched. "Damn, I ain't seen you— in a long azz time."

"Yeah, it's been a while. Nice to see you're doing good," she replied.

"I'm maintainin'. I still gotta ways to go though."

"Huh," she grunted. "Seems like you're doing more than maintaining. From the looks of this, and all the things I've heard here tonight. Look at this car!"

"Looks can be deceivin'. I ain't drivin' dis car by the way. I do aight, but, I ain't where I wanna be. Let's say dat."

Cortez relit the blunt and picked up the champagne bottle, taking the same position against the car, "Dis dat Sour Diesel. You wanna taste it?" Cortez jokingly asked.

"Nooo— I still don't smoke nor drink," Sophia reminded him.

Sophia did join him on the car, and they began to fill in the gaps since they last saw one another. Cortez was very impressed by what he was hearing. Several ideas began to appear in his mind's eye. Caught up in reconciliation, they weren't keeping track of the time. Nearly an hour passed before they knew it.

"I knew y'all two was together!" Megan exulted admiring the sight. "I couldn't find Sophie and everybody was looking for Cortez. I knew y'all had to be together."

"Lil' Sis we catchin' up on old times," Cortez told Megan.

"That's what's up. Are y'all going to get back together?" Megan bluntly asked.

"Megan gone!" Sophia angrily blurted out.

Cortez laughed at Sophia's reaction.

"I wouldn't mind. But we ain't seen each other in years. So, one day at a time, right?" he respectfully answered.

"Everybody lookin' for you inside," Megan told him again.

"I'm really ready to dip," Cortez replied.

"Cortez this your party," Sophia mentioned. "How you gonna leave?"

"Free alcohol, free drugs, free food, and shit. The majority of dem niggaz wasn't here to celebrate me no way. They don't need me to have a good time," Cortez told her. "I appreciate everythang, but I'm ready to get outta here. Can you take me home?"

"Ooh—" Megan said with an enormous smile.

"You make me sick girl," Sophia affirmed. "Yes, I can take you home."

"Don't do nothin' I wouldn't do," Megan suggested as she walked off.

They exchanged questions on the ride to Cortez's home. And every chance they got unnoticed, they were checking out one another. Sophia explained to Cortez that she's not a pediatric nurse, yet. However, she's earned her master's degree after five years, and now she's months away from her two years mark.

For two years she planned to work as a registered nurse, so she can take the National Certification Examination for Certified Pediatric Nurse. That was Sophia's ultimate goal, plus it made things official. They last saw one another almost eleven years ago. So, they're trying to figure out each other as well. Cortez was impressed she'd been committed enough to dedicate years to education, for a career.

Sophia parked in Cortez's driveway as she finished explaining her plan. Almost ten minutes had passed so Cortez invited her inside. She declined the invite but desired to continue their conversation. Cortez felt no type of way being declined; besides he's enjoying her company. Sophia managed to get Cortez relaxed before doing the inevitable.

"Lemme ask you something. Why did you stop talking to me?" she blatantly asked.

Cortez knew that before the night was over she was going to bring up the subject. He thought she would've asked during previous conversations they've had over the phone before tonight. Sophia had nothing to do with his decision. It was derived from Cortez's poverty-stricken upbringing, and he wanted his family to have finer things.

"I knew dat question was comin'!" he excitedly admitted. "I knew it!"

"Shouldn't be difficult to answer then," Sophia sarcastically replied. "You had ample time to think about it."

"I wouldn't say all dat, but I thnk you deserve an answer, though. Lookin' back, I can admit I handled the whole situation foul as fuck. It's no excuse for how I shut off all communication wit' cha. My deepest apologies," Cortez openly admitted. "I'm truly sorry I handled dat like a fuck nigga. Now here's where my mind was back den. My grandparents had just died six months apart, and shit got real hard, real fast! Granddaddy made up where my Daddy was bullshittin'."

"I agree, Mr. Surles was a good man."

"When Granddaddy died, money sho' nuff got funny, so I had to help out. It wasn't an easy decision, but back den, it was easier I did it dat way. Things had got crazy as fuck at the crib. And the first chance Bryon got, he went back home to Milwaukee," Cortez explained. "I wasn't 'bout to leave my mama and lil' sister here alone. Hell naw! I had to take on bigger responsibilities, but it worked out aight."

"It did?"

"I like to thank so. See Sophie I come from a fam, wit' a Daddy who had multiple families across the country. Who comes to the crib, maybe two or three days every month or two, and leave a lil' money before he dipped?" Cortez expounded. "I had to help my family. Shit, I still help my family! The only thang I regret for real is not includin' ya in the equation. But I'm tryna to make dat right now! Remember, we were kids. Check us out now!"

"So, is it true what I heard?"

"Depends on what you heard."

"Cortez O'Neal, the big-time drug dealer," Sophia stated with sarcasm.

When Cortez looked over at her, she had repositioned herself in the driver's seat. Sophia's back rested against the driver's door and her feet were propped up in the seat. She was staring at him, awaiting an explanation.

"Cut it out Sophie. Would cha?"

"Seriously! At least, that's what I've heard since I been staying in Montgomery."

"Don't believe everythang you hear love. I did what I thought was the best move for me and mine. Dat choice put me in a position to change the dynamics of my fam, and how my kids grow up. What kind of opportunities dats accessible to dem early in life. Dat shit's important!" hesaid, in hopes that she understood. "Ain't gotta worry 'bout basic survival no more. Niggaz able to save money now and make investments dat earns more money. Setting the lil' ones up to win."

"That's not the only way, though."

"Look baby. Now, I understand all I had to do was communicate wit' cha. But my immaturity, and the shame was really the determinin' factor for my actions. Like I said, I thank our hiatus was for a greater good. After years of not talkin', we still can have dese kinda talks." he told her.

"Really?"

"Hell yeah! Nowadays, I don't have any shame issues, so I can be honest 'bout shit. I saw it as, the Most High God guided us down our paths to get dat knowledge and experience to shape us. Sure, we traveled different paths to gain what was necessary, but yet an still, here we are together. Sophie, you were always more mature dan me. I promise! I promise I'll never make dat mistake again!"

"It's gotten late. I gotta be to work in a few hours," Sophia suddenly noticed. "Lemme take my butt home. It was nice seeing you again, and I'll give you a call tomorrow. Hopefully, it won't be another decade before I see again."

****

January 2009

The plane touched down at three-thirty a.m. and Cortez made his way through the corridor as he did any other time he'd visited within the past couple of years. The only difference this time was that he wasn't on business, and no one's expecting him. Cortez walked out the sliding doors of the airport carrying a bland Hermès night bag on his shoulder.

Cortez stood out front of the airport for a moment. He took in some fresh air while gathering his thoughts. Confidence exuded from him. The fact he manifests whatever he sets his mind to, Cortez felt was paramount to his success. Everything he thought a successful entrepreneur should embody. Cortez worked diligently to get a foundation laid. Also, he acquired like-minded individuals or those who possessed more ambition than himself.

Therefore, when he does have to get away for business or leisure there isn't a doubt in his mind, that business won't flow as usual. The first available cab that pulled out front of the airport, Cortez took to the Marriott. It was almost six o'clock a.m. once he laid back in the king-sized bed and dozed off.

Cortez awakened after about four hours of sleep. He got a good, hot shower that energized him for today's festivities. Although Cortez was unaware of exactly what the day holds, he got dressed and put on some black LRG stonewashed jeans, a black Nike hoodie, and some black and white Bo Jackson retros. Jewelry, he kept to a minimum. He had been to Orlando several times, still, he wanted to avoid unnecessary hassles.

Cortez was hungry and decided to put something on his stomach. He left the suite, making it to the dining area just in time for brunch. As he waited on his meal, Cortez called Enterprise Car Rentals to check on the car he had reserved. He finished his meal then took a cab to Enterprise.

He paid the deposit for Enterprises insurance, and payment for the next two days he planned to use the 2006 Lincoln Town Car. Immediately, Cortez turned the heater on to warm the interior. Cortez strolled through his iPhone in search of one particular number as he waited on the paperwork.

"Hello," a delicate voice answered.

"Yo' what's good! I'm here in yo' city!" Cortez exclaimed.

"Excuse me!" Amanda inquired making sure she heard him correctly.

"Wake up! I'm in Orlando!"

"You don't have to fucking shout! I'm already awake. Do you want me to come pick you up?"

"Naw. I'm gettin' a rental as we speak. Just lettin' ya know, I'm in yo' city. So, get yourself together. I gotta make a few stops but afterwards, we can link up. You should be ready by den."

"Sounds like a plan to me. I can't believe you came! I thought you were just talking shit after fifteen months. Seriously, I'm glad you came!"

Since that night they met in the lobby of the Omni, they've always kept in contact. Maybe not often, but periodically they would tap in with one another. In the beginning, Cortez intended to line her up for sex whenever he visited. In those early conversations, some indicators persuaded him that he may be looking at this the wrong way.

For instance, Amanda reminisced about this one episode when she helped a guy named Ronald get offloads of pills. She claimed one night to have distributed $80k worth of pills. She did it through an after-party for this volleyball tournament she participated in. Amanda has several stories about pills, but this one resonated with Cortez.

Maybe because Ronald had bought a couple of pill presses, and started pressing his pills. According to Amanda business went from $150k a month to $400k, and that got Cortez's attention. After almost a year and a half of conversing, they spoke on various topics from America to Zoology. The majority of the time, Amanda would be rambling over something that Cortez could care less about.

Then there were those times when she'll mention something that made his ears perk up. Also, through their talks, he acquired knowledge that Ronald sold exotic cars and weapons too. Cortez took into consideration that she could be running game. He only met her once, and she knew he was an out-of-towner. But intuition told him she was being truthful.

Amanda spoke vividly about these things as if she was there. Names, sizes, colors, and costs… They were detailed and accurate stories for her not to have been directly involved. Finally, Cortez felt comfortable enough about her to see if she was capable of producing these items, she vowed she could. He put this in motion perhaps two months ago. Amanda never expected him to show, although he often mentioned to her that he eventually would.

Cortez visualized another clientele base he could tap into back home. Cortez realized through observing the night scene, that pills were becoming the new crack. Anywhere there's partying, pills are going to be in the vicinity.

"Where are you? she asked.

"Where you at is the better question?"

"Out and about."

"How long will it take you to meet me somewhere?" he asked.

"Where you want to meet?"

"Dis yo' city. Ya tell me?" Cortez answered.

"Meet me at Barnett Park off West Colonial in a half-hour," she told him.

****

Bug shook hands with Alex, owner of the club Celebrations. That meant Bug was content with the conditions, and the price of renting the club. Whenever Bug got the notion he would host an exclusive party, at one of the local nightclubs. Who's not going to be in attendance for an all-you-can-eat and drink? One of many ways Bug showed love back to the city.

When he left the club and headed to Kinko's, Bug called two of the city's renowned radio personalities. Michael Long of Hot 105.7 and Bryan Corbett of 97.9 Jamz, guaranteed publicity over the airwaves. He ducked the blunt, quickly making his way inside evading the brisk breeze.

"Hi! May I help you today?" Desiree asked from behind the counter.

"Yeah. I'm throwin' a party right, and I wanna get 'bout five hunnid flyers printed up," Bug retorted.

"Okay. Anything particular you're looking for?" she inquired.

"Naw— just somethin' eye catchin'. It ain't gotta be no fancy shit. Just somethin' to get my point across. Ya dig?"

"What you have in mind? A birthday party, a graduation party, a bachelor party…"

"Nooo— cutie. Just a party to release some tension I'm feelin' throughout the city. Let people unwind and have a good time. Not dis weekend, but the followin' Saturday 'bout nine o'clock p.m. I tell ya what, what's yo' name?" Bug inquired looking for a name tag.

"Desiree," she modestly replied.

"Oh— okay. Desiree," Bug repeated. "Check it out! You come up wit' a funky azz flyer for my party, you can be my guest. No strings attached, just come out and have a blast. Cool?"

Desiree threw out a few ideas to decipher what direction Bug wanted to take. He let her do whatever came to mind for the design. Desiree used five colors, dividing the flyers into five groups of a hundred. After each process was finished, she consulted with Bug, whose nonchalance was evident. Desiree handed Bug the flyers once they were completed.

He took an ink pen laying on the countertop. Bug wrote his name and number on a yellow flyer atop of the pile, before handing it to her. Bug took out his money and after assurance that she'd be present, he paid for the flyers.

Chapter 11

■■■■

Kelt was dropping off a pair of Jordan sixesto his youngest son, in Smiley Court. He noticed Hard Duke and Lulu on the front porch of the flat across the street. He honked the horn of the '75 Chevy Caprice Vert so his baby mama could come and get the sneakers, along with the two warm-ups he bought. When he approached Hard Duke and Lulu, he noticed they were snorting cocaine out of a quarter ounce.

Kelt declined the invitation to the sack and gave both guys dap, before sitting in a white plastic chair. Lulu wanted to clarify the word in the streets about the shooting in Gibbs Village, a few months ago. Many different stories were circulating throughout the city, but Lulu would rather hear them from the horse's mouth.

Being active in the game for many years Kelt understood real street dudes wanted the facts about anything that could lead to jail, the graveyard, or war. He knew there were precautions to consider for his actions. So, everyone would be on point, in case of retaliation Kelt gave a brief re-enactment of that night. All the while, keeping in mind the advice his attorney shared with him.

This wasn't his first encounter, so he didn't need the advice. Although, he knew this conversation would be repeated amongst others, falling on many ears. Kelt made sure Corey was portrayed as the aggressor and that he simply defended himself. Agitated by their continuous questions, an eerie feeling overcame him and Kelt couldn't fathom why everyone wanted details. Whatever the reason, it sure wasn't in his best interest and intuition suggested he move on.

Weakness wasn't a part of Kelt's genetic makeup. Everything he'd been through, along with everything he's seen turned his heart callous. He still had malicious thoughts about those guys in Gibbs Village who shot at him. The dialogue between himself and Cortez was the only thing stopping retaliation. Kelt alleviated those reckless thoughts, realizing their hustle was going too well to be thrown away.

Kelt knew it would cost him a substantial amount of cash to eradicate the First Degree of Assault, along with Eluding the Police. His day-to-day life was still balanced, and his operation functioned as usual. Kelt still attended his usual hang-out spots. Also, the brotherhood between himself and his most trusted soldiers stood intact.

Especially, after his detainment. Kelt got word to Scooby Dum and Dae Dae to infiltrate B and R Wreckage Services and retrieve a backpack from the trunk of his car. The backpack contained $80k, and not a dollar was missing which convinced Kelt to place more responsibility on his protégés. Their diligence to make money had become a key asset for him, at least until he handled his legal woes.

****

Thank God for the inventor of the GPS. Cortez surveyed the spot where Amanda chose to meet him. Barnett Park was filled with a variety of people of different races and genders. There were young and old couples, families, some exercising, walking pets, while it was leisure time for others. *Smart and conservative.*

His cell phone rang, breaking his train of thought. Cortez noticed it was Amanda's number and immediately answered, "Yo', where you at?" he asked.

"I'm pulling in now," Amanda told him. "Where are you?"

"I'm towards the entrance. Parked on side of the street in a black Lincoln Town Car."

"I see you," she said ending the call.

Cortez's eyes darted to the rearview mirror watching an all-black Mercedes G Wagon pull up behind him. He focused on the face making sure it was her before he got out of the car and walked toward her vehicle. Amanda stepped out of the SUV with a huge smile, looking exceptionally gorgeous.

Amanda's 5'8 frame donned a white and pink Chanel jumpsuit, which complimented her perky breasts. The pink blazer perfectly exposed her curves too, by gaining a couple of inches from some white peep-toe slip-on. *Shawty tough! Muthafuckin' toned skin, hips, ass....*

They were delighted to see each other again, "We meet again!" Amanda mockingly said rushing to embrace him.

"You so silly. Good to see ya," Cortez whispered, hugging her tightly.

"I gotta confess. I didn't think you were ever coming back here," she admitted, looking him over.

"I told cha I was comin'."

"Dude— you've been saying that for a year and a half now! I said this fly azz dude be talking boss shit! Why hadn't he made that trip to come see me yet?"

"I'm here now. Damn— ya lookin' good baby! You all dolled up for me?" Cortez asked looking her over as he stood back off of her.

"I had business to handle this morning, thank you. It don't stop!"

"Sound like a good problem to have."

"I'm not complaining. Since you did show up, I'm clearing my schedule for today."

"Since I showed up! You funny as fuck!"

"Seriously, baby I didn't think you were coming," she reiterated. "Man, you was questioning me like you worked for Homeland Security. You hadn't acted on nothing. I thought you just wanted a phone friend."

"Ha-ha-ha!"

"Well, you're here. What do you have planned?"

"I plan to check on some of dis shit ya been talkin' over the phone."

"Here I was feeling fucking special. Like you're here for me, but you're on a business trip. My dumb azz," Amanda jokingly stated. "We talked about a lot of things over the phone. Refresh my memory."

"The pills and assault rifles, remember?" he asked.

"I remember. Shit, I was kidding around, but you're really here for business," Amanda said looking him in the eyes. "Well, what do you need?"

"I want both. I'mma be here two days. We can take care of dis lil' shit, and we can kick it the remainder of my trip."

"How many weapons?" Amanda inquired with a serious face.

"'Bout ten. Nothin' major."

"Pills?"

"A few thousand at the price ya told me. Also, it depends on what kind ya got."

"Again, I didn't take you serious, but I'll make it happen. I'm a woman of my word," Amanda said pondering how to fulfill the spontaneous request. "We're gonna have to take a ride to get them."

"Where?"

"Pompano Beach. A little further down south."

Amanda lived in Novel Lucerne, an upscale apartment complex on Main Lane Downtown South. She insisted Cortez wait in the car while she changed clothes because it wouldn't take her long. Cortez rolled a blunt, then stepped out of the car and stood next to it. It was almost dusk, and Cortez noticed the change in the temperature. Soon as he sparked the blunt and exhaled the smoke, Saundra met him.

"Hi, Cortez! I'm Saundra, Amanda's best friend. Remember we spoke quite a few times over the phone," Saundra reminded him. "Amanda told me you were down here, and I wanted to introduce myself."

"Oh— Okay. Of course, I remember you. A pleasure to finally meet cha," he replied, then offered his hand concealing the blunt in the opposite hand. "What she doin' in dere?"

"Showering and changing her outfit."

"She left me outside while she showered? It's a lil' chilly out here."

"I'm here to keep you company," Saundra seductively said. "Are you gonna at least offer me the blunt?"

Cortez snickered passing her the blunt. "Shid, I didn't take ya as the type to smoke," he told her.

"And what type is that?" Saundra asked.

"You know, good girl."

"I am a good girl! But I've been smoking pot since my eighth-grade volleyball team. Good girls get high too! We like to feel good too. Aren't you a good guy?" Saundra asked.

"Of course."

"You're getting high."

"Gotta point baby."

Amanda returned wearing black Seven7 denim jeans, a light grey Louis Vuitton shirt, with black and grey Louis Vuitton peep-toe pumps. She anticipated whatever the night had in store, "You're ready to go?" Amanda asked when she approached them.

"Yeah, let's ride," Cortez answered. "Saundra, it's a pleasure finally meetin' ya in person."

"Pleasure meeting you, too. Where you taking my girl, anyway?" Saundra asked.

"I ain't too familiar wit' the city. So, wherever she wanna go," he told her taking Amanda's hand. "As long as it's a laid-back environment, where we can have a good time. I'm good."

"Hmmm. Well, girl have a great time. I sure hope y'all come back here to cap off the night," Saundra blatantly suggested heading back inside.

Pompano Beach, Florida is located south of Orlando, just north of Ft. Lauderdale. Cortez drove the rental because of the unexpected, and when he was ready to ride he wasn't waiting on anyone. Amanda didn't take Cortez seriously at first, but she managed to hook up the deal on short notice.

Besides, that's her hustle, brokering deals. She would middleman deals for whatever products are in demand, for a twenty percent cut. Amanda called Ronald before leaving her apartment. Amanda told him she's on the way with company, and to have everything accessible he's ready to sell.

Amanda informed Ronald they've made it to town and were at the Miami Grill getting a bite to eat. Cortez observed his surroundings and remained colloquial. Normally, he doesn't work on blind faith alone. Also, a few times he questioned Amanda's authenticity.

Sure, her stories over the phone had been entertaining and relatable. Surely the figures she conveyed were believable and meticulously explained but still, there's the unknown. Towards the end of their meal a tall, slender, casually dressed white man in his mid-fifties approached their table. Cortez's first thought was that he was the manager or owner of the establishment until Amanda raised to hug his neck.

"Uncle Ronnie!" she excitedly said.

Cortez thoroughly looked him over this time.

"Hi, Amanda. Glad you made it safely. You must be Cortez?" Ronald asked hand extended.

"I am. Pleasure to meet cha. I've heard alotta 'bout cha," Cortez replied shaking his hand.

"Well, I can't say the same. Amanda made this whole thing happen. She gotta really like you or she's trying to impress you. Either way, I could care less," Ronald explained. "I have other things to do besides watching you two dine. If you want to do business, I suggest you follow me."

Cortez paid the bill and they followed Ronald outside. His awareness was still on high alert. Ronald wasn't anything like Cortez imagined. He was very clean-cut, exuded professionalism, calculated, and soft-spoken. Cortez didn't want to misconstrue Ronald's appearance. He has seen some notoriously violent individuals matched the same profile.

Ronald suggested Cortez ride with him and let Amanda trail in the rental car. Ronald's driver had the backdoor opened once he saw them exiting the eatery. Ronald and Cortez sat in the back of the Yukon. Ronald instructed the driver to go to the dealership.

"You're from Montgomery, Alabama?" Ronald asked Cortez in a mellow tone.

"Right," Cortez replied.

"Montgomery's such a small city. I do a lot of business in Alabama. Mainly, the Birmingham and Mobile areas, but I often travel through Montgomery," Ronald told him. "A couple of months ago we ate at Wintzell's Oyster House downtown Montgomery. Guess what I want to know is, why you need assault rifles? Montgomery's so quiet and peaceful."

"Ronald, there's another side of Montgomery they don't like to talk about! This side they don't advertise on tv."

Ronald nodded his head in agreement.

"Once you purchase anything from me it's no longer my business what you choose to do with it. My only concern would be anything coming back to me."

"Hey, me and Amanda been kickin' it for a lil' while now, and I took her up on an offer. I consider myself a biznessman too. And I like to thank men like us, honor the etiquette we chose to live by."

"So, these weapons you're purchasing aren't going to revert back to me?"

"I'm gettin' dese weapons at a good price. They can't come back to ya if I don't talk. Believe me, I won't talk!" Cortez admitted. "Dats a worst-case scenario. I'm gettin' 'em for protection. One of the lawful things they're for. Nothin' foolish."

"Alright. I trust Amanda's judgement."

"What kinda pills ya got?" Cortez inquired.

"Whatever you desire."

They arrived at the New Toy Store, one of Ronald's exotic car dealerships. The driver opened Ronald's door assisting him out as Cortez exited. Amanda pulled into the parking space next to them, which somewhat put Cortez at ease. He had no other form of protection besides his hands. This weighed on his mind and was why he'd been on edge, but Cortez felt he wouldn't need them tonight.

Ronald unlocked the entrance, and hastily entered the security code before it triggered the silent alarm. Inside the showroom was dimly lit, although, the cars on display were illuminated that they were visible. Cortez was enchanted by the Lamborghini Aventador the moment he laid eyes on it.

Amanda tapped her uncle's hand to watch her work. "You must be feeling this one baby?" Amanda asked when she approached. "You over here daydreaming and shit!"

"Ya already know I'm visualizin' myself, pushin' dis bitch back in the Gump! Dis bitch hard!"

"Baby— my Uncle will make that happen. Just talk to him. He's a businessman that's always willing to negotiate."

Cortez put his arm around Amanda's waist as they followed Ronald into the garage.

"See you were checking out the Aventador," Ronald stated. "You're into exotic cars?"

"I am. I don't own one yet, but I've been in and around 'em."

"You hadn't driven nothing until you're behind those horses. A symbol of power, success. These cars indicate you're on another level," Ronald told him.

"I don't like pretendin' Ronald. I suck at it!" Cortez replied. "I don't thank my city is ready for dis yet. Most definitely gonna keep ya in mind when it's time. I've been checkin' out those new Porsches though."

"What model? I may have exactly what you're looking for." Ronald mentioned.

"He got a Porsche dealership a few blocks away," Amanda whispered to Cortez.

"I like dat 911 Turbo, but I've had my eye on dat Cayenne," Cortez admitted.

"Come with me," Ronald instructed him. "Let's handle this first. Then we can go over to the other dealership and see if you like my selection of Porsches. I have about six Cayennes left on my other lot."

Ronald led them to the back of the garage where his driver pulled up on a forklift, carrying a wooden crate. The driver took an impact wrench and removed the screws revealing ten new, black, and wood grain Kalashnikov AK-47 assault rifles. The driver removed one assault rifle handing it to Cortez.

"Russian AK's! Kalashnikov's the best of the best. The originator," Ronald boasted.

"Russian AK's?" Cortez inquired, inspecting the assault rifles.

"Look at the brand! Kalashnikov USA. Tullytown, Pennsylvania is where these weapons were imported directly from Moscow. Sixty rounds per minute," Ronald informed him.

The driver handed Cortez a clip with a few live rounds and began letting down the garage door in case he wanted to test the weapons.

"Wait— Let me get back!" Amanda anxiously blurted out.

"Aim at the foam on the wall," Ronald instructed Cortez pointing to the specific spot.

Cortez looked behind him making sure Amanda had her distance before letting off six rounds. "Ooh weeee!" Cortez excitedly shouted. "Dis baby gotta kick too. They say dese ain't accurate."

"They need an excuse for such a shitty shot," Ronald blatantly retorted.

Cortez chuckled.

"Have my man box them back up for you?" Ronald curiously asked.

"Yeah, $1000 each?"

"Right."

"What about these?" the driver asked Ronald holding four gallon-sized zip lock bags filled with pills.

"Do you still want these?" Ronald asked pointing to the zip lock bags. "I told you I had whatever you desired. But on such short notice, all I have on hand are these Oxys, Roxis, Percocets, and X-pills."

"Gimme a thousand each."

Cortez and Amanda rode together in the rental to Champion Porsche. Ronald's driver stored the pills inside the crate with his weapons and securely screwed it back. Awaiting Ronald's arrival, they looked through the window at some cars on display. Cortez fell in love once laying eyes on the Porsche Cayenne. After twenty minutes of shooting the breeze, Ronald arrived opening the car dealership.

Once inside, Cortez went directly to a Black Porsche Cayenne Turbo S which had him mesmerized looking through the glass window.

"Baby, you like this one?" Amanda asked.

"Yeah. Dis it right here!" Cortez proudly responded.

"That's the 2010 Porsche Cayenne Turbo S. Fully loaded, all-wheel drive, 550 horses, 4.8 liter, V-8 twin turbo, 180 miles per hour is the max speed," Ronald explained when he walked up.

"What's the askin' price?" Cortez asked him.

"A $118k," Ronald replied.

Cortez's unenthused look spoke volumes.

"How long are you in town? Or do you plan to drive the car back home?" Ronald inquired.

"Nope! I don't have the time to drive back. I'm flyin' out in two days."

"The least I'll take is $105k, plus have it transported to you."

"$105k?" Cortez pondered. "How long will it take before it arrives?"

"I told you, I pass through Montgomery regularly. Two or three days tops. Also, your merchandise will be delivered with the vehicle."

"Look, I'll pay you for the car, but I need you to tweak the paperwork as if I'm makin' monthly payments. If you can make dat happen, we gotta deal," Cortez explained.

"No problem. I'll handle that."

"Gimme your information so I can wire the money. Hookup the paperwork. I'll register it back home. I'mma get the car! You'll have your money in the mornin'."

Tomorrow the money would be wired to Ronald's account, and they'll go back to tighten up all loose ends on the paperwork. Amanda anticipated receiving her twenty percent from brokering the deal. Now, she just wanted to go home. Cortez and Amanda drove back to Orlando after they handled business.

They arrived at Amanda's apartment at about three-thirty a.m. Cortez had to awaken her, "Yo' Amanda, we're here." Cortez calmly said tapping her arm.

"Huh?" she asked a little woozy.

"We're back at your place."

Amanda yawned while stretching and said, "Saundra been texting me all night to see if you're gonna hang out with us. Are you coming up?"

"Sure. Why not?"

Amanda escorted Cortez to her bedroom when they entered the apartment. She let him know to make himself at home. Cortez sat on a king-sized platform bed checking out the organization of her bedroom. It reminded him of a furniture store ad how orderly everything was placed. Amanda got comfortable kicking off her pumps and removing her shirt. Saundra knocked at the door once, then entered the bedroom.

Saundra was braless in a long, pink tank top. Her nipples pierced through the thin t-shirt, with some maroon panties that failed to do their job. Amanda was fine, but Saundra is what you called thick. Redhead stood 5'9, 165 pounds, built slightly thinner than Coco, with a tan. Saundra laid across the bed on her stomach as Amanda applied facial cleanser.

"Cortez, I'm glad you came back," Saundra told him, then shouted. "Bitch come tell me about your date!"

"I'll be back. Let me wash off this makeup," Amanda responded before going into the bathroom.

"Cortez what did y'all do? Did I miss anything exciting?" Saundra asked.

"Nothin' for real! Just took care some bizness, but tomorrow we gonna go have some fun. You should join us!" Cortez told her removing his top. "Amanda said cha been askin' 'bout me. Wonderin' if I was comin' thru or not! I'm here now! What's happenin'?"

"I think you know why!"

"I wanna make sure," he said grabbing a handful of ass.

Cortez stood to unbutton his jeans, dropping them and his boxer briefs in one swift motion. Saundra stood true to her word. She didn't hesitate to take Cortez's manhood in her mouth. Cortez kicked off his shoes and jeans, then laid back on the bed. Saundra continued where she started. Amanda came back into the room amidst the oral session.

"Y'all didn't have to start without me!" Amanda playfully shouted.

****

Cortez and Sophia were talking over the phone more frequently since they've been reunited. In an attempt to get reacquainted they agreed to meet up a couple of times. Seemed like they picked up, where they left off. The fondness they once shared has suddenly resurfaced. Sophia wondered was she acting off emotions from a teenage relationship in hopes of fulfilling a fantasy. While Cortez vowed not to blow the opportunity of proving she's always been important to him.

The Harriott II Riverboat was built in 1981 and extensively refurbished a few months ago upon its arrival to Montgomery's Riverwalk. The Harriott II was one of the many elements placed in the entertainment district downtown. Cortez gathered the info about what the riverboat consisted of and that it could be privately booked. After doing a walk-thru he privately reserved it for a night.

He acquired Sophia's favorite foods, wines, and music... so the chef and band could have everything perfectly prepared. Cortez thoughtfully planned the night out, down to their attire. Earlier that week, he ordered Sophia a black Vera Wang evening dress, also a small gold necklace with a diamond-studded heart-shaped charm. He got confirmation that Sophia liked the ensemble yesterday when she called him elated after receiving the gifts.

He arrived at her home well-groomed in a navy-blue Dolce and Gabbana suit, carrying a dozen red roses. Cortez pressed the doorbell expecting to see Sophia, instead, it was Megan who greeted him. She was there helping Sophia with her hair and makeup. Cortez followed Megan to Sophia's bedroom and handed Sophia the roses.

"Damn— ya lookin' good as fuck!" Cortez unhesitatingly told her.

"Don't she look good bro-law," Megan reiterated.

"Thank you for the roses. They're beautiful," Sophia mentioned then gave him a peck on the lips. "Lemme get a vase to put them in and I'll be ready."

"Bro-law where y'all goin' tonight?" Megan asked.

"Downtown, to the Riverfront. 'Bout to get on the riverboat," Cortez informed her. "I reserved the whole thang just for us. Show my baby how special she is to me."

"Awww. She gonna love that!"

"Dats the plan."

Cortez parked his Jaguar close to the entrance of the tunnel that leads to Riverfront Park. They held hands exiting the tunnel to witness in the distance, a ninety-six-foot, triple-deck riverboat docked on the Alabama River. They walked through Riverfront Park, down to the illuminated boat, and were kindly greeted while being helped abroad. They entered the riverboat on the lower deck which was the dining room.

Cortez was observing the layout, assuring it was as he instructed. Chef Gill along with his assistant Rachel came and introduced themselves. Also, Cortez hired Fernando Mack and his band The Mack Attack, instead of the house band. He took Sophia's hand and escorted her to the middle deck. The band played Jagged Edge's "Walked Outta Heaven" when they entered.

Cortez led her to the dance floor in front of the band. He held her closely, grooving to the music. An employee approached them informing Cortez they were about to cast off.

"We're about to move?" Sophia shockingly inquired.

"Right— We headed up the Alabama River."

"Just us!"

"I don't wanna see nobody but you!" Cortez exclaimed. "I reserved the boat for you. The band, the chef, Pinot Grigio, convenience… all for you Sophie."

Sophia began to realize what was taking place and could no longer suppress her smile.

"Yeah. Chef Gill gotta fresh, clean, and delicious meal for us! Whenever you're ready to eat," he informed her. "Hope ya enjoy dis evenin'!"

Sophia reached up with her hands on both sides of his head. She stared Cortez in the eyes for at least ten seconds, before planting a real wet one on his lips. *That's what I'm talkin' 'bout.* She then removed her shawl, setting it across the back of a chair. Sophia strutted back to Cortez on the dance floor, with a devilish smirk.

He finally got a complete view of how well the dress fit. It's been some time since she's felt this carefree. Feeling at ease with him, Sophia let her hair down embracing whatever else the night had in store. Cortez led Sophia back to the lower deck. He had the lights dimmed and a candlelit table awaited them, with a chilled bottle of Pinot Grigio. He assisted her into a seat adjacent to a window.

It's dark outside, so there isn't much of a view. Besides, what Cortez wanted to see was sitting directly across from him. Being a gentleman, he poured them a glass of wine.

"Sophie you good?" Cortez inquired as he sat down.

"Yes, Cortez! I love it! And the fact we're in this place by ourselves, is crazy!" she gloated. "Guess Megan was right. I did need a night out 'cause I am enjoying myself. I can't lie!"

"Cheers— to dat then," he declared wine glass suspended in the air. "Toast to us being reunited, and the promising future ahead of us."

Sophia paused a second. She flashed a grin before following through with the toast. Chef Gill stepped out of the kitchen looking for his cue to prepare their meal. Cortez gestured with his head that they were ready to eat.

"I was hopin' you didn't spazz out 'bout being on the water," Cortez mentioned.

"Honcstly, I didn't know how I was gonna feel once they said we about to cast off," Sophia admitted. "You got me on cloud nine. And I'm having so much fun, I haven't had time to really think about it."

"Sophie dis just the beginnin', trust me," Cortez informed her reaching over and taking her hand. "It makes me happy seein' dat smile again. I wanna regain yo' trust like before. I promise I won't violate dat again!"

"I forgive you. I understand what you was going thru," she unhesitatingly revealed. "There aren't any pressing issues now, are there?"

"I don't claim to live in a perfect world, but it's a helluva lot better than when I was eleven, twelve…" he admitted gripping her hand tighter. "It wouldn't be life if it wasn't no problems, but I can promise ya dis! I don't have those kinda problems no more. I want my friend back. I want my baby back! You turned out just like I imagined, too."

"I can't say the same about you," she nonchalantly responded. "Can't say I saw you being a drug dealer. I knew you would be somebody though."

Cortez stared at her with perplexity. Chef Gill and Rachel exited the kitchen with large server trays carrying four plates each. Chef Gill served Sophia first. The menu had an assortment of dishes, so Chef Gill chose to make a few of them. Sophia received shrimp scampi, baked cod, tempura vegetables, and rice with stir-fried vegetables.

Cortez had the smoked salmon, seafood tostada bites, and mac and cheese, with fresh asparagus. They were left to their meal and Cortez refilled Sophia's glass with wine.

"Okay, they're gone now. You can answer my question," she told him before sipping the wine. "And don't be trying to get me drunk!"

"Sophie dat was a means to an end," he said. "I already got legit businesses baby. Plus, I've partnered wit' a few local business owners, too. Me and a coupla my partners 'bout to do somethin' real major. The game over wit' baby."

"Good! 'Cause I don't know where you and Marcus get that from. Y'all granddaddy would be mad as hell."

"Shid— Dats where we get it from," he informed her. "Granddaddy was a straight hustla! Bootlegged corn whiskey, Georgia skinned, ran crap houses, loan sharkin'… How you thnk he bought all dat land and set up testamentary trust funds for all six grandkids? Granddaddy wasn't bullshittin'."

The two of them continued their dialogue as they dined. Enjoying one another's company with unrestrained laughter that felt genuine again. The Harriott II Riverboat docked at Riverfront Park. Cortez conversed with Chef Gill as Sophia used the lady's room. Cortez placed Sophia's shawl on her shoulders and gave her a passionate kiss, before leading her off the vessel.

The employees continued to shower them with flatteries until they exited. They held hands and conversed about their evening strolling through Riverfront Park and headed to the car.

"I really enjoyed myself tonight Cortez O'Neal," Sophia jubilantly admitted.

"I did my thang!" he boasted. "Naw— real talk. Anythang for you baby. Ya deserve it. It's only gonna get better from here."

"I have zero complaints."

"Word. You comin' home tonight or ya gotta be to work early in the mornin'?" he sarcastically inquired.

Sophia giggled.

"Yes," she said looking up at him. "I'm comin' home tonight, baby."

****

"Cuzz where the fuck you been!" Marcus asked intrigued by Cortez's whereabouts. "Niggaz been tryna to get at cha bwoy. What's the deal?"

Marcus and Bug unexpectedly showed up at the new home, out in Mount Meigs, which Cortez had built from the ground up. No one had heard nor seen Cortez in a few days and his people were beginning to get worried. This was the last known place to check before they put out an A.P.B.

"Yeah, nigga I hit ya up a few times too," Bug added.

"I had to take a trip. I couldn't talk no way," Cortez told them, "What's happenin' though?"

"Shit for real. I hadn't heard nothin' from ya. Normally, you would've been holla'd at me by now," Bug retorted.

Cortez lounged around in a white wife-beater, some black and white Adidas slides, and black Adidas warmups. He darted outside onto the manicured lawn to retrieve the daily newspaper, "Shit bwoy! It's officially winter 'round dis bitch! Colder than a mu'fucka out dere!"

He led them into the spacious living room, tossing the newspaper onto the couch and flopping down. His eyes redirected to the 60" that hung over the fireplace, as the guys took a seat. "Make yourselves at home."

"Dis my first time out here since ya had dis built," Marcus mentioned, obviously impressed by the luxurious mini-mansion. "Dis bitch nice too, Cuzz! Really though! Dis what's up nigga!"

"Oh, bruh caked up for real!" Bug expressed to Marcus.

"Just tryna live, my niggaz," Cortez replied.

They sat around perhaps another half hour conversing about miscellaneous trends. Amidst the madness, Cortez's cell phone rang.

"Hello. Dis is he. Right. Correct. You're out front now!" he spoke into the cell phone attempting to restrain his enthusiasm. "Drop it where you're at! I'm comin' out, right now!"

Ply Car Fine Automotive Transportation was another one of Ronald's businesses. The one he agreed to deliver the Porsche Cayenne because Cortez wasn't in the mood for the trek back home. Cortez slipped on a pair of Jamaican-colored Air Forces and grabbed his black hoodie off the back of the couch, "Check out dis new toy I copped!" he told them and headed outside.

"Dats the Porsche Cayenne ain't it, Cuzz?" Marcus asked as all three walked down the driveway.

"Oh yeah! I saw dat bitch and had to have her!" Cortez replied.

Marcus and Bug inspected the vehicle through the window while Cortez signed the required documents and received essential paperwork. He shook the driver's hand and wished him a safe trip to his next destination.

"Hold up! Lemme put on some," Cortez exclaimed. "We 'bout to hitta few corners and ride dis bitch!"

Chapter 12

■■■■

Cortez has set the standard, along with his lifestyle, it's no shocking revelation that his influence swayed others to follow suit. Marcus headed the operation in Lowndes County and the surrounding rural counties. He and his team are the most profitable out of Cortez's organization.

Money was abundantly coming at such a fast pace that Marcus couldn't help but re-evaluate things. Lowndes County would forever be home but there's Megan and the kids to consider, too. *As a whole, what's best for them?*

Montgomery has a slightly better school system, much more opportunities as well as resources. Still, he would maintain the units in the projects for those late nights when he's unable to drive back to the city. He's the boss of a multi-million-dollar operation. He knew this wouldn't abruptly end, therefore he decided it was time to uproot his family and relocate.

Sophia spent the majority of her morning chauffeuring Megan and her kids around town. Megan was house shopping, and narrowed it down to two homes, out of twelve. One is located on Fisk Road, and the other off of Carmichael Road. Both were four bedrooms, two and a half baths, big front and backyards, and also extremely spacious. She couldn't distinguish which of the two homes would be the best for them. So, she decided to bring Marcus along one day to help decide.

They started house shopping, which turned into girls' shopping. Something the sisters have in common. Sophia took Megan to DiVa Nail's Salon on Ann Street.

"You talk to Cortez lately?" Megan asked her sitting side by side soaking their feet. "Y'all tryna rekindle that old flame?"

"We talk every day! We had a blast the other night. Kinda had that feel like when we was younger. That friendly, carefree feeling. But Cortez got too much going on though," Sophia affirmed.

"Girl— you know that nigga gonna hustle."

"Nooo— not that. Well, that too. 'Cause if I get back with him and he gets locked up, I'm still gonna be by myself. I don't want that to happen, but it's a possibility though!" Sophia expressed to her sister. "You told me you've heard about all the different women. I ain't got time for that either. We're adults now, not horny teenagers."

"Sophie girl— you gotta claim what's yours!" Megan declared. "You can't be passive wit' dese triflin' azz bitches or niggaz! They'll trample all over you. You're my sister, and I love you to death. I just want you to be happy and I see how he lights ya up. Sophie you deserve to be happy."

Sophia sat in silence. She intently thought about the advice her baby sister had just provided. They finished their pedicures, got a clear coat on the nails then loaded the kids up. They headed to The Shoppes at Eastchase, purchasing a few shirts, and bags, along with some outfits for the kids. It's been a while since they all hung out, so they dined at Red Robin's to get the kids something to eat.

"Marcus tried that shit! I showed my azz!" Megan willingly expressed. "I immediately checked them skank bitches! Wrapped that up real quick. I didn't spare Marcus azz either! I let that nigga know he ain't gonna be disrespecting me. Have me looking crazy out here!"

"I don't know if I can really take him serious anymore. He cut me off before. That shit hurts! What says he won't do it again?"

"Sophie y'all were twelve, thirteen years old. And you said he told you why he did it. Not making excuses for him, but I think he for real. What other reason would he be taking your greedy azz out?"

"Whatever. We'll see," Sophia responded.

"I know you got some the other night?"

"Sure did! Much better than before! This time, it'll be on my terms when I give him these goodies!"

******

Cortez hadn't been this excited about something materialistic in some time. He wasn't anxious in the sense of flaunting the vehicle. Cortez was more like that kid on Christmas morning, eager to test out their new toy. Cortez opened up the Porsche on I-85 trying to get a feel for it. They rode around the city before pulling up on Kelt.

"Put dis bitch on the slab, my nigga!" Bug shouted from the backseat.

"Bwoy ya gettin' it in," Kelt said leaning up behind Cortez in the backseat on the driver's side. "My nigga got cribs, mini-mansions, and shit. Foreign whips, an arena wit' his name on it. Bwoy ya puttin' on like E-40, in a major way!"

"Ain't it, mane!" Marcus exuberantly agreed looking back at Kelt.

"Cut it out. I'mma take advantage of my opportunity. Dats why I stressed dat shit so hard wit' y'all niggaz. All dis shit can be gone tomorrow. Shit happens!" Cortez earnestly explained to his crew. "Everybody's in a helluva position to stack some real bread. Dats how I designed it. Wit' y'all in mind! So, ain't no animosity amongst us. Dat shit destroys cliques, and we don't do dat."

"Ain't nobody in dis crew flaw," Bug asserted.

"Managin' yo' guap right y'all can do exactly what I do. Stop trickin' off on dese buzzard azz bitches Bug—"

"I'm the only one ya puttin' on blast?" Bug intervened.

"I ain't puttin' nobody on blast. I'm tryna hip ya 'cause I fuck wit' cha. 'Cause I got love for ya," Cortez said distinguishing the two. "My first cousin sittin' up here on the side of me. Two sisters kids, and he ain't no more important than anyone of y'all. Kelt my dawg! Ask him what I told him. Bruh don't blow dis 'cause you don't wanna leave the street shit alone. Shootin' niggaz over bullshit, we did dat years ago."

"Facts," Kelt admitted.

"Why risk goin' to prison over some goofy shit? Sittin' in dat bitch, sick as fuck! Wit' a million reasons how ya could've prevented being dere," Cortez affirmed.

"Real shit!" Kelt agreed. "But everybody ain't the same though, Cuzz. I'mma street nigga! A real street nigga! Dis what I do. I hustle in the slums and live damn good. I can't knock the next man on how he eats. It's certain shit nobody can duplicate."

"You right, to a certain extent. Some niggaz ain't comfortable on another playin' field, so you gotta let 'em do they thang," Marcus said voicing his opinion. "Dat was me up until lately. Seein' the moves niggaz makin' forced me to look at my life differently dese past few months. Splurgin' and fuckin' off my bread ain't gonna be 'bout shit in the end. Nothin' but some memories."

"I'mma real street nigga too! And the streets respect what cha got nigga, not what cha had!" Cortez told them.

"All of us eatin' good nigga! All of us!" Marcus said respectively looking at the clique. "I don't know what y'all stash lookin' like, but every nigga in dis circle should at least be a millionaire."

"Multi! All of y'all should be playin' wit' a few million," Cortez admitted.

"I'm straight! Ya dig? The bizness suits and shit just ain't me, dats what I'm sayin'. I'mma stay in my lane," Kelt explained.

"It ain't 'bout what cha wear. You missin' the point. Y'all grown. Do what cha wanna do. But why jeopardize everythang ya grind for over some bullshit?" Cortez pleaded.

"We ain't you Cuzz," Kelt snapped. "'Cause, it worked for you don't necessarily mean it's gonna work for the next man."

"Where ya headed anyway?" Bug asked deterring the direction of the conversation.

"Shit, we might as well ride to the A. Ball a lil' bit. Unless y'all got some other shit to do?" Cortez replied.

"Cool," Marcus said.

"I'm wit' it," Bug stated simultaneously tapping Kelt on the arm. "What's happenin' my nigga? Let's show dese niggaz how to ball!"

"Let's ride," Kelt responded dropping a pill in Bug's palm.

"The A-Town it is!" Cortez yelled mashing the accelerator.

****

"Y'all bring them bags inside," Po' told the kids.

North Pass is a residential neighborhood that has fallen into ruins throughout the years. The high volume of drug activity and violence helped destroy the community. Po' and Katrina have been on and off in their relationship since middle school. Katrina's older sister, Mary went on random binges and oftentimes used her house as a trap. Which deprived her kids of necessities to live.

Po' knew this and would gather the kids, whose ages ranged from five to fourteen. He took them shopping for clothes, groceries, and toys. He would leave Katrina a quarter-brick to grind at Mary's house, while he and the kids were shopping. Once Po' was assured the kids were at ease he'd post up on the front porch, scoping the scenery.

He mainly watched the flow of traffic, as well as Johnny Law. In previous months, Jumpstreet has tried to take back control over this area. But the fact remained that the children needed to be provided for. Po's theory was relatable to them and justified it as being worth the risk.

Although his lifestyle had tremendously changed, Po' still considered himself an ordinary guy. It's probably why the hood embraced him and showed so much love. His kids were cheerful as they ran around and played. Because their day was coming to an end, as the sun began to set.

Laquanda, the eldest of the five kids was in the back, bathing a younger sibling. Po' was in the kitchen dicing veggies for the tacos he was preparing for dinner. Mary staggered in the side door, looking horrible with both hands on her hips and eyes deadlocked on Po'.

They silently stared at each other, "What up?" Po' asked.

"Move! I'll cook for my own kids!" Mary blurted out.

"Shawty, go 'head on."

"Nigga— dis my sister's house! Those my muthafuckin' kids," she slurred.

"Mary I ain't goin' dere wit' cha tonight."

"Move— I'mma fix my kids somethin' to eat. Tryna make me seem unfit," Mary said trying to bump Po' out the way.

"I ain't tryna do shit! Ya doin' a helluva job all by yourself! Ya should've been fixed dese kids somethin'. Fuck you sayin'! All ya concerned 'bout is gettin' geeked. So, miss me wit' dat shit."

"You the reason I'm like dis," Mary snapped. "Got my sister over dere at my house, now, sellin' yo' shit."

"Bitch lemme tell ya somethin'," Po' said infuriated. "She's sellin' my shit, to take care yo' kids, bitch! I ain't trippin' 'bout dese kids, but don't ever front me wit' dat bullshit. You the one fuckin' up! So, don't blame me for yo' shit! A better yet, get the fuck out wit' dat goofy azz shit! We coolin', enjoyin' ourselves. Ain't nobody goin' for dat sympathy reel you tryna run. Get yo' azz up outta here!"

****

The guys arrived in Atlanta in a little under an hour and a half. As they're entering downtown, Cortez reminisced about his first trip to Orlando. The hospitality bestowed upon him by the family. He felt obligated to show appreciation to his team for fulfilling their roles in the organization.

First, the guy's stopped at Lenox Square Mall because this was a spontaneous trip, and no one had a change of clothes. Before they exited the vehicle Cortez was uncompromising about the guy's money not spending, and all expenses being covered by him. They reminded you of middle school boys meeting up at the mall.

They're high as a Georgia pine tree and interactive with some of the south's most attractive women. Also, they're in and out of department stores purchasing gear from world-renowned designers. The guys then cruised the city in search of a hotel to stay in, until they leave. Cortez decided on the W.

The guys were treated with courtesy by the hotel staff. All they wanted was to be alone amongst themselves to unwind. Cortez and Kelt drank a couple of shots of brandy. Bug and Marcus smoked a blunt as they enjoyed the view of the city. Even that was brief before they chose Ruth's Chris Steak House to sit down and have a meal.

Feeling amped with food on their stomachs the guys anticipated what the night had in store. Cortez drove around unsure of exactly where to go, and by happenstance drove into a traffic jam. Cortez eased along in traffic close enough to read the illuminated billboard: Cleveland Cavs-vs-Atlanta Hawks.

"Let's go watch the King get off!" Bug eagerly suggested.

Cortez navigated off I-20 to Phillips Arena. They momentarily sat in the car, as Marcus did surgery on a blunt wrapper stuffed with Sour Diesel. He rolled it as if it came from the factory. They stood aside the Porsche smoking the blunts before approaching the arena. Cortez noticed there was a multitude of people who filled the gym in support of their team.

It didn't matter how many shots the guys drank. It wasn't gonna change the fact that Lebron James torched Atlanta for forty-two points, twelve rebounds, seven assists, three blocks, and two steals, with the win. A typical night for the King, and yes, they were entertained.

After the game, they went back to the W to freshen up and get a change of clothes. Everyone had been eating pills throughout the day, except Cortez, but he's ready to party now. He took a pill and a half, then escorted the crew out into the nightlife of the ATL. Indecisive about where they desired to go, Kelt suggested Strokers. The other guys agreed in unison.

Cortez popped the hatchback and opened a black leather satchel bag concealed behind the back seats. He produced several stacks of hundred-dollar bills. Cortez handed them $10k apiece and stuffed $50k in the front pockets of his gray Sean John jeans. The guys bum-rushed the strip club like they owned it.

The atmosphere was electrifying, with scantily clad women everywhere. Some women danced on stage. The other women gave lap dances, worked the room, or prepared for their act. The city's elitist dope boys occupied the club, along with a group of athletes and a couple of entertainers. The majority of the money was converted into dollar bills. They also had quite a few twenties, and fifties, for the women they deemed worthy of bigger bills.

Popping bottles as they threw money the guys felt they were exactly where they belonged. They weren't going to be modest amidst all the excitement. Once they located a spot to set up, everyone except Cortez got a lap dance. His mind began to operate when he noticed certain entertainers were in attendance tonight.

With the grand opening of the O'Neal Amphitheater scheduled in a few weeks, this was the perfect opportunity to lock up some quality acts. Cortez introduced himself to The Youngbloodz, Too Short, Lil' Jon and The Eastside Boyz, Young Jeezy, and Slim Thug. He didn't crowd them. He has a tremendous amount of respect for all of them. Cortez considered it an honor to personally meet Short Dogg. Not to mention, smoking a blunt with him was a moment that'll last for ages.

Throughout the night Cortez and his clique popped bottles, smoked blunts, and showered the dancers with money. Cortez's alcohol consumption was kept to a minimum. He wanted his guys to enjoy themselves, but that's not why he didn't overindulge. They're out of bounds and anything's subject to happen. Therefore Cortez stayed on point in observing their surroundings.

He conversed with some of the local guys in attendance, networking as he kept his eyes on his comrades. Cortez managed to gain insight into a few dancers who privately perform. He needed to show the clique a good time, plus it was overdue. Cortez got four of the baddest dancers that guaranteed satisfaction and gave them his suite number.

****

As the sun began to set, the temperature started to drop. Sherry hugged Po' inside of his navy-blue pea coat. He leaned against his Porsche Cayenne out front of his grandmother's house in Newtown. They're engaged in conversation when Po' realized the same police squad car drove through a few times. Really he hadn't given it much thought because that was the norm.

Shortly, a white Dodge Ram 2500 abruptly pulled up. Po' tried to decipher whether or not it was Jumpstreet or a hit. Within a few seconds of capturing Sherry's reaction, Po' was able to decipher what just occurred. The decal with Knox Construction Company plastered on the door was the confirmation needed.

Harrison bolted out of the truck clutching a chrome revolver. Sherry met him before he could get near Po', but Harrison was determined to get him. He vigorously tried getting past Sherry, to no avail.

"What the fuck are you doing?" Harrison shouted looking past her eyes deadlocked on his target.

"Harrison! He's just a friend!" Sherry responded.

"A fucking friend! You're out here in this fucking place hugged up on this son-of-a-bitch, and you expect me to believe he's a friend!"

At that point, Po' eased behind the Porsche in case Harrison managed to let off some rounds. Some of Po's soldiers were posted up in the vicinity and began to approach with weapons drawn.

"Baby please put the gun away and let me explain," Sherry pleaded.

"Please do! Please fucking explain!" Harrison shouted in her face. "Before you say a word, I know everything! You even co-signed for the fucking car that coward's hiding behind."

Sherry was extremely shocked by the statement. Furthering her confusion was how did Harrison know of her whereabouts?

"How could you? You're my wife! After all I do for you," Harrison murmured.

Po's soldiers formed a wall between them. The only thing stopping a barrage of gunfire was the two police squad cars slowly closing in from both directions. Po's soldiers concealed their weapons and dispersed toward Mrs. Gordon's property.

"Sir— put down the weapon!" an officer yelled out gun pointed at Harrison.

Harrison immediately complied.

"Get face down on the ground!" the officer instructed him.

The other policeman moved in to subdue Harrison. They placed handcuffs on him, then brought him to his feet.

"This motherfucker sleeping with my wife!" Harrison pleaded.

"Hey my man! You got the wrong idea," Po' said.

"I know what I saw!" Harrison snapped.

One of the officers placed Harrison in the backseat of the squad car, while the other scrutinized the revolver. Po' got in the Porsche to get away from the scene. Officer Hart, who drove through before this incident flagged him down.

"You're lucky I was here, or you'd be a dead man," Officer Hart told Po'.

"Whatever," Po' replied before driving off.

How the fuck this chump find us?

Officer Hart noticed Sherry wasn't your typical white woman that frequented these drug-infested areas. He was intrigued to find out who this attractive woman was hugged up with a known drug dealer. Those times he rode past them, Officer Hart ran Sherry's plates.

After revealing who the vehicle belonged to, Officer Hart whose job is to protect and serve, further investigated. He found out Sherry was a married woman. Officer Hart felt obligated to divulge the affair to Harrison Knox. Officer Hart assured Harrison it was true, then gave him the location where he could see for himself.

Chapter 13

■■■■

November 2010

Since Cortez's release from federal holding Sophia hadn't given her husband much room to breathe. She haven't experienced anything of that magnitude before and was overwhelmed by the possibility of Cortez having to do a bid. After everything they've accumulated this wasn't how she envisioned them enjoying life together.

Therefore, she did everything within her power to see that Cortez doesn't do anything else that'll be detrimental to his freedom. Cortez and Sophia were spending a lot of time together, but he received a call that wouldn't be ignored. Driving to Shorter, Alabama he was still puzzled about why Milton McGregor wanted to meet with him.

Cortez heard a lot about the legendary casino owner. But only had the pleasure of meeting the guy, once, briefly at a fundraiser about two years ago. Mr. McGregor came up with his phone number and also invited him to the Oasis, Mr. McGregor's Five-Star Hotel and Restaurant adjacent to VictoryLand Casino.

Must've made a helluva first impression.

Balling on another playing field Cortez not only dressed the part, but he also made a conscious effort to be mindful in all discussions with Mr. McGregor. Cortez stepped out of the Range Rover clad in a steel gray Salvatore Ferragamo suit, a white shirt by the same designer, and black cap-toe laced shoes.

He strolled into the restaurant to be met by a serious, but polite older black woman. She showed Cortez to the table where Mr. McGregor was wrapping up a conversation with the young lady that accompanied him.

"Glad you could make it," Mr. McGregor told Cortez when he stood to shake his hand. "This is my daughter, Tabitha."

"Pleasure to meet you," Cortez said gently shaking her hand, "I'm Cortez O'Neal."

"Pleasure to meet you," Tabitha replied. "I have pressing business to attend to."

"Call me later and let me know the outcome," Mr. McGregor told her as she positioned her purse onto her shoulder. "Have a seat Mr. O'Neal."

Cortez unbuttoned his blazer and took a seat.

"Nice suit. Business must be good," Mr. McGregor stated.

"Thank you. Not doin' quite as well as you, but we keepin' the lights on."

Mr. McGregor couldn't contain his chuckle. "You've had lunch?"

"No."

"Great! You can join me for lunch. I truly don't like dining by myself. How do you like your steak?"

"Mid-well."

"Okay. We serve a fine cut New York Strip you'll love," Mr. McGregor informed him signaling for a waitress. "Bring us two New York strips. One medium rare, and the other mid-well with a bottle of Betts and Scholl's."

"Mr. McGregor you gotta nice set up here. The last time I was here, none of this was here," Cortez admitted.

"You hadn't been here within the past couple of years."

"Somethin' like dat."

"I wanted my guests to be comfortable. People come from near and far to see us, all up I-85, and down I-65. Some might've had too much to drink, and really shouldn't get on the road. Others may want to finish playing and are just too tired," Mr. McGregor explained. "Now they have a spot to get some rest or a decent meal before they continue. Gotta give the people what they want. They're the ones who make us. Kinda like what you're doing over off of Fleming Road."

The waitress returned with their bottle of wine and meal, "Appreciate ya. Smells delicious," Cortez told the waitress.

"Hope you enjoy," she replied.

The two enjoyed their meals while engaging in small talk. They spoke on different ideas that'll help the city flourish, also who's who throughout the city. They picked each other's brains and tried to get a feel for one another. Mr. McGregor offered dessert, but Cortez declined, stuffed by the entrée.

Instead, they drank another glass of wine and Mr. McGregor led the way to his suite, which oversees the entire compound. He handed Cortez a Cuban cigar, lighting it before he lit his own. Mr. McGregor stood in the window gazing down on his empire, then excessively exhaled smoke.

"Kid I think you know why I asked you to come here," Mr. McGregor said in his distinctive southern accent.

Cortez scanned the room.

Dis ain't no muthafuckin' hit, is it?

"I been wonderin' since I got the call," Cortez responded.

"Don't you have some legal woes?" Mr. McGregor asked still looking out the window.

"Yeah. Why you ask?" Cortez curiously inquired.

"You wanna know why you have these issues? Kid, you affected alotta income for some of the top political figures in this city. And they're peeved at you."

"How?"

"That amphitheater you own stopped a bunch of revenue for the Montgomery Civic Center and Garrett Coliseum. Son you didn't grease none of the upper echelons palms," Mr. McGregor explained to him. "How do you think they felt about a young, black kid making a power move like that?"

"I don't give a fuck how they felt," Cortez blatantly expressed. "When me and my team was starvin', didn't nobody give us nothin'! So, you tryna put the press down on me?"

Mr. McGregor stared at Cortez with this smirk on his face. "Perhaps you've got the wrong idea. It's obvious I have money and don't need, nor want, a quarter of yours. Truthfully, everyone's impressed you pulled it off. I'm telling you, you were targeted, young man. I have been greasing palms in this city twenty-five years before you were born!"

Mr. McGregor had Cortez's undivided attention. He sat there carefully listening.

"You're in the big leagues now and the rules vary. These parasites aren't alright when your livelihood changes for the better and theirs remains the same. Kids' college tuitions, vacationing for the Misses, and gifts for the Mistresses depend on guys like us."

Cortez contemplated everything he'd just heard.

"Kid I felt obligated to let you know why this was unexpectedly happening, and I wish you the best. We have some disagreements on how we conduct business, but I admire you kid. I really do. You're the future!" Mr. McGregor told Cortez and extended his hand.

Cortez looked him in the eyes and shook his hand, "Why ya felt obligated to let me know?" he asked.

"You remind me a lot of myself when I first started."

Cortez drove directly back to the city. He replayed the entire conversation in his head, trying to decipher every angle behind the meeting. If it wasn't a trap to incriminate him, what was Mr. McGregor's motive for telling him what they've done? Cortez couldn't be too trusting at this point. Especially after what Judith warned him about the other day. He never mentioned it to Mr. McGregor, but some palms did get greased. Cortez felt like he got played. Several violent thoughts ran rampant through Cortez's mind over this debacle.

****

February 2009

The whole hood came out with several others throughout the city once they got wind of Bug's Bash. He knew this would be one to remember. Club Celebration's, Gator's, Office Depot, and the entire Vaughn Plaza parking lot were full of cars. The guest began parking on the other side of the plaza.

Bug was at the door fluctuating the price of admission. No less than $40, up to $100 for the more obvious hustlers. The most attractive women got in free. Trying to impress the women made the hustlers less concerned about expenditures. Towering over Bug we're two ex-gangbangers, reformed prisoners who every waking moment was on the weight pile.

Big Melly and Bull weren't ones to shy away from the action. So, getting paid to kick ass was right up their alley. The line was still long, and the club's capacity has almost reached its apex. Bug already decided to allow five more before cutting it off and going to enjoy himself.

"I never called, and honestly I didn't know if the invitation was still good," Desiree candidly stated.

"Hey, Lil' Mama! Ain't no pressure you didn't call," Bug replied, recognizing Desiree. "I been doin' so much since I last saw you. But your invitation is always good wit' me love."

"Oh. Okay. 'Cause I sure was gonna be pissed the fuck off! Gettin' dressed for nothin'.'"

"Naw— None of dat! And ya lookin' hot as fuck tonight, I can't lie!" Bug said before taking her hand. "Yo', she the last one. Come on baby. Let's get outta dis air and go enjoy dis bangin' azz party."

"Dats it y'all! Can't no more fit in here!" Big Melly shouted in a deep baritone.

Killa Kat was the D.J. for the party and had the club rocking. Right next to the D.J. booth were Cortez, Sophia, Megan, and Marcus. They were chilling with a couple of bottles of Dom Perignon on the table, absorbing the energy in the club. Megan loved every minute because she was with her man, and Sophia was with the man she was destined to be with.

Sophia looked refreshed as she uncontrollably smiled and laughed. Cortez always did bring out the best in her. Across the club Po' and his affiliates occupied a section. Some of his guys stood on the chairs rocking along with a Small Time Ballaz classic. Po' was incognito underneath a black Gucci bucket hat, twisting a blunt. Although his eight solid golds, four tops, and bottom, were a dead giveaway.

The dance floor's packed and there's a crowd of women within Po's view. They showed zero concern for the two women sitting beside him. These women's erotic dance moves were captivating enough to garner Po's attention.

Clubbing wasn't something Kelt did frequently. He's the epitome of the term hood nigga. Since they've formed their clique, this was the most he'd ever partied. Honestly, it's been therapeutic for him. Gradually, another passage opened that was non-existent in him before. Kelt got a single table in the center of the club with a bottle of Patrón, and a six-pack of Corona on ice. At this point, Kelt's complacency led him to get a lap dance.

Bug and Desiree approached Cortez and the others with an unlit Cohiba Siglo I in his mouth, and a bottle of bubbly in hand. With his free hand Bug retrieved another cigar from his Evisu jeans pocket, handing it to Cortez.

"Dis my big bruh. Dis Marcus. And dese they old ladies," Bug respectively introduced them. "First cousins, by two sisters. They family! Y'all dis Desiree."

Cortez looked over his Versace frames for a better view of Desiree, as they greeted her in unison, "Hello. She pretty, Bug," Cortez admitted then took Sophia by the hand to the dance floor.

Killa Kat had T Pain's "Buy You A Drink" playing. Cortez was grooving to the song while holding Sophia closely in his arms.

"Baby dis feels so right to me."

"Ummm," she delightfully sighed, burying her head in his chest.

"Sophie, I need to apologize…"

"Cortez don't," Sophia intervened. "It's not necessary."

"It's so necessary! I was young, priorities outta order, and I just didn't know what I had when we was together. Second chances don't present themselves too often, and I wanna make thangs right dis time," Cortez expressed. "I plan to stick wit' what we have, and I promise to never again take ya for granted baby. You're the one piece missin', dat'll complete my life."

The party was officially on the way once the Deuce Komradz banger "We Rollin'" got played. Men and women alike swarmed the dance floor, performing the local dance create for the song. Many could relate because they were in the zone, rolling on x-pills. Everyone's energy in the club intensified by a hundred. The women were provocatively dressed, showing no shame in shaking their asses.

Some guys assumed their position behind the women. Being the host of the party, Bug maneuvered throughout the club with Desiree on his arm. He assured every guest in attendance was enjoying themselves. Bug did a splendid job juggling everything while being very attentive to his special guest.

He made Desiree feel extremely special. Bug introduced her to different individuals he considered relevant, also they'll run on the dance floor to certain songs. This treatment made her feel like the center of attention. Whatever she desired, Bug made it his business to fulfill the request.

Cortez came out to support Bug, and secretly oversee the party in hopes of things not getting out of hand. Satisfied with the results so far and confident no madness would transpire, he decided to call it a night. Cortez conversed with a few people from Regency Park and elsewhere, along with Marcus and Megan. He even confided in Bug about how proud he was of him.

Bug openly admitted his unhappiness over the early departure, but he understood. Cortez and Sophia exited the nightclub. Cortez gave Big Melly and Bull an additional $200 to make sure the party ended with no incidents of violence. He knew the significance of not attracting unwanted attention from law enforcement, or the media, due to violence. That'll be detrimental to the overall plan if any of his clique got jammed up.

Cortez's Porsche Cayenne was parked in the first parking space, directly in front of the nightclub. Cortez being a gentleman, opened the passenger door for Sophia. Walking behind the vehicle, Po' mysteriously appeared. Reacting off impulse, Cortez upped with his .45 Automatic Colt Pistol.

"Whoa—" Po' shouted both hands raised in the air. "It's just me Cuzz!"

"Bwoy you 'bout to get two in ya, bullshittin'!" Cortez aggressively stated. "Dese the spots where niggaz be tryna lick. I'm on point!"

"Is it safe to put my hands down?"

"Mane, what the fuck ya want anyway?" Cortez irritably asked putting the pistol back on his hip. "I'm 'bouta go lay up."

"I see ya snatched ya a nice— lil' piece up outta dere. I ain't want shit, my nigga, I was just blowin' at cha. Fuckin' wit' cha."

Cortez cranked the Porsche and turned on the heater, so Sophia would be nice and comfy. Their conversation continued, "You must've saw the Cayenne I copped?" Po' inquired.

"Naw—"

"Yeah I got the '09 a coupla months ago. My white bitch got it."

"Dats what's up. I had dis probably a month now," Cortez replied pointing at the vehicle, "a 2010 Turbo S. I copped dis bitch when I was in Florida. Off the showroom floor."

"Cuzz since I been fuckin' wit' cha heavy, shit been good! Bwoy I gotta keep it hunnid. My nigga I really 'preciate the opportunity," Po' openly admitted in a drunken slur. "Real talk, I was gettin' guap, but fuckin' wit' cha introduced me to another lifestyle I was unfamiliar wit'. But damn sure been envious of. I ain't had the chance to thank ya Cuzz."

"Dats what love is bruh. You ain't gotta thank me for no shit like dat. Dats what real ones do. Looky here, lemme get dis girl outta dis cold. I'mma fuck wit' cha tomorrow."

"Bet it up," Po' told Cortez giving him dap.

Cortez sat in the driver's seat a second contemplating, before his train of thought was broken, "What's wrong?" Sophia asked him.

"Nothin'," Cortez immediately answered. "You ready to go home?"

"I'm ridin' wit' you."

"Let's ride, baby."

Chapter 14

■ ■ ■ ■

Being relentless was the main attribute that positioned Cortez, with the status he's acquired. True enough he retained Kelt the best attorney in the city. Cortez still wasn't content with the possibilities that lingered in the wing.

He never mentioned his intentions so no one wouldn't have prior knowledge, nor act out of character. Early Sunday morning Cortez left home carrying a Louis Vuitton satchel. He left Sophia asleep because he planned to be back before she awakened.

He showed her a new exercise after they left Club Celebration earlier. So, she's expected to sleep in a little later today. Cortez took I-85 to the Fairview exit, in route to Gibbs Village. When he entered the housing projects, he passed a patrolman on duty for the Housing Authority.

He parked out front of Monesha's unit. Cortez placed the pistol in the lining of his Evisu jeans, covering it up with a forest green Ralph Lauren RLX fleece. Headed up the walkway Cortez observed a handful of kids out playing. Cortez kept his defenses up as he knocked on the door.

"Who is it?" a female grumbled.

"Dis Cortez. Monesha here?" he asked.

"Who is you?" she asked through the door.

"Baby it's breezy out here. Can I talk to ya?"

"No! I don't know you, nigga!"

Cortez's giggle was unrestrained, "Love one, I don't mean no harm. You know Kelt? Dats my nigga! I just wanna speak wit' cha 'bout the shit dat happened out here."

"Hang on!"

He stood on the front porch a couple more minutes before the front door opened. A petite redbone, with menacing cat eyes pierced through the screen door at him.

"I ain't never seen you with Kelt before," she affirmed revealing her four open-faced gold teeth. "You the police?"

"Shawty lemme in out dis air! I ain't no muthafuckin' police!" Cortez snapped, peeved by the insult.

Monesha gave this coy look before removing the latch to let Cortez inside.

Damn dis lil' bitch fine as fuck! Jazzy lil' broad. See why Kelt and dat nigga bumped heads.

"Check dis out. Kelt said yo' bwoy rushed him and left him no choice, but to bust him."

"Kelt know he supposed to call before he came over here," Monesha said in a whiny voice.

"The first thing he said shawty—"

"Now he wanna get mad at me. He won't answer my calls nor call me."

"Shawty he gotta take care of dis case," Cortez said planting a seed once sensing her affection for Kelt. "Dats why I'm here. Corey pressed charges on my nigga and dis was just a big misunderstandin', for real. I wanna holla at lil' buddy and see if I can lace his pockets, plus take care his medical bills so we can put dis behind us."

"I don't know."

"Lemme blow at him and see what he talkin' 'bout."

"You want his number?"

"Yeah. Where he staying at?"

Monesha recited the number as Cortez punched it into his cell phone, programming the address in his head. He apologized for the disturbance and tried smoothing things out by giving Monesha a fifty-dollar bill, along with a few grams of purp.

Cortez didn't waste any time already on the west side of town. He opted not to call because he had no idea what was going through Corey's head. He chose to show up unannounced. That way no surprises would be waiting upon his arrival. Cortez trekked through the different neighborhoods, buying time to prepare his approach.

Cortez took a left off of W. Jeff Davis Avenue onto Holcombe Street and parked aside the curb in front of the duplex house. Same routine as before when he visited Monesha. As he moved toward the front door a guy stepped out onto the porch, gingerly moving, which indicated this was his man.

"Corey what's good hustla?" Cortez greeted and attentively watched him.

"Who the fuck is you?" Corey asked.

"Call me the fixer. I wanna blow at cha 'bout somethin'. I ain't here for no bullshit, straight bizness! Come sit in the truck a minute and let's chop it up."

Corey glanced at the Range Rover then stared at Cortez, from his Polo boots, up to his Cartier frames. Intuition told him money was involved which made Corey limp to the SUV. Cortez adjusted the heater to a more comfortable temperature. Cortez sat the pistol on his lap in plain view.

"First, my nigga don't be intimidated by this fire, it's for protection, not you," Cortez thoroughly explained. "You smoke?"

"Sometimes," Corey replied.

"Here. Fire dis up," Cortez instructed Corey passing him the blunt. "The reason I came thru, was to holla at cha 'bout dat lil' situation, out in Gibbs Village."

Cortez cell phone rang.

"Hey baby," Cortez answered.

"Where are you? Why you left me here alone?" Sophia inquired.

"You're at home baby! I had to make a run, and you was sleepin' so good, I didn't wanna wake ya. Gone make some breakfast. I'll be dere in 'bouta half an hour."

"What you want?" Sophia asked him.

"Whatever ya hook up baby," he said ending the call. "'Cuse dat Cuzz. As you can see, I got other shit I'm supposed to be doin' too. But dis just how important it was. I wish he wouldn't have shot cha, but I'm glad it wasn't more serious. He said you rushed him, so he had no choice."

"He could've knuckled up!" Corey mentioned.

"Niggaz playin' to win out here! Ya gotta defend yourself. Y'all was dealin' wit' the same woman and dat shit happens wit' fly niggaz. But it's bullshit to lose yo' life over," Cortez explained. "Me and dude close and he's needed out here. So, what I'mma do, I'mma pay your medical bills, put $10k in your pocket to completely forget 'bout dis shit. Feel me?"

Cortez lifted the console and retrieved $10k and sat the cash atop the leather console.

"A street nigga can work miracles wit' dis bread," Cortez mentioned in an attempt to persuade him.

"Fuck dat! Dat nigga shot me! And his pussy azz goin' to prison!" Corey shouted.

"My nigga, what you gain by him goin' to prison? You still got shot! Can't take dat back. I'm makin' ya an offer you can't refuse. Tell you what. Thank about it, and I'll call ya later to see if ya came to your senses."

"Ain't shit to thank 'bout! Fuck dat nigga!" Corey said with such disdain he was trembling when he slammed the door of the SUV.

Shit'll be cheaper dis way anyhow.

Cortez drove up the road a piece before calling a number that was programmed on speed dial. He made a right on Mildred Street as the phone rang.

"Been a while," the guy said in a low baritone.

"Right. I need to see ya," Cortez replied.

"Bet dat," he responded then ended the call.

****

Blissful and stress-free would be the best words to describe life for all parties since Cortez formed this alliance. Being in this position enabled these young men to accumulate money inconceivable to most people, generated luxuries, along with a lifestyle. Observing Cortez influenced Kelt to re-evaluate how limited his potential had been. Questions began to arise within him, and a revelation occurred.

How much longer could he stay off the radar? Especially, with the amounts of money rapidly coming. Never purchasing anything of significant value, where would he have to invest this money? In this game, being on top meant you're targeted and could have your life

*taken any day to obtain your riches. What's the reason of acquiring
wealth and you can't enjoy it, due to death or incarceration?*

Ja'Lisa Grissom is from Jackson, Mississippi. She's a sophomore
at Alabama State University and majoring in architectural design.
She chose Alabama State because she earned an academic
scholarship, plus to get away from home. Ja'Lisa and Kelt met about
a year and a half ago, at a tailgate party outside of the Multiplex at
Cramton Bowl. They started out inseparable, then the flame fizzled,
up until about nine months ago.

They reunited, tightening their relationship and things have been
flowing smoothly ever since. Kelt felt an undeniable connection with
Ja'Lisa. Perhaps the relationship was attributed to their similar
upbringing. Ja'Lisa's relentless about bettering her situation. Not
permitting her past to dictate the future.

Kelt has so much admiration for her, based on that simple
principle. Money was never the topic of their conversation when they
were together. Being a part-time waitress at Ruby Tuesday's, along
with doing students' hair was how Ja'Lisa survived. Kelt took notice.

It's three-fifteen a.m. and Kelt was still cruising in his newly
purchased Cadillac CTS-V. He's been driving around the city for
over an hour, debating should this next step be taken. He pulled up
to the security gate of Bristol Downs, punching in the access code.
When the gate rolled back, Kelt slowly drove through. He took the
first right and navigated around the curve, then backed into a parking
space that faced the apartments.

He grabbed the .40 cal, concealing it underneath his black LRG
hoodie. Kelt then popped the trunk retrieving a black Gucci
backpack. Observing his surroundings he walked upstairs to the
apartment and rang the doorbell.

"Who is it?" she asked.

"It's me baby!"

He heard the unlocking before the door crept open. A chocolaty beauty in a short ASU t-shirt, displaying thighs and ass reminiscent of a quarter horse stood there. Ja'Lisa swayed her hips down the hallway, back to the bedroom. The television had the room dimly lit, so Kelt hit the light switch on the wall.

"Baby—" Ja'Lisa whined.

Kelt didn't say a word. He snatched the comforter off of Ja'Lisa and dumped the money on top of her. Realizing what has been dumped atop of her, those almond-shaped eyes got big as fifty-cent pieces.

"Keltric what you do!" Ja'Lisa asked hastily sitting straight up in bed. "Where did you get dis money!"

"Calm down baby," Kelt managed to answer in complete laughter. "I been had dis bread. Get yo' stuff together, you're comin' wit' me!"

"Where are you goin'?" she curiously asked.

"Daybreak we gonna find us a nice crib. So we can stop playin' house." Kelt told her removing his top displaying his chiseled, tattooed body, and the pistol stuck in his jeans.

"Keltric why you got dat?" Ja'Lisa asked him.

"For protection," Kelt blatantly answered. "Got alotta money on me."

"You're scarin' me."

"Scarin' you? Baby, I'm the same guy you opened the door for and didn't look back once to see what I was doin'. You came and got right back in bed. Ja'Lisa I ain't never done dis before. Met a woman dat I cared 'bout so much, that I want to protect her. Baby, I wanna be wit' cha!" Kelt explained before he got atop of Ja'Lisa and kissed her.

She embraced him wholeheartedly. Kelt removed the t-shirt revealing her small oval breast. He grabbed handfuls of money and let it shower down on her. "You ever made love on a quarter million dollars before? he asked her.

Ja'Lisa's smile was unrestrained, "No—" she modestly replied.

"Let's make it a memorable moment den!"

Kelt began to passionately kiss her lips, before moving to her neck and chest. He licked and sucked on her nipples until they became erect like pen tips. Slowly he moved down to her belly button snatching off her pink laced panties. He was flattered by her manicured pubic hairs. But what got his undivided attention, was the bulge, favoring a camel toe between her thick thighs.

He used his right thumb to skin it back so the clitoris could peek out. Using his pointer to open the passage revealed the inside of her pleasure spot. Ja'Lisa's insides are pink like a salmon fillet. Without any thought, Kelt let his tongue go into action. He kissed, licked, and sucked her clitoris gently, which drove Ja'Lisa insane.

He squeezed her breast and occasionally came up for air to plant a kiss on her luscious lips. Kelt could feel her juices flowing after teasing her with half an hour of four play. The sensation between her legs was unbearable. Ja'Lisa nudged Kelt to the side removing his camouflaged cargo pants and boxers together, before she pushed him back into the pile of money.

"You ever made love on top of a quarter million dollars?" she playfully asked him.

"It's a first time for everythang," he replied.

Ja'Lisa straddled Kelt. She reached beneath her to guide the tip of his erection into the spot in need of attention. Gently gliding the head in and out, Ja'Lisa slowly eased down on his manhood and began picking up the tempo.

Ja'Lisa moved similarly to a centipede. She tongue kissed Kelt in unison with her body movements and talked shit during intervals. Kelt enjoyed every minute! Even when her juices spilled all over his pubic hairs and thighs. She was exhausted from grinding. Perspiring with hundred-dollar bills stuck to them, Ja'Lisa laid back in the money, legs agape, inviting Kelt to close out the show.

He gracefully obliged to the grand finale. Kelt placed the head of his tool back inside, grasping her thick thighs before sliding in and out a few times. As usual, Kelt grinds inside just to let her know he's working with something. He loved the way she squealed in his ear when he does that.

Kelt completely stretched out. He pinned Ja'Lisa's legs back and jabbed her womb repeatedly with constant long strokes. Sweat dripped off his forehead onto her stomach as she uncontrollably moaned. Not to mention, this was their first-time having sex without protection. The moisture of being skin-to-skin, mixed with her womb's warmth was overbearing.

He stroked faster, and faster, until the urge to relinquish all his fluids inside her couldn't be resisted. Kelt put every inch of his manhood inside her as he released everything. The two lightly kissed as they lay across the bed panting, both with noticeable smiles on their faces.

Chapter 15

■■■■

April 2009

This Thursday evening had been a busy one for Cortez. He was at Destine's Connection munching on a piece of sea bass. He's trying to reach a mutual agreement with Big Bruh and Chize Money of Deuce Komradz, to open Saturday night at the grand opening of the O'Neal Amphitheater.

Their discussion had reached its apex about compensation for a scheduled performance. A local rap artist definitely won't get the same amount as an established artist. Out of respect and being supportive of the group, Cortez offered to pay them $7500 to open up. Cortez felt that was a reasonable amount to pay the group, plus the publicity from performing at this event.

Cortez didn't show any signs of agitation as he finished his meal, although Chize Money continued to unnecessarily ramble on about what Cortez considered absurd. Cortez admired his persistence, but Chize Money's argument fell on deaf ears. He was touched on his shoulder towards the end of the talk.

Cortez turned around and excitedly jumped to his feet when he recognized the person's face, "Bwoy what it is! When ya come in town!" he asked giving Lil' Derek dap and a half hug.

"I got here 'bout ten o'clock dis mornin'," Lil' Derek told him. "Ya lookin' good! I like to see ya like dis."

"I'm maintainin'," Cortez responded nonchalantly.

Lil' Derek laughed out loud, "The big debut Saturday, huh?"

"Yeah," he replied. "Nigga how ya know dis?"

"I'm connected like WC and Mack-10, nigga. Plus, they're advertisin' dat shit crazy on the radio. And ya got the Snowman comin' thru. Dats what's up! All I wanna know is why you ain't call me and lemme know dis shit was goin' down?"

"I wanted to have dis bitch jumpin' before I invited y'all up," Cortez explained sitting back down.

"Cuzz you know I'mma support ya regardless. I just wanna be here to see the look on your face when dis shit pop."

"Well, you here now. You're not leavin' before Saturday, right?"

"Fuck naw!"

"Dats what's up. Dis Big Bruh and Chize Money. Two members of the infamous Deuce Komradz," Cortez told him. "They're the openin' act to get the party jumpin'. Fellas, dis my folk, Lil' Derek."

The guys exchanged handshakes.

"How the fuck you knew I was here?" Cortez asked.

"On the real my nigga! They advertisin' dis bitch as hard as they promotin' the O'Neal Amphitheater on the radio. So, I stopped to get me a plate and noticed yo' long head azz," he told him.

****

Po' and E Boy, Po's childhood friend were out all-day shopping before they made it back to the hood. When Po' pulled into the driveway, he immediately recognized his trap had been infiltrated. He noticed that the curtains in the back bedroom were awkwardly positioned. Po' doesn't permit anyone in that room, and he hadn't been anywhere near the window today.

Po' got his .40 cal from underneath the seat. He instructed E Boy to shoot anything that came out the front, as he went around back. Po' made his way to the backdoor looking for anything suspicious. Pistol in hand, he eased the curtains back and crept inside. Po' tried not to make much noise when stepping on the shattered glass from the backdoor, where the culprits entered.

He glanced in the kitchen. Po' then went around to the living room; both were empty. Momentarily, he stood there looking down the hallway listening for any type of movement. The first place he checked down the hallway was a bathroom, on the left side of the hallway. He turned on the light switch and no one was there. Walking out of the bathroom Po' went directly across the hallway to a relatively empty bedroom, besides the queen-size bed and recliner.

Po' opened the closet door making sure there was no one hidden inside. The master bedroom door was open too, and the first place Po' crept to was the bathroom. He repeated the same routine from the previous rooms by opening the closet door and flipping the mattress to check underneath the bed. His temper began to rise, simply because he knew the intruder was gone.

Directly walking towards the bedroom that raised his suspicion, Po' vigorously kicked the door open. The room was empty. Still, he opened the closet door, and it was empty as the rest of them. Po' squatted down, lifting two pieces of the wood floor, and found the contents he had hidden there, remained.

He went to the front door to let E Boy know the house was empty. Po' reverted into the first bedroom because there was the most rummage. Recognizing the mattress had been shredded, Po' felt the ten pounds of marijuana were gone. He realized a gold chain and diamond ring were missing in the next room, which he thought wasn't anything of value.

"What they took?" E Boy asked him.

"Fuck niggaz got 'bout ten bows and $40k worth of jewels. Bitch azz niggaz missed a $250k and four bricks though," Po' revealed. "I wanna know who had the nuttz to come up in here! All dese niggaz 'round here I feed Cuzz, and a nigga wanna do me!"

"Straight up! Somebody seen somethin'."

"Somebody seen some too! Cuzz go out dere and see who seen a muthafucka 'round my shit. Tell 'em I got five stacks for anybody who can point me in the right direction."

E Boy was outside gathering information while Po' loaded a gym bag with money and cocaine. He walked out the front door with the bag over his shoulder and locked eyes, with the pesky Officer Hart driving by. *His bitch azz might've had somethin' to do wit' dis bullshit. 'Cause dese niggaz ain't lost they muthafuckin' minds.*

Po' didn't break his stride nor eye contact with the policeman. He opened the trunk of his Porsche Cayenne, placing the bag inside. Po' asked the young ladies across the street, "Y'all ain't seen nobody 'round my shit!"

"No— we just got back home, Po'. I can't believe a nigga tried cha like dat. Everybody knows you feed the hood," she affirmed.

"Dats what pissin' me off the most," he confessed. "Come on E, let's get the fuck outta here."

"My nigga ya gonna let dis shit ride?" E Boy asked walking back across the street.

"Hell naw—! Dis pussy azz police ridin', so I can't act out how I wanna, right now. I gotta get the fuck from over here. It'll come to the light, and I'mma deal wit' it. Let's go!"

****

Cortez convinced Lil' Derek to get a to-go box because he was eager to show him the state-of-the-art facility. Cortez led the way to the O'Neal Amphitheater as Lil' Derek, and Deuce Komradz ensued. Cortez punched in an eight-digit security code before they entered the building. He guided them upstairs to his private office. They were in awe of the place and all its splendor.

At the office door, he punched in another four digits before entering. Big Bruh was startled by the blinds. Cortez hit a button that activated the blind's departure and revealed the entire amphitheater through the translucent plexiglass. Lil' Derek, Big Bruh, and Chize Money stood there marveled. They gazed down on the facility, while Cortez poured four glasses of Louis the XIII.

Glass in one hand, and a gigantic remote control-looking device in the other, Cortez touched a button activating the Jumbotron. It displayed Young Jeezy videos heard crystal clear in the office, as Cortez motioned for someone to give him alight.

"Bwoy you puttin' it down like dis!" Lil'Derek exclaimed. "When you told me 'bout it, I didn't thank ya was gonna do it dis big though!"

Cortez puffed on a blunt as he looked out over the place, "Dere y'all some dranks over dere. Cuzz, I told cha when I do it, it's gonna be somethin' the city won't never forget bwoy! And I meant dat too!" Cortez exclaimed.

The guys got their drinks then stood next to Cortez. "Dats the stage y'all gonna perform on in two days," Cortez said pointing down at the stage, passing the blunt to Lil' Derek. "Young Jeezy a major nigga. He certified, right now. But ain't no muthafuckin' way a nigga ain't from the Gump, gonna grace dat bitch first! Keep dat in mind! Dis for the city and Gumptown niggaz gotta be the first ones to perform on stage."

"I'm feelin' dat Cuzz. Dats real shit and we gonna represent for the Gump Saturday night." Big Bruh stated slapping hands with Chize Money.

"Real shit!" Chize Money replied.

"I'm proud of ya," Lil'Derek told Cortez.

"Hurry up and smoke dat, so I can give y'all a grand tour," Cortez replied.

Playing the role of a tour guide, Cortez took them down to the stage. Chize Money and Big Bruh commenced a mock performance of what they planned for Saturday night. Cortez and Lil' Derek continued with the tour. Cortez showed him the fully stocked bar before briefly expounding on the operations, projected earnings, and estimations of what the bar should generate.

Cortez pointed out a few V.I.P. sections and LCD monitors so everyone could enjoy the show. Next, was the area where the photographs would be taken, also Cortez had different cameras positioned to record performances.

"Mane dis bitch gonna be blowed," Lil' Derek assured Cortez. "And dis spot here should cleanse plenty bread for ya, too."

"My nigga I'm straight, ya dig! I been manipulatin' dis bread, makin' dat shit work for me. Makin' good investments and gettin' great returns on my investments while steadily easin' dis drug money in on they azz. But dis shit right here gonna set us up straight!"

"Dats what's up. Now, I see why ya ain't been down to show yo' face. You been handlin' yo' bizness!"

They stood close to the entrance of the amphitheater where the seating area began and Cortez received a call, "Yo' what the deal?"

"Shit my nigga. A bitch azz nigga just broke in my house." Po' disgustedly answered.

"Straight up!"

"Yeah— mane."

"Who?"

"I don't know."

"What they took?"

"Shit! 'Bout $40k worth of jewelry and ten bows."

"Ah— dat ain't shit."

"Fuck niggaz missed a $250k and a few squares!"

"For real! Broke azz niggaz got 'em ten bows and got over excited. Missed a blessin'!"

"Ya feel me! Tripped me out they missed it. What tripped me out for real though, was a nigga tried me like dat!"

"I tell y'all all the time, niggaz gonna pump they nuttz to try ya. Even though ya put yo' murder game down, some thirsty sum-of-a-bitch gonna check yo' nuttz, Cuzz."

"Real shit."

"Feel me?"

"Yeah, I feel ya. I called ya because I needed a spot to crash. I'mma handle dat other shit."

"What you mean crash?" Cortez asked.

"Lay for a minute, Cuzz. 'Til I get dis situated."

"I gotta spot you can chill at, but I don't do no trappin' at dis spot. So dat mean you don't do no trappin', either. Ya understand me?"

"I got cha, Cuzz. I'm just tryna lay for a minute fam. Dats all," Po' assured him.

"Meet me in Carriage Hills; 4133 Bridle Path Lane."

"Bet it up," Po' responded putting the address in his GPS.

In the process of Cortez's phone conversation, Lil' Derek went back to the office and finished off the plate he purchased earlier. Cortez went upstairs to get Lil' Derek and to lock up his office. Cortez deactivated the Jumbotrons after pouring up another drink. As they descended the stairs Chize Money and Big Bruh had just made it to the lobby.

Cortez apologized for the disruption but assured them Saturday the stage would be all theirs. Everyone exited the facility, and Cortez secured the amphitheater. He and Lil' Derek got in his Range Rover. Chize Money and Big Bruh followed them in a square body Chevy until they reached the entrance.

Cortez merged onto the East South Blvd. and received another call from B.A. He informed Cortez that the job he'd been hired for had been fulfilled. Cortez inquired about B.A.'s whereabouts, so he could pay him. B.A. was with his wife at the Winn-Dixie Promenade on Eastern Blvd. grocery shopping. Cortez considered it perfect timing, although it's a bit past his destination but still in the vicinity.

He let B.A. know he'd be there in fifteen or twenty minutes and would call once he's in the parking lot. Cortez positioned the SUV to see B.A. exiting either door, before making the call. Cortez left the fog lights on as he and Lil' Derek continued conversing. Cortez blinked the car lights, getting B.A.'s attention as he walked out of the grocery store.

B.A. approached the vehicle as Cortez unlocked the door pointing to the backseat. B.A. climbed inside behind Lil' Derek. "What's good?" Cortez greeted him.

"Everythang good. Out here pickin' up some grocery wit' the wife," B.A. replied.

"Gotta eat!"

"No doubt. Dat job you gave me, I took care that lil' bit early dis mornin'. I was kinda busy, so I ain't had a chance to call."

"Everythang straight, though?" Cortez seriously asked.

"Like twelve-thirty."

Cortez didn't say another word. He simply retrieved $7k from his pocket and handed it to B.A. B.A. knew it wasn't necessary to count the cash, so he tucked it inside his jeans pocket before exiting the vehicle. Cortez left Winn-Dixie in route to Carriage Hills to find Po' sitting in the car out front of his house. Cortez pulled up directly in front of Po's car. He and Lil' Derck got out of the car.

"Cuzz what's happenin'?" Po' asked Cortez slapping hands.

"Shit. Just kickin' it wit' my folk. Lil' Derek dis my nigga Po', and Cuzz dis my people," Cortez said introducing them.

The two exchanged greetings and shook hands.

"Now what happened, Cuzz?" Cortez asked Po' while he deactivated the ADT home alarm.

"A fuck nigga broke in my trap I got in Newtown," he told him.

"Ain't nobody seen shit?"

"I really couldn't put the press down 'cause dis rookie police ridin' hard, and I got $250k dat the bitches missed. So, I had to get on for dis hoe azz police got to harassin'. Feel me?" Po' explained.

Cortez turned the lights on throughout the house. Also, he went and checked his stash spots, making certain everything had been removed. "How long you need to lay?" Cortez asked when he entered the kitchen.

"'Til I find a duck off spot. I'mma get down on dat ASAP, my nigga," Po' briefly answered. "I gotta start gettin' cribs in neighborhoods like dis. Soon as I get me somethin', I'm out."

"Come here, lemme blow at cha," Cortez said showing him to the back patio. "Hey what cha do wit' your bread is yo' bizness, but Cuzz I know ya a million-dollar nigga or should be. A coupla times over as a matter of fact."

"Facts!"

"You mean to tell me you ain't bought a crib! Ya gotta Porsche, and several other whips. Jewels, clothes, hoes, and ain't gotta crib to call home?"

"I got some spots I can lay, but I just wanna hideaway for a minute. Get lost! Somewhere dat nobody knows about," Po' assured Cortez.

"Bruh— handle yo' bizness! Handle yo' bizness bruh—! And shid don't do nothin' dat'll get ya jammed up! But cha gotta make an example outta dem niggaz dat violated," Cortez informed him. "And yo' dese people in dis neighborhood ain't off into dat shit we into. So ain't no trappin' out my house! I'm off the radar and I wanna keep shit just like dat. Feel me?"

"Bruh, I'm tryna duck off, and lay low, too."

"My shit should be just like I'm leavin' it, too," Cortez declared.

"My nigga I ain't gonna fuck up yo' shit!" Po' assured him.

"Aight," Cortez said before walking back inside. "Let's ride Cuzz. And I know ya comin' Saturday night to check out Young Jeezy and show ya partner some love."

"Most definitely!"

Chapter 16

####

Despite getting home almost five hours ago after a night on the town with Lil' Derek, Cortez managed to get three hours of sleep. Anxiety wouldn't allow him to get a second more. Cortez eased from underneath Sophia who laid comfortably on his chest. He sat up aside the bed contemplating the day ahead of him.

Cortez adjusted the shower to a perfect temperature, removed his Sean John boxer briefs, and stepped into the spacious walk-in shower. Getting dressed, Cortez admired Sophia as she slept plus how she embellished his world. He knew that she was the only thing missing in his life at this point. Walking down the hallway he peeped into his daughters' room, who spent the weekend, finding them sound asleep.

He stood there smiling before going downstairs to the kitchen. Cortez decided to surprise everyone with an appetizing breakfast. Remembering Lil' Derek stayed in the guest room, Cortez went over and woke him. He sat at the kitchen table busting down a cigar when Lil' Derek came in and took a seat. Cortez passed the blunt wrap to

Lil' Derek so he'd finish rolling up as he dropped the pan sausage into a skillet.

Cortez ran upstairs and woke Sophia, so she could get Kenya and Cheyenne together. He and Lil' Derek smoked during the process of them attending to their hygiene. When everyone gathered at the table, Lil' Derek introduced himself and gave the girls hugs. He has heard a lot about them, but this was officially their first meeting.

Everyone enjoyed a great breakfast, conversing about whatever came to mind. This small gathering delighted Cortez, being with people he unconditionally loved.

****

Cortez's entire day was based on developing a spectacular debut for tonight's main event. That's why Cortez's street team showed up everywhere throughout the city, promoting. Every fifteen minutes the radio personalities reminded the entire city and all surrounding areas. Cortez had already laid the groundwork. His family, friends, and associates already received invitations. He understood there was only one thing left, and that's for the show to begin.

Cortez and Lil' Derek made it to the O'Neal Amphitheater at six-thirty p.m. The parking lot was empty, except for the rental car Lil' Derek had left there Thursday night. The guys entered the venue and went straight up to his office. Cortez flopped down in the executive chair, propping his feet up on the desk, while Lil' Derek fixed a drink.

"Nigga you nervous as fuck ain't cha?" Lil' Derek bluntly asked.

"I'm straight, Cuzz," Cortez responded.

"Shittin' me," he told Cortez handing him a drink. "Here. You got butterflies like a muthafucka. Drank dat, it'll calm yo' nerves. All ya gotta do now is chill out, and let dis shit do what it do. The hard part over."

"Naw it ain't. I done hit dis nigga twice tryna make sure he comin' to perform. The whole city expectin' Young Jeezy to be here. Ya feel me?" Cortez nervously mentioned. "Muthafuckaz ain't answer or hit back. The success of tonight depends on whether or not dis nigga shows up."

"I know how your feelin', but, ya gotta relax. Dis bitch gonna jump! Trust me, Cuzz I've been here before. You good! And I'm proud of ya, too."

Cortez refused to show how grateful he was for the pep talk. It calmed his nerves some but didn't alleviate the thought of his headliner being M.I.A. He and Lil' Derck casually talked while smoking a blunt, as they looked down on the employees who began to perform their duties. Cortez made his rounds and consulted with his personnel.

Cortez appointed Big Melly head of security. He assured Cortez if any physical altercations occurred, he or the security crew would handle it. The bartenders, Ligon and Tina, stocked their stations with ice and glasses because they were anticipating a busy night. Cortez figured admissions was an adequate spot to place the neon stampers for the hands of guests, under the age of twenty-one.

Cortez assured every facet has been covered. He stepped out front to smoke a cigarette and to get some air. Standing out front he watched a caravan of headlights progress across the parking lot. Bodies bailed out of the Chevy Tahoe's and Yukon's, but Cortez wasn't ecstatic until he recognized the leader of the entourage. He felt like the weight of the world had instantly been lifted off his back.

Now it's official, like a referee wit' a whistle!

"What's happenin' hustla?" Cortez asked Young Jeezy. "Glad you ain't changed yo' mind on me!"

"I'm all 'bout dis money. Dat'll never change," Young Jeezy replied.

"Know dats real!"

"Where the money at?" Young Jeezy candidly asked. "I gotta get mine before I hit the stage."

"Follow me," Cortez told him.

Young Jeezy entered the venue and his entourage ensued. Big Melly approached them curious to see what was happening and Cortez instructed him to show them to their dressing room. Two of the guys didn't digress, they stayed with Young Jeezy as they went upstairs.

Cortez looked back with an awkward expression.

"Dis my security," Young Jeezy said.

They entered the office to Lil' Derek looking down on the venue rolling a blunt, "Oh shit! Ya got some of dat for sell?" Young Jeezy asked Lil' Derek.

"You can smoke, but it ain't none for sale," Lil' Derek informed him.

Cortez went directly to his biometric fingerprinting safe, behind an oil painting of the iconic Malcolm X clutching an AK-47. He retrieved $40k, along with a nickel-plated .45 that he tucked in the small of his back. Cortez handed Young Jeezy the stacks of money and then leaned back against his desk. Just as the purp began to rotate, Deuce Komradz entered the office.

Cortez introduced the group to Young Jeezy, informing him that they would be opening the show. They exchanged courtesies and then found them a spot in the rotation. The artists were taken to their respective dressing rooms before Cortez maneuvered throughout the facility. He witnessed an influx of people.

Reality began to register at this point, and the anticipation of this event happening diminished. Just as it was planned, everything manifested right before his eyes. Cortez stopped by the bar for a single shot of Patrón. He threw back the tequila and sat there watching the seats fill by the minute. Delighted by the crowd of people, Marcus, Megan, and Sophia closed in from the blindside.

"Nigga we been lookin' everywhere for you!" Marcus stated giving his cousin dap.

"I been in the back wit' Young Jeezy," he modestly responded.

"Bruh-law you somethin' serious! 'Been in the back wit' Young Jeezy'!" Megan repeated.

"Baby I'm so proud of you," Sophia told him with her arms around his neck simultaneously kissing him. "I'm so— happy for you!"

"Thanks. Y'all don't know how much dis means to me. Cuzz take them to V.I.P. The show 'bouta start in a few minutes. Y'all drank whatever ya want! I'mma be up dere in a minute!" Cortez instructed.

Cortez made his way down to the lobby. Big Melly's indecisive about whether or not he should allow Bug, Kelt, and Po' to enter without a cover charge. Big Melly had them grouped up just inside the door. One of his subordinates watched them so they wouldn't wander off.

"Ain't no need of lookin' crazy! Y'all ain't special. Y'all gotta pay, too! Big Melly, I like dat! You ain't showin' no favoritism," Cortez jokingly said.

"Y'all come on back outta here," Big Melly demanded.

Cortez's laughter was unrestrained. "Naw. Naw. They good, homie. They aight dis time," Cortez playfully told him.

"Ya sure Cuzz?" Big Melly insistently asked. "Dis the Grand Opening! I know ya gotta get yo' bread back outta dis shit."

"Ole big dumb azz nigga! Go 'head on wit' all dat jeffin'!" Bug snapped.

"You gonna be the first nigga to getta pumpkin head," Big Melly told Bug.

"I got 'em homie," Cortez said. "Follow me. We in V.I.P. The show 'bouta start, too."

Just as the guys were about to top the small flight of steps to V.I.P., someone tugged the back of Cortez's Prada button-down. The lights were dimmed, and Deuce Komradz local hit, "Certified" pervaded the venue. Cortez turned around to see Melissa. He unhesitatingly hugged her, giving her a peck on the cheek.

Sophia and Megan both took notice. He took Melissa's hand, assisting her to his section where everybody sipped Dom Perignon. Cortez poured himself a glass, followed by Sophia and Melissa reserved strictly for this moment. Unsure of what to think of Melissa but reluctant to jump to conclusions, Sophia kept quiet and continued to enjoy herself.

Not only was the V.I.P. jumping Cortez observed, but the entire venue was rocking and singing along with Deuce Komradz. They performed songs from their catalogue such as Down Wit' The South, 100 Elbows, and Ride Smokin'. Duece Komradz gave a stellar performance and prepped the crowd for the headliner.

Tightly holding Sophia from behind Cortez poured them another glass of bubbly. "Baby I love you. I wanna spend the rest of my day's wit' cha. I don't think ya understand how much cha complete my life. Sophie, will you marry me?" he whispered in her ear over the blaring music.

Caught off guard by the question, Sophia completely turned around. She looked into Cortez's eyes for assurance that he was being serious, as everything else became mute. "Are you serious!" Sophia asked in disbelief.

"As cancer," he responded maintaining eye contact.

"Yessss—!" she jubilantly yelled leaping into his arms.

The O'Neal Amphitheater became completely dark, "I went from old school Chevy's, to drop-top Porsche's. You couldn't walk a mile off in my air forces...." The amphitheater illuminated and Young Jeezy gracefully paced across the stage. The crowd erupted. Men and women alike sang along to the songs. "Sky's the Limit," "Soul Survivor," and some mix-tape bangers he randomly selected.

The crowd got its money's worth with a live performance that lasted an hour and a half. After the show, Young Jeezy felt the love permeating throughout the facility. He prolonged his stay, appearing in the photo area. The majority of the guest had departed in route to their next destination. A few did hang around for an opportunity to get an autograph, a picture, or meet the rap star.

Cortez and his guest remained in V.I.P. enjoying one another's company when Cortez announced the engagement. Kelt managed to get Cortez alone after everyone's congratulations.

"Bwoy I been tryna get at cha all day! Congrats on pullin' dis off, too. Dat was huge, for the city! And nigga— ya took everybody by surprise wit' the engagement," Kelt openly admitted. "But I wanna ask ya somethin'. I saw ole girl Monesha yesterday, and she told me ya came thru a couple weeks ago, askin' 'bout ole bwoy."

"I did."

"They found lil' buddy slumped over in his car outside his crib, wit' two to his head. Is dat yo' work?"

"You askin' me did I kill him?" Cortez asked confused by the abrupt inquiry. "Cuzz, I hate another brother got murdered, but you my dawg and shit gotta way of workin' itself out. By him gettin' killed, dat frees you. But to answer yo' question. No, I didn't. Me and Lil' Derek been together since Thursday tryna make sure dis shit here was a success. But, if I did do it, what's up?"

"Shit! I just was puttin' two and two together, after shawty told me ya paid her a visit. Fuck dat nigga!" Kelt told him. "Plus dem crackaz gonna be on my azz, swearin' I hit him!"

"Just be cool! You're good! Anythang you wanna tell me?"

"No!"

The crowd began to dwindle. Cortez along with the crew took pictures with Young Jeezy. He took one by himself and the rapper for the wall of guest performers that'll grace the stage soon. Also, there's a picture of himself and Sophia snuggled up to always commemorate the night he proposed. He and his team took a picture on the strength that these were the ones to help him build an empire.

He and Deuce Komradz took one because they kicked off this enormous night. Then there's the final one of himself and Lil' Derek, who allowed him to make all of this a reality. For future references, Young Jeezy gave Cortez an email address, a contact number, along with his road manager's cell phone number.

"What y'all talkin' 'bout? Glad to see y'all met," Cortez said approaching Sophia and Melissa.

"You. You put somethin' together," Melissa told Cortez as she hugged him. "I'm proud of ya. Also, congratulations on the engagement. She's perfect for you."

"She sure is!" he responded taking Sophia in his arms.

Everyone gathered outside talking about the events of the night before the crowd started to fade. The employees were finishing their respective duties, and the clean-up crew would be the last to disperse. Marcus and Megan left, then Lil' Derek and a female, along with Bug and Po'. Kelt left with Deuce Komradz leaving Cortez and Sophia alone.

"Baby lemme run up to the office to put dis money, and receipts in the safe. I'll check 'em tomorrow. It ain't but one thang that'll complete my night," he told her.

"And what's that?" she inquisitively asked.

"I'll show ya when we get home. How 'bout dat!" Cortez told her.

Over the next few months, the O'Neal Amphitheater was responsible for numerous musicians visiting Montgomery. Cortez made Fridays and Saturdays hip–hop nights. Young Jeezy stood on his word, coming back to perform a couple more times. So did T.I., Lil' Boosie and Lil' Webbie, and Trick Daddy, just to name a few. He dubbed Sunday nights, Ladies Night. Featuring renowned R and B artists, like Gerald Levert, Keith Sweat, Stephanie Mills, and Ginuwine.

Cortez didn't discriminate by only catering to his people. He's operating a business for profit; therefore, the only color of significance was green. He made Thursday nights for Country Music fans, along with square dancing. It came to a point where the O'Neal Amphitheater was where all major events in the city were held.

The rumor mill began to churn that some political officials were offended by the success of the O'Neal Amphitheater. Some people claimed the venue has caused the city to lose lots of revenue. Others proposed that the City of Montgomery should have part ownership of the facility. These rumors, if there was any validity to them, Cortez considered absurd.

He relinquished the thought of being extorted by anyone. Especially, about something he expended so much into and built from nothing.

Chapter 17

■ ■ ■ ■

May 2010

The next course of months was incredible for Cortez, whether it be business or his personal life, respectively. Southern Way Trucking, an independent trucking company Cortez established has proven to be productive. He has accumulated a fleet of fifteen Peterbilts that's constantly on the road.

Cortez and Melissa collaborated with some of her constituents in developing River Region Real Estate Management Firm. Also, Cortez became a silent partner in a plethora of local businesses, where he eventually bought the owner completely out. Not to mention the O'Neal Amphitheater was producing a substantial amount of revenue, plus it had the entire city buzzing.

Cortez shelled out money for a Carolina Herrera gown and veil, with blue Manola Blahnik bridal heels, a bejeweled wedding day clutch, along with an Ermenegildo Zegna tuxedo. Sophia hired a caterer, cake decorator, florists, photographers and videographers, a stylist. She ordered the customized CumuLLus wedding bands from Lester Lambert.

Plus, a two-week-long honeymoon in the Grand Cayman Islands, was an indication of how lucrative every facet of business had been. When Sophia was informed to coordinate their union, she was also instructed to design her dream wedding. Sophia did just that! She even made provisions for the first addition to their newly acquired family.

****

Sherry had become a vague memory for Po', since the run-in with her husband. He knew any further affiliation would bring unwanted troubles. Yet and still, Po' went against his better judgment and the outcome was detrimental. This Saturday afternoon he sat around watching the Celtics vs Heat in the Second Round of the Playoffs.

He received an unexpected call from Sherry. Sherry grieved about how much she missed him and couldn't bear not seeing him another day. Envisioning their XXX sex acts convinced Po' to let her come visit. Po' stared at her. Amazing was the only word to describe how Sherry looked standing on the front porch. Sitting in the den, Sherry meticulously explained the whirlwind she'd been in since that dreadful day Harrison caught them together.

Having feelings for two men, she realized it'll be best to salvage her marriage, because Po' only considered her for great sex and benefits. Sherry expressed that the fire in her heart for him would never subside, but she must do what's best for her livelihood. Po' intently listened while Sherry continued expressing her feelings.

He agreed, that might've been the more logical decision. Sherry knew he had no problem moving on with life. The familiarity of Po's embrace led to caressing and kissing, before enacting the specific connection that built their relationship. Their intimacy wasn't ignored. Nor did either of them put up resistance, which made the experience everlasting.

Afterward, Sherry laid in his arms and relayed what she'd heard about his house being burglarized. *How she knew about that?* Instead, Po' boasted about how nothing happened on the North Side, let alone in Newtown, that his hands aren't in or got his signature of approval. A foolish move by two young knuckleheads, which he implied ended with death sentences.

If he only knew his boastfulness had single-handedly destroyed a burgeoning dynasty. A multi-million-dollar empire that's on autopilot. He'd give anything to recant what he just confided in her. It shouldn't come as a coincidence, nor a surprise that three weeks later the D.E.A., A.B.I., a few of Montgomery's finest raided at sunrise.

They caught Po' comatose, in a heavy drug-induced sleep. When he did awaken, it was to multiple flashlights, and pistols pointed in his face. He was laid face down on the bedroom floor then swiftly handcuffed, and detained. Next to the bed, a chrome .45 pistol was retrieved off the nightstand, along with a hundred Lortab 10mg, and seven grams of purp.

Po' knew that's nothing money couldn't make vanish. He was assisted off of the floor. One D.E.A. Agent put Po' on some pants and shoes, then laid a shirt over his shoulders before escorting him to the front of the house. Po' was suddenly engulfed by panic once the K-9 Unit brought in two husky German Shepherds.

Po' tried maintaining his composure because he didn't want the agents to read his body language. Now, Po' regretted making the trip to Atlanta and coming back with 500 pounds of marijuana. *My house ain't a trap!* That's all Po' heard Cortez emphatically telling him.

The federal agents flashed a search warrant, then took turns bombarding Po' with questions about drugs, and a host of other accusations. Forty-five minutes into the search, that confidence Po' had the K-9 Unit might've missed his stash, shattered. An agent came upfront with a compressed bale of marijuana and assured them there was more.

A D.E.A. Agent assisted Po' off the couch where he nervously awaited as the search was conducted. He escorted Po' to the back of an unmarked car. For the past few months Po' had been low-key. Once discovering Cortez's old stash spots he stored the majority of his work at the residence. No one knew he resided there, so Po' was complacent storing 500 pounds and four kilos he copped earlier that week.

Po' was transported to the Narcotics Division, placed in an interrogation room handcuffed to a table, and put on ice for about an hour. He sat there plotting, mind running rampant over the possibilities of coming from underneath this untarnished. Sgt. Malcolm "Radar" Johnson, the supervisor on duty entered the interrogation room.

"Vanshon Gordon. The last time you came through here was 1999. On possession of a lil' over four and a half grams of crack cocaine," Radar reminded Po' reading from a manilla folder. "Now a decade later you're back in possession of four kilos of powdered cocaine and 500 pounds of wacky weed. I must say, you've officially graduated from nickel and dimin'."

"Mane what you talkin' 'bout," Po' somberly responded.

"You have the slightest clue to what I'm talkin' about? Let me refresh your memory then," Radar told him. "There was a raid at your home. Where you were in the bed, and narcotics was found inside the wall of your residence. Does that help you remember?"

"Yeah I was asleep," Po' admitted. "But dats not my house, so I don't know shit 'bout no drugs!"

"Really? What about the firearm, pills, and the small amount of marijuana next to the bed, where you were asleep? You don't know about that either, huh?"

"Nooo— mane," Po' nonchalantly answered.

"So, whose house is it, if it isn't yours?" Radar inquired.

"A friend asked me to house sit for 'em," Po' replied.

"So, everything found inside the house isn't yours, it belongs to this friend you're house sittin' for?"

"I don't know nothin' 'bout nothin'. I know I ain't had no mu'fuckin' drugs! I know dat!"

"Vanshon perhaps you don't understand the seriousness of what's happening. You're not going to Air Base Juvenile Detention or released to your Mama like before. You're lookin' at some real-time! And a lot of it!" Radar explained to Po'. "Also your name keeps coming up in some other major offenses. So, you should think about this carefully, and consider cooperating. Try making things more lenient on yourself."

Po's mental state was disoriented. He unconsciously involved Cortez in this debacle, especially after being forewarned about that kind of activity in his home. He tried non-stop to come up with a reasonable explanation, that'll justify his actions. Po' was still contemplating when Radar returned.

"Vanshon you were telling the truth. That residence belongs to a Mr. Cortez O'Neal," Radar informed him. "Where is he?"

"I told cha he went outta town! I ain't got no reason to lie to you mane!"

"Where did he go? When is he due back in town?"

"'In a coupla days," Po' answered agitatedly.

"So, you're saying the drugs were Cortez's?"

"I don't know! They wasn't mines!"

"Well, a firearm and narcotics were next to you. So, you're charged with that, too. Plus, the both of you will be charged with the rest of it, until someone own up to it. They'll transport you to headquarters," Radar explained cuffing Po's hands behind his back.

Two officer's escorted Po' into booking, and he reminisced on the last time he'd been to this place. The officers took Po' upstairs unlike before when he went downstairs, to the Juvenile Division. Po' noticed Homicide Division plastered on the wall as they exited the elevator, leaving him baffled. Po' scanned the offices passing through, before being placed in another interrogation room.

Shortly after he was handcuffed to a chair, a burly, black detective entered.

"Mr. Gordon, I'm Detective Armstrong. Seems you've had a pretty action packed morning. And I promise it won't stop there, trust me," he told Po' showing him some pictures. "I've been investigating an unsolved double homicide. Do you know these two young men? They were found dead in a car over in Hunter's Walk?"

"Yeah, it's been a helluva mornin'! No, I don't know those guys. And what dis got to do wit' me?" Po' replied upset.

"Your name came up. Actually, it keeps coming up! These were the two guys that broke into your home and you retaliated with murder."

"Hey mane, I'm really havin' a fucked up day! Somebody broke into my house, but, murder I don't know nothin' 'bout," Po' retorted.

"That's funny because there's witnesses, also someone made a statement you admitted that you killed these guys. Now we can fuck around, and I promise ya, I'll make you wished you never fucked with me. Or you can cooperate, and I'll make sure the judge knows to show you some leniency." Detective Armstrong declared.

"Sir yo' witness bullshittin' you! And nobody couldn't have told cha nothin' like that 'bout me. Whoever broke into my spot ain't get nothin' but some jewelry. And dat ain't shit! I got more jewelry," Po' responded grappling the chain around his neck.

"Where were you on the seventh of April last year?"

Po' pondered the question a moment. "I don't know. Dats been over a year ago. Ain't nothin' special happen dat day. How the hell I'mma remember dat, outta the blue? What I did on dat specific day, a year ago? Mane, I ain't killed nobody!" Po' pleaded.

"I don't have all day to mess around with you," Detective Armstrong said. "You're being charged with double homicide, in the first degree, and we'll let the courts deal with you. I'mma set your bond at $250k, an additional $60k for the firearm… Not to mention the other charges from the drug raid. And I hope ballistics come back with something on the pistol found, that'll be tacked on, too."

"So you just puttin' some murders on me?" Po' blatantly asked before Detective Armstrong walked out.

****

August 2010

An extravagant trip to the Grand Cayman Islands was exactly what the newlyweds needed to commemorate their union and honeymoon. That time alone allowed them to brainstorm about the direction of their lives together while tightening their bond even more.

Back home a few hours now, Sophia laid across the king-sized sleigh bed, in a Victoria's Secrets set. She networked with family and friends. Cortez was unpacking his luggage. Sophia began calling credit card institutions and terminated utilities to her old home. She was looking forward to starting the journey at her new residence.

The doorbell repeatedly rang. Cortez's focal point became who dared to ring his doorbell like they owned the place. As Cortez descended the stairs he got a glimpse of unmarked cars, and D.E.A. Agents through the translucent glass. Confused about the unexpected visit, he couldn't think of a logical explanation.

His six-sense implied this was going to be an unpleasant experience. Cortez slowly opened the door with an unemotional facial expression. Immediately, the field supervisor introduced himself by flashing his badge, before presenting a search warrant. Two federal agents put handcuffs on Cortez, while twenty more stampeded inside.

Cortez called out to Sophia, alerting her to get dressed as he was placed on the couch downstairs. Moments later she sat next to him. Sophia's nonverbal expression implied alarm, due to the knowledge of activities her husband partook in. Cortez was infuriated more than anything but didn't show it. Because these agents finding anything was the least of his worries.

Cortez never kept anything illegal at his home. Perhaps a half-pound of presidential for personal use, a P-89 handgun, along with some assault rifles which all were licensed and registered. Neither would require him to have to go away. *What suddenly made dese mu'fuckaz raid my home?*

The Agents searched the house from top to bottom. Also, the Agents searched his vehicles and the property grounds, finding nothing. All they found was a half-pound of marijuana, registered firearms, and two million cash. The D.E.A. confiscated two laptops and one desktop. Agent Welch apologized to Sophia for the inconvenience and removed her handcuffs.

Agent Welch informed Cortez that he would be taken into custody. Sophia began to frantically behave, but Cortez swiftly interceded. He assured her this was some sort of mistake. That his attorneys would straighten out the issue and he'll be back immediately.

Chapter 18

November 2010

Judith and her staff showed resilience by filing an appeal to get Cortez released on bond from federal custody. Being confined for the past ninety days, Judith understood Cortez needed to spend time with his loved ones. To help him get back in his comfort zone. Judith thought Cortez's best chance of getting acquitted was with him being on the outside, enabling her to paint a picture for jurors in a whole new light.

Judith already had the discovery but felt it wasn't the right time to inform Cortez, so she called him to her office. "Good morning. How are you doing this morning?" Judith curiously asked Cortez. "You know why I asked you to come here?"

"Can't say I do, but it sounded urgent," Cortez replied.

"My investigative team were right and wrong. Initially, you were going to be discredited and your image tarnished. The narcotics found at the residence were much more than what I expected. So now they're going to vilify and defame you in the media daily."

"So, what you sayin'?" he anxiously asked.

"Calm down. I want you to understand what's going on, Cortez. Do you know Vanshon Gordon?"

Cortez dropped his head. "Yeah," he somberly answered looking up at her.

"This was your involvement with the narcotics," Judith stated placing the discovery on her desk.

Browsing over the discovery Cortez shook his head in disbelief. He slammed his fist atop the desk, merely out of frustration of being betrayed by someone he considered a brother.

"Yeah… I know dis dude! I let dis sum-of-a-bitch stay at the house, for free 'cause somebody broke in his," Cortez blatantly explained, enraged by the disloyalty. "I specifically told him don't bring dat shit dere, 'cause the neighbors aren't those kinda people. Now, I'm caught up in dis bullshit."

"First, I thought perhaps someone convinced him to plant it there, but that wasn't the case. A police officer had it out for Vanshon, and found some leverage," she confirmed. "Come to find out Mr. Gordon was sleeping with this guy's wife, and she had gotten pretty close with him. So, a police officer took it upon himself to inform her husband of the affair."

"Uh huh," Cortez uttered.

"Her husband caught them together and drew a pistol on both of them. The same Officer Hart stopped the husband from shooting. Vanshon Gordon's house was burglarized shortly afterward, and the two guys suspected of the B and E were found murdered. Officer Hart convinced the husband to have his wife pump info from Vanshon. In hopes of reconciling their marriage." she expounded.

"So, they got me caught up in they love triangle?"

"Basically! It's a ploy to rid Vanshon of their lives. That's my conclusion. From my understanding, Vanshon confided in her then she checked in with Officer Hart. Shortly afterward your property was raided. It was orchestrated to get Vanshon Gordon off the streets."

"I can't believe dis shit!" Cortez stated with disgust. "How I got involved though?"

"Read this right here," Judith told Cortez pointing to the section where Po' cleared himself. "He claimed to have no prior knowledge of the narcotics being inside the wall. Also, Vanshon said, he was house-sitting for a friend. Which, technically he was because not one bill has his name on it. He owned up to the firearm and a controlled substance, and a misdemeanor count of marijuana. A hundred Lortab 10 mg. He was also charged with a double homicide. Unrelated."

"So, he threw me under the bus for his shit. Judith, I just got married! We hadn't even made it back from our honeymoon good, to come home to dis shit! Everythang goin' swell for me right now. You gotta beat dis shit! Dat shit wasn't mine!"

"I promise I'm going to do everything I can to prove that," she assured him.

"You can't get the wife he was cheatin' wit' to testify, on my behalf?"

"First, let me get all the facts. I wanted to inform you of what's really going on. Just calm down and let me handle it. Right now, it's not looking good because Vanshon's willing to testify. So, let me gather all the facts and strategize a viable defense, while you stay off the radar. Alright?"

"Yeah," he responded with dryness in his tone. "Run me off some copies of dese documents."

****

Now, with a better understanding of this debacle and who's responsible, Cortez sought to make others aware that Po's cooperating with the Feds. Cortez's main objective was to tarnish his street credibility because that's where the majority of Po's money was earned. Plus, he doesn't want to see Po' take down anyone else. He felt the ultimate betrayal. Cortez's motive was to impact Po's cash flow until he could deal with him accordingly.

Cortez and his goons drove through some of Po's hangouts. No one had seen him in weeks. After some investigating, Cortez discovered Po' made bond on the murders and the likelihood of him being convicted was slim. One charge that stuck was the unlawful possession of a firearm, which carried up to five years for ex-felons. He could possibly walk on that charge for his cooperation.

Cortez stopped by E-Tax to inform Melissa of what he'd just found out from Judith. She was disappointed seeing how devastated Cortez was by the ordeal. She knew her friend and saw how infuriated he was behind this, which normally meant tragedy for all parties involved.

Melissa suggested that he calm down because it'll cloud his thinking. Then she inquired about how to help. Ironically, his sole purpose for stopping by was so she could share online the information Judith gave him. She immediately downloaded the information, along with a photo of Po' on a Lexar flash drive, followed by the documents.

Snitch.com, You Tube, Myspace, and Facebook; the main social media outlets was where she posted the information. Melissa made sure it spread like wildfire. She emailed certain people instructing them to share and for clarity, anyone could go check out the websites.

Cortez's next move was to alert his team of the informant, so they would be on point. He and Bug sit in his Range Rover outside of

Joe's Burgers awaiting Marcus, and Kelt to arrive. Shortly, Marcus arrived and got in the backseat of the SUV.

"What's happenin' wit' y'all niggaz?" Marcus asked sensing something wasn't right. "What the fuck up!"

Bug handed the paperwork to Marcus in the backseat.

"Tell Kelt to get in on my side," Cortez stated.

"Go on the other side, Cuzz," Bug told him then let the window back up.

"Bruh glad to see you back wit' us," Kelt told Cortez. "What's the deal?"

"Mane, I called y'all, to let y'all know dis bitch azz nigga Po' ratted on me," Cortez admitted.

"What!" Kelt bellowed in disbelief.

"Marcus got the paperwork back dere. My lawyer gave me dat shit dis mornin'. It's in black and white Cuzz! I ain't talkin' 'bout no rumors. Dis fuck nigga, the cross!" Cortez told them.

"Four bricks and 500 bows, dats automatic Feds. Who shit was it?" Bug inquired.

"Are you listenin'? The nigga crossed me out! The dope was his— The shit wasn't mine!" Cortez shouted.

"How they charged you den?" Bug asked.

"Bitch azz nigga asked to stay at my crib 'cause some niggaz broke in his shit. And like a damn fool, I let him," Cortez disgustedly explained. "My first mind told me not to! Niggaz gettin' too much bread not to have 'em a coupla spots to lay. Feel me?

"Facts," Marcus said.

"But y'all my squad. We gettin' guap together, and I would've done that for anyone of y'all. I told him though! Don't be trappin' outta my crib, 'cause the neighbors ain't on dat shit! Dat ain't a hood. Mane y'all know what it is."

"Where he at?" Kelt asked proofreading the papers.

"Nigga disappeared. He ducked off somewhere. He got two pendin' murders he gotta go to trial on, so he still 'round here," Cortez answered.

"Who he murked?" Bug asked him.

"I guess dem dudes who broke in his shit. Dats what triggered all dis bullshit. Well— really the white hoe he was fuckin'. A police officer told the white hoe husband, Po' was fuckin'. So the bitch picked Po' lame azz to give up, and save face wit' her husband. All dis, to get his stankin' azz out the way. Fuckin' wit' dem crackaz."

"Fuckin' wit' dem crackaz!" Marcus repeated. "Cuzz, the fuck nigga might go free on the murders for givin' you up!"

"He put dis on you, tryna escape dem murders?" Kelt asked.

"Gotta find dat bwoy! He gotta get dealt wit'!" Bug mentioned.

"Know what's so fucked up 'bout it? I specifically told dat nigga not to fuck off at the crib Cuzz. And he did it anyway! Put me in the mix. I would've tried to help him come from under the shit, 'cause I fucked wit' the nigga," Cortez told them.

"Ain't no excuse for dat shit! Cuzz it's inexcusable!" Marcus admitted.

"I knew shit was goin' too smoove. We eatin'! Bruh, ya got everybody eatin' good and dat fuck nigga crossed ya! Bwoy— dat shit don't sit right wit' me," Kelt said.

"It's all good though. I wanted to put y'all on point 'bout dis chump. Lemme say dis, and listen carefully," Cortez said, which got their attention. "Y'all lay low, keep your ears and eyes open. 'Cause the nigga might've called y'all name and the Feds could be watchin'. So, chill for a minute and thoroughly clean up y'all house!"

"Ain't gotta tell me twice," Kelt blatantly stated.

"I was told he might beat the case 'cause they ain't got shit, but the white bitch sayin' he admitted that he did it. The pistol case solid, so he might use y'all to work it off. Feel me?" Cortez expounded. "Close down shop for a minute, 'til shit smoove out. Plus, don't mention to no one what's gonna happen when he resurfaces. Just put the word out dat bitch poison, so that'll fuck his paper up and maybe that could flush his bitch azz out."

The media had a field day with the story. It's being driven by some political figures, who were relishing at the moment. They loved the fact Cortez was in between a rock and a hard spot. Cortez used his resources and tried to combat the slander, but the onslaught was excessively pursued until it became futile.

Federal prosecutors attempted to tack on additional charges, accusing Cortez of badgering a witness with the internet stunt. They claimed Cortez was jeopardizing their witness's life. Judith quickly nipped that in the bud and refuted this claim, simply because the information given was public records. The stunt was viewed by some as Cortez incriminating himself. This caused animosity between certain crews throughout the city.

Cortez's daily life went on as usual. Despite him facing a lengthy prison sentence if found guilty. The businesses proved to be profitable and operated normally. The O'Neal Amphitheater continued to bring some of the music industry's most renowned artists to the city.

An undisclosed amount of money was given as gratuity to certain individuals, like Melissa, Marcus, Mona, and Malik, his home inspector. Malik was another person Cortez formed an alliance with, devising a business partnership over the past couple of years. Cortez urged them to invest the money wisely. On paper, his philanthropy was a gift. In reality, it made him an investor/silent partner in their respective establishments, and future endeavors

Some bank accounts and assets were frozen, until after the trial, but a real hustler always creates a way to make money. A few pieces of property, businesses, and money was given as gratuity to his pregnant wife. Cortez was playing chess and made preparations for the future. Over the past couple of years, Cortez secured the livelihood of the people he's employed.

Cortez and Bug were posted up in the hood one evening. They're on Oakleigh Road talking to some guys they grew up with about these turbulent times. Out of the blue, a youngster approached Cortez in hopes of consignment. Everyone got silent, while Cortez stared the kid up and down. Bug commenced to straighten this situation, but Cortez intervened.

"Youngun what cha gonna do wit' some work?" Cortez asked him.

"Get me some money, OG," he abruptly replied.

"Get money, huh? You want some work? So, when ya bubble dese fuck niggaz go to hatin' ya. No matter how much ya help 'em, muthafuckaz still plottin' against ya. Or ya wanna put your life in jeopardy daily, 'cause dese niggaz wanna rob or kill ya? Or maybe you wanna be like me facin' all dis muthafuckin' time, huh?" he stated to the youngster.

"No," the youngster uttered.

"You want some work? I'mma give ya some work! Go get your CDL's. And when ya get 'em, call Mr. Perry at Southern Way Trucking Company. Tell him I said give ya a job," Cortez told him. "Trust me, you'll get some money drivin' trucks, wit' out all the bullshit dat comes along in dese streets. Dats the work I got for ya."

Chapter 19

May 2011

Day one of the trial, Cortez arrived at the Frank M. Johnson Jr. Building and United States Courthouse wearing an azure three-piece Brooks Brothers suit. Sophia's on his arm clad in a smoke gray Vera Wang business suit, strutting in a pair of four-inch Jimmy Choo heels, toting a bag by the same designer.

The couple displays a united front and confidence as they top the stairs of the courthouse, where the major news media awaited to do their job. Camera-men and photographers snapped photos as they passed through the metal detector. On the elevator, Cortez joked about making Sophia famous because they'll be shown non-stop, for weeks on the news.

He tried bringing humor to the situation, to no avail. Judith Kidd and her associates waited out front of the courtroom for their client. Stepping off the elevator they're bum-rushed by more cameras. Cortez noticed it was fairly empty in the courtroom, besides a marshal and some agents that partook in the raid.

Judith sat on the left side of the courtroom rehearsing with Cortez, as people began to fill the courtroom. Many of these people were supporters of Cortez. The ones that came over to him, either shook his hand or hugged his neck wishing him the best. Assistant United States Attorney Jonathan Adcock and his assistant eased in setting up at the opposite table, after eloquently trading amenities with Judith.

"All rise, for the Honorable Judge Myron Thompson," the marshal commanded standing next to the bench.

"Good morning. Please be seated," Judge Thompson addressed the court taking his seat. "Counselors, you're ready to get this on the way?"

Both attorneys agreed.

"Bring in the jury," Judge Thompson stated.

He addressed the jury before acknowledging counsel. He stated case numbers and charges, so the clerk could make things official.

Mr. Adcock was first in presenting the government's case to the jurors, "Today we're going to show that the defendant, Cortez O'Neal is the head of a criminal enterprise, dealing in illegal narcotics, homicides, money laundering, embezzlement, and a host of other crimes to try the defendant under the RICO Act."

"Today, I'm going to show how the powers that be used a conniving ex-associate of my client. Whom the government chose to conspire with, in an attempt to incriminate my client, despite his generosity," Judith hastily responded, refuting prosecution.

The Government called DEA Agent Jeff Welch to the stand for his testimony of what took place, the morning they raided the house in Carriage Hills. Other agents were called to testify, and Judith wanted to get their testimonies out of the way, to cross-examined them. She planned to make their testimonies contradict one another.

"Agent Welch you were ranking officer, right?" Judith asked.

"Yes," Agent Welch answered.

"First thing I want to know is, who discovered the narcotics, and what was found inside the home?" she inquired.

"Agent Merriweather and I were the first to engage, presenting the search and arrest warrants," Agent Welch explained. "Agent Merriweather led the search on the east side of the residence, and I did the same on the west. I didn't record finding anything. Everything was found on the east side of the home. Five hundred pounds of marijuana and four kilograms of powder cocaine."

"Also wasn't other drugs and firearm's found?" she asked.

"Yes, there were," he answered.

"Wasn't those items found in the room with Vanshon Gordon, the friend Mr. O'Neal allowed to live on the property, as a favor? He did admit to those drugs and weapons, right?"

"Yes, there were. And he did eventually own up to the items found in his vicinity."

"Is it possible everything found could've been Vanshon Gordon's?" Judith promptly asked.

"Anything's possible."

"How did Mr. O'Neal's name come up as the person housing these narcotics found?"

"Vanshon Gordon."

"The same guy that's been charged with these kinds of charges in the past."

She was giving the jurors room to question Po's character. Also, her intention by mentioning Po's pleaded guilty to drug charges. She wanted to highlight Cortez's background was the complete opposite.

Bitch azz nigga, got me in here fightin' for my mu'fuckin' life!

Judge Thompson recessed court until tomorrow. In Judith's opinion, that round she won only by a small margin. Cortez and Sophia walked down the stairs of the courthouse holding hands. Cortez locked eyes with B.A., an indication he still hadn't seen the mark. News reporters diligently tried getting a word from Cortez, as they gingerly waltzed to the car.

Once inside the car behind the tint, Cortez leaned his head backward and took some deep breaths. Sophia took his hand comfortingly being supportive, doing her best to make this situation less stressful. Being in court for the past five hours their appetites wouldn't be denied any longer. Already downtown, they dined at Davis Café, one of Cortez's favorite restaurants in the city.

He and Sophia were seated in a recluse area, off in a corner of the soul food restaurant. Sheila Davis, along with her younger sister Val, were childhood acquaintances of Cortez. They sat with them a while and expressed their concerns, also assuring them they'll keep him in their prayers. Sheila even went to the extent of giving them a meal on the house.

"Hey there! How y'all feelin'?" B.A. asked them. "Mrs. Lady I know you tryna enjoy your meal wit' cha man, but I need to speak wit' him a second about somethin' important. Can I borrow him a second, please? Promise it won't be long."

Sophia stared at B.A. very peculiarly before giving Cortez the same look.

"I'll be right back baby," Cortez told her then walked out the front of the restaurant.

"Hey, sorry to interrupt y'all, bruh. Dis nigga done vanished. Mane, ain't nobody seen dis nigga for months. I thank dem folks hidin' him out," B.A. admitted.

"Dats what it is. Damn, I was hopin' dis rat azz nigga would've popped up before dis court shit," Cortez said.

"On the real fam. If the Feds hidin' him, me or my folks probably can't touch him. I'mma stay at it 'cause I know how major dis shit is."

"Do dat!"

It was day four of the trial and the media circus still lurked around the courthouse waiting for Cortez and Sophia's arrival. The media weren't going to pass up the opportunity to cover this high-profile case. Trying to ignore all the unwanted attention, they still represented a united front as they walked through the crowds of cameramen and reporters. They topped the stairs and were met by Marcus, Megan, and Bug, who came to show their support.

Judith and her team were conversing when they entered the courtroom, "Good mornin'. This my family right here. Y'all dis my lawyer, Judith Kidd," Cortez introduced them. "What's yo' take on the direction of the trial? And what's the plan of defense for today?"

"It's still too early to definitely know the direction of the trial, I could get a better analysis once Mr. Gordon takes the stand," Judith assured him. "And since we decided on you taking the stand, please maintain a humble and calm demeanor, or else the prosecutor is going to insinuate a lot of falsehoods. Also, no menacing stares towards the witness because the jurors will be observant."

Judge Thompson entered the courtroom from his chambers, and the marshal announced, "Court is in session."

"You can bring in the jury," Judge Thompson told the marshal.

Judge Thompson took care of the formalities with the court's clerk, making this session an official court document. They concluded yesterday with Judith cross-examining witnesses. This morning, the defense was first to call witnesses. And Judith decided to play offense. She started with Cortez, by building his character as someone to whom most working citizens could relate.

Allowing the jury to hear about Cortez, the human being, and how he'd been betrayed for his generosity. "Mr. O'Neal how long have you known Vanshon Gordon?" she asked.

"Since we were kids," he replied.

"Okay. So, he's someone you considered trustworthy?"

"I did."

"How long have Vanshon Gordon lived in or on your property?" Judith inquired.

"It supposed to have been a week or two that turned into several months."

"So you were Vanshon's landlord?"

"No. He didn't pay me anything. Neither was he supposed to," Cortez confessed. "Like I said earlier, it was supposed to be a couple weeks, max. He said his home had been burglarized so he needed somewhere to stay."

"So as a favor to a friend, you allowed Vanshon to live on your property, rent free?"

"Correct."

"The home was vacant until this situation with Vanshon?"

"Yes. The home was for sale or rent-to-own, but when Vanshon called needing a place to stay, I let him stay there."

"Was the home empty or was it furnished?"

It wasn't completely empty," Cortez admitted. "It wasn't fully furnished either. There were a few pieces of furniture I never got around to gettin'."

"How much furniture would you say you left inside the home?"

"Not much. A bed in one room, sofa and loveseat, a television."

"That's it?"

"Yes."

"No narcotics hidden in the wall of the home?"

"No ma'am."

"Mr. O'Neal how well do you really know Vanshon Gordon?" Judith curiously asked.

"Obviously, not as well as I thought I did."

"How do you feel about a so-called friend placing you in a predicament like this?" Judith sincerely asked. "Something that can cause you to lose everything you've worked so hard for."

"Objection Your Honor!" AUSA Adcock intervened. "Misleading jurors, Your Honor."

"Overruled," Judge Thompson stated.

"You can answer, Mr. O'Neal," Judith told Cortez.

"Honestly, it's disheartening! A guy I considered a brother," Cortez openly spoke to the court. "I'm not braggin' nor tryna embarrass anyone. I've helped this man so much I lost count. And that's all I was tryna do, was help him. If he would've owned up to his drugs, I still would've helped him."

"Defense rests, Your Honor."

Judith tried placing doubt and influencing jurors to question the logic of Cortez's dabbling in illegal narcotics. It didn't make any sense that a successful businessman would have a house full of drugs. Especially, when it's documented the figures his businesses accumulated. The IRS audited all of Cortez's businesses finding much of nothing. She elaborated on Cortez's philanthropy, and the positive things he does for the community.

She was doing her best to portray him as not just a model citizen, but a pillar in the community. Judith laid the canvas exemplifying Vanshon Gordon as this devious person, whose only concern was his well-being. Once she rested, AUSA Adcock didn't hesitate to take the floor donning a pristine navy-blue power suit.

Immediately, AUSA Adcock attempted to ravage the same businesses that others spoke so highly of, by claiming they were funded by drug money.

"Mr. O'Neal I don't want to speak about the illegal narcotics found at your residence, yet. I'd like to speak about the businesses," AUSA Adcock told him. "I'm curious to how did you get started in business?"

"Watchin' my grandfather and that encouraged me."

"Were the business your grandfather owned handed down to you?"

"No."

"Did your grandfather legally own a business?"

"No. More of an experience. Watching him manage money, reinvest into his business," Cortez answered.

"Okay. How long have you owned the property where the illegal narcotics were found?" AUSA Adcock asked.

"A few years," Cortez replied.

"Have you ever lived there?"

"Yes."

"And how long has it been since you last stayed there?"

"Maybe three years or better."

"And how long did Vanshon Gordon stay there?"

"Almost six months."

"So, in a few months Vanshon meticulously designed compartments in your wall, filling them with illegal narcotics?"

"Yes. I didn't do it! Who else could've done that?"

"Perhaps the previous resident."

"No one else had been in the house."

"The previous resident could've left it behind. Completely forgot about it."

"That space in the wall wasn't there at all," Cortez said. "When me and my home inspector checked the place, everything was intact."

"I have another question. How did you finance your business? Because it shows you never worked a job in your life," AUSA Adcock mentioned. "How did you acquire the money to start these businesses? Being that you've never been recorded as having a job. Perhaps from what was found in the wall of your home?"

"Relevancy Your Honor!" Judith objected mainly to cease the onslaught.

"No further questions, Your Honor."

AUSA Adcock had accomplished what he'd set out to do. Making the jurors aware that the defendant may very well be involved in something illegal before the government rested. Judith did her best to repair the collateral damage. She asked Cortez many rhetorical questions to counter-attack the barrage of questions from the prosecution.

The defense called Vanshon Gordon to the stand. Po' was being escorted by two agents in designer suits, flanked on both sides of him. The entire courtroom turned around to witness the man of the hour. Gingerly walking down the aisle, he and Cortez made eye contact briefly before Po' disengaged. Cortez unconsciously stared him down until he sat on the stand. Even then Cortez looked at him with this blank expression.

Judith took to the floor like a tigress with prey insight for her young, "Mr. Gordon, I see you started dealing in illegal narcotics early in life," she opened, so Cortez could hear any discrepancies in his testimony. "Did some digging and stumbled up on a couple businesses. A One-Stop Detailing books aren't quite matching up, also the Hair Salon your kid's mother, Katrina owns. Guaranteed after some serious probing, we can determine if it's funded by drug money."

Judith walked over to the table reviewing her notes. "Let's get to the reason Mr. O'Neal was gracious enough to let you live in his home," Judith stated looking at Po'. "Mr. Gordon were you a paying resident? Did you sign any binding agreements?"

"No. I was house sittin'," Po' answered.

"House sitting. No binding agreements. No rent payments. Mr. O'Neal being a real friend, let you live in his home, and this is the thanks he gets," Judith blatantly said. "Did your home get burglarized?"

"Yes."

"A known drug house?"

"Not my house."

"A known drug house gotten broken into, and the two males who committed the B and E soon after, murdered. You know anything about that? You were charged with their murders, right?" Judith asked.

"Objection Your Honor!" AUSA Adcock intervened. "The witness is testifying about illegal narcotics found in a raid. Not murder."

"Overruled," Judge Thompson told him.

"You can answer Mr. Gordon," Judith said.

"No. I wouldn't know anything about it. I am charged with the murders, but I'm confident of my day in court."

"Mr. Gordon, was the house completely empty or did you have it furnished?"

"I didn't have it furnished. I wasn't going to be there long," Po' answered. "It was basically empty. A few pieces of furniture that was already there."

"A known drug dealer, whose dope house was broken into, and you wanted to relocate. You called a friend for help, then turned his house into a drug hub," Judith bluntly stated. "Were you charged with other crimes that day too?"

"Yes."

"What were those charges?"

"Felon in possession of a firearm, a Possession of Marijuana and Controlled Substance," he replied.

"All these charges on the premises, but you expect the court to believe the other illegal narcotics weren't yours too?" Judith harshly asked.

"The court don't have much choice, 'cause I'm tellin' you the truth."

"We have a choice! Logic should prevail in this trial," Judith declared. "An honest, tax-paying businessman jeopardizes everything with a house full of illegal narcotics. Oppose to a convicted felon with a history of illegal narcotics. He's pending two homicides, found in possession of a firearm with narcotics, and the bulk of drugs discovered isn't his either. Hard to fathom. Huh?"

"I don't know what you want to hear, ma'am."

"The truth! That you killed those two young men for burglarizing your dope house. That you misused a friend! Using his property as a hub for drugs."

"You're wrong ma'am."

"The murders garnered law enforcement's attention, making you the focal point," Judith expounded. "You're recorded bragging about being the leader on the north side of the city. And it seems like everywhere you go trouble follows. The house was raided because you were wanted in a double homicide. What kind of friend are you?"

"A real one."

"I beg to differ. If you let this generous man possibly perish on account of you, then you're the worst kind of friend. Defense rests, Your Honor."

She tried raising the possibility that Po', with the felonious activities he partook in, may have easily stored the drugs found on her client's property. Judith believed history generally pointed in the direction of the guilty. She tried her damnedest to evoke reasonable doubt within the jurors.

"The witness past shouldn't force him to take the fall for something that didn't belong to him," AUSA Adcock immediately clarified. "Mr. Gordon, it's been established you two have known each other for some time. Real friends! My friends wouldn't want me to go down for their wrong-doings. You still consider him a friend?"

"No."

"Did you have knowledge there were illegal narcotics on the property?"

"No!"

"How often did Mr. O'Neal visit?"

"Periodically, but he has a key. He could've come by when I was gone."

"So, it's a good chance the narcotics were there when you arrived?"

"Yes."

"No further questions Your Honor," AUSA Adcock stated.

Judith cross-examined Po' once more in the last attempt to pry something incriminating out of him or to prove he's a dishonest individual. Before the attorneys made their closing arguments, Judith called some material witnesses to the stand, in an attempt to adorn any blemishes to Cortez's character the prosecutor may have caused.

Judith started closing arguments by briefly touching on Cortez's ownership of some pretty lucrative businesses that have created jobs for many local people. First, she spoke about the O'Neal Amphitheater and the number of people it employed. Cortez, Lil' Derek, and Marcus were partners in this endeavor. They grossed thirty-seven million their first year, forty-nine million the second year, and projections showed seventy-nine million by the end of this fiscal year.

Southern Way Trucking Company tremendously picked up speed generating a substantial amount of revenue, itself. Cortez finally recruited some qualified dispatchers with knowledge of the industry. Also, there was Déjà Vu, a pool hall and bar that did its best numbers on the weekends. He had four professional billiards, along with six regular pool tables. Realizing alcohol was where he made his money, Cortez implemented weekend specials.

For the past couple of years, Cortez had been investing in various vending machines. Honestly, he didn't expect it to flourish until he gained access to some local warehouses and plants, a couple of hotels, and a hospital. That's when he started seeing profits. That prompted him to expand into a full-fledged business. Whatever the demand for that facility he provided. All of Cortez's establishments had some sort of vending machines, from an ATM to gum ball machine.

He even saved some local businesses that were in a financial crisis. Cortez became a silent partner who'd invested money in renovations, quality inventory, and marketing, enabling these business owners to finally get out of the red and see some profits.

The majority of the business owners Cortez partnered with; he now owns the business outright.

AUSA Adcock agreed with Judith Kidd's statement about history repeating itself. The witness's previous convictions, he was accountable for by pleading guilty. So why wouldn't he own up to the narcotics found in a distinct location of Mr. O'Neal's home? Perhaps because those weren't his drugs.

The law stated, that if anything unlawful is found in or on your property, then the person, the property owner shall be prosecuted. The prosecution felt it was pretty much an open and shut case. A witness testified that the illegal narcotics were the homeowners.

Judge Thompson recessed court as the jury deliberated. Cortez, Sophia, and the others were leaving the courthouse to get a bite to eat when B.A. pulled Cortez off to the side. B.A.'s facial expression spoke volumes. He informed Cortez that he did see Po'. Po' had the protection of so many federal agents, it would've been insane trying anything.

B.A. would've been committing suicide. For the inconvenience, he genuinely apologized, because B.A. knew how badly this problem needed to be exterminated. Cortez shook B.A.'s hand. Cortez assured B.A. he appreciated the time and effort expended trying to carry out the job. B.A. informed Cortez he wasn't giving up yet.

The jurors deliberated three hours before they came back with a verdict. In the hallway of the courtroom, a crowd patiently maneuvered inside. Waiting for the crowd to decrease, Bug lured Cortez away from the others and inquired, "What you think the outcome gonna be?"

Cortez was perplexed and couldn't quite find an answer. The entire time they've known one another, Bug couldn't recall Cortez ever having such a dubious facial expression. Bug didn't exchange any words. He just gave his friend a comforting hug before leading Cortez back inside.

Judge Thompson took his seat and the jurors entered from deliberation. "Have the jury come up with a verdict?" Judge Thompson questioned.

One of the jurors, a white guy stood up with an envelope in hand, which indicated they had. The marshal retrieved the envelope handing it over to Judge Thompson. In turn, Judge Thompson read the contents of the envelope silently. Judge Thompson read out the jury's verdict on an excess of charges. All of which the jury found him not guilty, except for one.

"Count number five. Drug Trafficking. The jury has found the defendant guilty beyond a reasonable doubt."

There was tumultuously chattering throughout the courtroom, and Judge Thompson slammed the gavel to regain order. Cortez held his head high while the marshal placed handcuffs on him. He turned around to see Sophia sobbing. He's facing a sentence of up to 240 months to life, in a United States Penitentiary.

"Sentencing will be June twenty-seventh at nine o'clock a.m. Court is adjourned," Judge Thompson stated before banging his gavel.

Cortez's supporters shook their heads in total disbelief at what just happened. Cortez took a deep breath and looked at Judith whose response to this injustice was, that they were going to file for an appeal. In a state of confusion, Cortez was taken to the back and handcuffed to a wooden bench. Another marshal retrieved Cortez's paperwork to transport him into federal custody.

The reality of what just took place in the courtroom he was now beginning to register. "All 4 Nuthin'," a cut-off 8 Ball's Lost was the first thought that came to his mind. Cortez prided himself on being strategic. Making a way for his friends and himself to prosper. In his wildest dreams, he couldn't have seen this move coming.

A guy he respected and entrusted to help build a multi-million-dollar empire, suddenly altered the trajectory of every member affiliated. With Cortez's future being bound to federal prison, everyone began strategizing their next move. Cortez's incarceration will directly impact the livelihood of many people.

Of course, the family down in Orlando will continue to handle their affairs. What about the people Cortez businesses provide income for? How about his newlywed wife and family who are disheartened by this travesty of justice? Then there's the clique. Will they be able to bounce back from the unfortunate turn of events?

Cortez's mind was currently cluttered due to this whirlwind he found himself in. He does know they worked too hard to reach this status, unscathed, just to lose it in this fashion. Once he gets settled in and reaches out to the world, he planned on orchestrating some ways to protect his assets.

Coming Soon

Honor Society Publications Presents

Chronicles of a Hustla:

Greed Masquerades As Ambition II

■ ■ ■ ■

Unfinished Bizness

May 31, 2011 was the day Po' took the stand, and willingly testified as a government witness against Cortez. Also, that was Po's last day in the City of Montgomery. For the past four years, he's lived in a few different states, all expenses paid for courtesy of WITSEC. For his cooperation and fabricated testimony against Cortez, he receives a government allowance. Po' was ashamed to bring anyone with him into WITSEC, so he entered by himself and the solitude was driving him insane.

Nebraska, Minneapolis, Wisconsin, and Seattle was the final destination before Po' decided he's had enough of this monotonous, square lifestyle. As of late, Po' was in frequent communication with his soldiers back home. The Feds informed Po' that Cortez was still incarcerated in a United States Penitentiary. Po' unhesitatingly signed the waiver to be released from federal protection, once he heard Cortez was still on lock.

He got his ducks aligned before returning to Montgomery, after disappearing four years ago. Nothing much had changed about Po' that anyone could visibly notice. He's still flamboyant and fly, looking like he's up, as usual. Po' had everyone under the impression that he'd relocated to Miami, Florida, in pursuit of better opportunities.

In actuality, frustration began to creep in with the living arrangements of being housed in WITSEC. It was inevitable Po' requested to be released from protection. Being back in Montgomery for six months, at certain times Po' started moving around more throughout the city. Being a living legend in Newtown, he could move around at will. Back in his comfort zone, Po' got complacent being home. He hadn't heard about any foul rumors of himself being a rat, so he figured to steer clear of the south side, and he'll be good.

****

Cortez was almost four years into serving a 240-month sentence at a US Penitentiary located in Tucson, Arizona. The Family, down in Orlando got the news of what led up to Cortez's incarceration, including the outcome. Lil' Derek conveyed the message that his dad chose to terminate their business affairs, until further notice. He made sure Cortez knew he had no say so in the decision. There was one thing Lil' Derek could control, and that was retaliation against Po' for his treachery.

Lil' Derek promised Cortez he would get a location on Po's whereabouts, and when he does he guaranteed to take care of the rat. He moved Hot Boi and Glokk, two of his most trusted hitters to Montgomery. Lil' Derek wanted them on the ground when Po' reappeared. Lil' Derek had a hunch that Po' would resurface after some time. Hot Boi and Glokk represented the streets. They navigated throughout the city and were only seeking acquaintances with the major players on the north side.

Hot Boi, Glokk, and TD had become associates from frequently crossing paths at Club Big Boy's, and many other places. Hot Boi was at TD's trap in Newtown one day buying some gas. As usual, TD would smoke a blunt or two with Hot Boi before he left. TD and Hot Boi were smoking as TD talked on the speakerphone. Hot Boi wasn't really ear hustling, but he was sitting right there, and the invaluable information fell in his lap.

"I ain't seen him yet, but too many niggaz sayin' it's so," TD said on the iPhone.

"It's back on den!" the guy on the phone excitedly pointed out. "Nigga ya bullshittin'?"

"Po' back in the city!" TD assertively told him. "Nigga I'm from the hood! Too many real niggaz already said dat shit. I'mma see 'fore the night out though."

Before tonight Hot Boi and Glokk felt they'd overextended their stay and were griping about returning home permanently. "O.G.," Hot Boi said into his iPhone. "What cha got goin' on?"

"Takin' care some bizness. What's happenin'?" Lil' Derek concisely replied. "I know y'all niggaz ready to come back to the crib. Gimme another…"

"O.G. I don't mean to cut cha off," Hot Boi said interrupting him mid-sentence. "Ole bwoy, he back in town! We comin' home for good!"

"Ya, sure! How ya know it's him?"

"O.G. it's him! His name been rangin' out in the city, like a muthafucka!"

"The faster y'all murk dat rattin' azz nigga, the faster y'all get back here."

"Say less!"

The comfortability of being back on familiar soil enabled Po' to continue running his operation as if he hadn't left. Therefore, Po' was posted up in Newtown daily. Hot Boi and Glokk were regularly hanging out in Newtown, too. They would sporadically cross paths with Po'. That's when it dawned on Hot Boi how to complete the mission. A bad lil' baby from around the way captured Po's attention. Having O.G. status encouraged him to shoot his shot, multiple times.

Hot Boi garnered all of this young lady's attention and decided to use it to his advantage. He convinced the young lady that if she did this favor, she'd forever be in good graces with him. After she agreed to let Po' take her out, Hot Boi knew he had this in the bag. Well aware that she's young, Po' wooed her by taking her to places she's never been. He took her to Kobe's, a Hibachi restaurant, where he could pick her brain while planning the remainder of the night.

Po' decided to flatter the young lady by taking her to a rental property, where he lived in the gated community of Deer Creek. Po' fixed them a nightcap before taking her upstairs to his bedroom. She left the front door unlocked and texted Hot Boi: "We upstairs. The front door open. Give us fifteen minutes." Po' pulled the young lady closely, fervently kissing and caressing her.

When they were finished, Po' went into the bathroom to wipe himself off. She texted Hot Boi again. Hot Boi and Glokk were already inside the house, basically awaiting the confirmation. The guys cautiously entered the bedroom wearing all-black, including their gloves and ski masks. Hot Boi motioned for the young lady to get out of the room, literally catching Po' with his pants down. Po' walked out of the bathroom, completely taken aback by these men abruptly appearing in his bedroom.

"Courtesy of our partner, you sent away. Rattin' bitch!" Hot Boi told him.

Glokk's first shot was to the head, and the next one was to his torso. The guys casually walked back downstairs to where the young lady was now fully dressed, and panicky. "Let's go baby! You did good!" Hot Boi assured her.

In the foyer at the front entrance of the house, Hot Boi shot the young lady in the back of the head, tightening all loose ends.

Acknowledgments

First and foremost, all praises to the Most High, who empowers me with words that conjure up lucid images. There are several people I've encountered along my journey, who've all played a significant role in shaping me, in some form or fashion. For that, I'm grateful. I would like to take this time to personally thank Damien "Lil 'D" Jenkins, a Birmingham, Alabama author of The Wrong Side Of Midnight. The thought of writing festered for some time until I read his rough draft, and that motivated me to write my own. Also, double salute to Tre Carter and Megan B. Joseph of Joseph Editorial Services, for their roles in helping this novel materialize.

About Author

■ ■ ■ ■

Sed Green always had a desire for writing. That desire increased the instant he began reading stories that were similar to the reality he overcame. Sed Green is the CEO of Honor Society Publications, also he's an author of Urban Fiction. His company's first release Greed Masquerades as Ambition and his upcoming novel, Jackboyz. He was born in Montgomery, Alabama, and lived there most of his life. He randomly attends the Cloverdale Writing Group, located in his hometown. When he's not honing his craft, he can be found spending time with his family and friends, sporting events, live music events, hustling, and reading.

You can contact Sed Green on:

Instagram or Facebook @sed.green

or check out his website www.honorsocietypublications.com